"Everyday Use"

B. Affinity Identities;

ii. Black

Women Writers
Texts and Contexts

VOLUMES IN THE SERIES

"Everyday Use"

ALICE WALKER ■

Edited and with an introduction by
BARBARA T. CHRISTIAN

Rutgers University Press
New Brunswick, New Jersey

Library of Congress Cataloging-in-Publication Data

Walker, Alice, 1944–
    Everyday use / Alice Walker ; edited and with an introduction by
Barbara T. Christian.
       p.   cm. — (Women writers)
    Includes bibliographical references.
    ISBN 0-8135-2075-4 (cloth) — ISBN 0-8135-2076-2 (pbk.)
    1. Afro-American women—Southern States—Fiction.
    2. Quiltmakers—Southern States—Fiction. 3. Quilting—Southern
States—Fiction. I. Christian, Barbara, 1943–
    II. Title. III. Series: Women writers (New Brunswick, N.J.).
PS3573.A425E9   1994   93-35018
813'.54—dc20   CIP

British Cataloging-in-Publication information available

❏ Contents ∎

❑ Introduction

Introduction

Although Alice Walker's "Everyday Use" was published in 1973, in the early phase of her writing career, it is a cornerstone in her large and distinguished opus—one that consists, to date, of five novels, five volumes of poetry, two essay collections, two children's books, and two short-story collections. For it is in this story and in her classic essay "In Search of Our Mothers' Gardens" (1974) that Walker first articulates the metaphor of quilting to represent the creative legacy that African Americans* have inherited from their maternal ancestors. Walker's exploration of that metaphor is not only an abiding contribution to African American literature, as well as to American women's culture, it is also the basis of the forms she has used in her works, especially in her novels, including *The Third Life of Grange Copeland* (1970), the Pulitzer Prize–winning *The Color Purple* (1982), and her most recent, *Possessing the Secret of Joy* (1992).

During the twenty years since this story was published, critics have explored the quilt as the major metaphor in Walker's works. In *Black Women Novelists, The Development of a Tradition, 1892–1976* (1980), I called Walker's first two novels "quilts" and named the chapter on these works "Novels for Everyday Use."[1] In "Alice Walker: The Black Woman Artist as Wayward" (1981), reprinted in this volume, "Everyday Use" is pivotal to my reading of Walker. Houston Baker and Charlotte Pierce Baker critique my analysis of the quilt motif in African American culture and in "Everyday Use" in their es-

---

* "African American" appears with or without a hyphen according to the style used in individual articles. Similar variations are respected in the capitalization of "black."

say, "Patches: Quilts and Community in Alice Walker's 'Everyday Use'" (1985), also reprinted here.

In the 1980s, partially inspired by Walker's works, many studies, including those by cultural and feminist critics such as Elaine Showalter, explored the relationship between the quilt as metaphor and American literature and culture. In her book *Sister's Choice,* named after Walker's name for Celie's quilt in *The Color Purple,* Showalter investigates the history of the quilt in relation to American culture, ranging from nineteenth-century women's literature to the AIDS Quilt so important in contemporary culture.

African American women writing today have also responded to Walker's metaphor of the quilt as an articulation of women's culture, notably Toni Morrison in *Beloved* in her subtle use of the orange piece in the quilt that Baby Suggs looks to for color,[2] and Gloria Naylor in *Mama Day* in her dramatization of the construction by the "matriarch," Mama Day, of her quilt as the history of her family and community.[3] In her essay, "Sister's Choice: Quilting Aesthetics in Contemporary African American Women's Fiction," included in this volume, Margot Anne Kelley traces that motif in the novels of Walker, Morrison, and Naylor.[4] Even a popular magazine, *Newsweek,* has acknowledged the importance of the quilt in its articles on African American writers, as, for example, in Margo Jefferson's review of Toni Morrison's *Song of Solomon.*[5]

In her essay "In Search of Our Mothers' Gardens," published in 1974 before the rise of Cultural Studies, Walker celebrates the creative legacy, symbolized by the quilt that women like her mother had bestowed on her and other contemporary black women writers. In this essay, Walker searches for literary models of her own, as Virginia Woolf does in *A Room of One's Own*. Instead of analyzing the reasons why women had not created great art, as Woolf—an upper-class British white woman—does, Walker wonders whether, instead of looking for a clearly defined African American female tradition of 'art,' perhaps we should look for the female folk creativity that sustained our maternal ancestors. When she looks "low," Walker finds quilts like the one she saw in the Smithsonian Institution, composed by an "anonymous black woman" who lived in an almost invisible past, yet who created a work of art valued for its passion and imagination. What Walker, a contemporary black woman writer, stresses in her appreciation of such examples of the creativity of nearly anonymous black Southern women like her mother is their ability to devise something beautiful and functional out of throwaways, from what the society considers to be waste. "In Search of Our Mothers' Gardens" beautifully complements Walker's short story "Everyday Use." In both pieces she uses the metaphor of the quilt to represent the pivotal role Southern black women played in the development of African American culture. The ability to transform nothing into something, central to these women's creativity, is the critical theme of "Everyday Use."

In "Everyday Use," as in "In Search of Our Mothers' Gardens," Walker alludes to the process of quilting as a basis for "high art." Walker's own literary process is, in fact, developed on that model of quilting, for she consistently stitches together short units in patterns of recurring imagery to create her novels, the first three in particular: *The Third Life of Grange Copeland* her patchwork quilt,[6] *Meridian* her crazy quilt,[7] and *The Color Purple* her sister quilt.

In *The Third Life of Grange Copeland*, Walker uses the novel form to explore the complexities of the relationships between poverty, racism, and gender oppression in the life of a black Southern sharecropping family, the Copelands. More generally, Walker confronts the question of how to change the destructive pattern comprising the lives of many black sharecroppers to a pattern of creativity and wholeness.[8] In *Grange Copeland* she demonstrates the ways in which the oppression the men face sometimes results in cruelty to wives and the destruction of children. In the first part of the novel, Walker graphically lays out the bleak pattern of life for Grange, the father, who comes to hate the white man so much he has no space to love his own family. In the second part, Grange's son Brownfield repeats that same pattern of despair, resulting in his murder of Mem, his wife. But in the third part of the novel, Grange, now a grandfather, is able to change the motifs in the pattern that had made up the quilt of his life. He learns, in his third life, that the possibility of "surviving whole" resides not in his hatred of whites but in his love for his granddaughter, Ruth, his reverence for the land, and his African American Southern heritage.

In *Meridian*, published in 1976, two years after "Everyday Use," Walker improvises more freely to create a crazy quilt, juxtaposing the histories of Southern blacks and Native Americans, and the motifs of violence throughout American history as well as in the decade of the 1960s, with the life of Meridian, an "ordinary lower middle class Southern woman." At first the quilt of change she constructs seems incoherent, but by arranging a pattern of patches for Meridian's growing up (one being the way in which girls are made to feel that their only goal is to be biological mothers) in apparently random relationship to patches evoking the collective, often violent history of the sixties (with the assassinations of President Jóhn F. Kennedy and the Reverend Martin Luther King, Jr.), Walker in fact creates a quilt of the Civil Rights Movement. As she focuses on the Movement's refusal to violate life and extends its philosophy of non-violence to include the nurturing of life, she creates a pattern that suggests a quality usually ascribed to mothers as central to all those who would be revolutionaries.

Walker employs another pattern of quilting in *The Color Purple* to embody the history and culture of women, for the entire novel is written as a series of letters, a form which feminist historians have found to be a major source of women's history. Walker's composition of a quilt of sisterhood is signalled in the novel by her choice of the name "Sister's Choice" for the quilt her central character, Celie, is stitching.

Walker's choice of these various quilting techniques for her three novels is related to the project she proposed for herself in the early 1970s. In her interview in 1973 with critic Mary Helen Washington, Walker described the three "cycles" of black women that she was about to explore in the early seventies. The first type of black woman character Walker felt was missing from pre-1970s American literature were those "who were cruelly exploited, spirits and bodies mutilated, relegated to the most narrow and confining lives, sometimes driven to madness"—a succinct description of the Copeland women in Walker's first novel as well as of many of the young protagonists of *In Love and Trouble*. The women of Walker's second cycle are those who are not so much physically abused as they are psychically conflicted as a result of wanting to be part of mainstream American life—for example, Walker's sister in the poem "For My Sister Molly Who in the Fifties" (reprinted in this volume), or early twentieth-century writers Nella Larsen and Zora Neale Hurston, who suffered from "contrary instincts" in their need to be recognized as "real" writers in order to express themselves and their people. In Walker's third cycle are those black women who come to a new consciousness about their right to be themselves and to shape the world. The title character in Walker's second novel *Meridian* is a woman who moves in that direction, but who suffers from the restrictions imposed by the world in which she lives. Thus Meridian's need to be a part of a Movement, a struggle for change. It is Celie, Shug, and Sophia in Walker's third novel, *The Color Purple*, as well as some of the women in her second collection of stories, *You Can't Keep a Good Woman Down* (1981), who achieve the wholeness of Walker's third cycle of women. Yet, while most of the third-cycle women appear in works published after *In Love and Trouble*, there are some older women in Walker's early fiction, Washington notes, who are clearly and completely themselves.

As early as 1973, in "Everyday Use," Walker presents women of all three cycles. Maggie is the scarred sister who does not know her own worth. Her mother tells us that she walks like "a lame animal, perhaps a dog run over by some careless person rich enough to own a car." In contrast to Maggie, Dee is very much like the women of Walker's second cycle. It is true that she does not want to assimilate into white society, and that at first glance she appears to have a sense of her own selfhood. Yet it is clear from her mother's description of her growing up that she detests her family and her people's past—until it is fashionable to appreciate them. While her mother is, from time to time, fascinated by Dee's desire to win in the world, Mrs. Johnson understands Maggie's value and her love for her family, and she is critical of Dee's denigration of her past. As someone who understands herself, her right to be herself, Mrs. Johnson is one of those older women in Walker's fiction who prefigures the women of the third cycle she would so beautifully portray in *The Color Purple*. And it is significant that in "Everyday Use" it is the older mother figure, a woman who must have learned much about her own worth from her grandma Dee, who passes on that tradition of selfhood to the scarred black women of Walker's first cycle.

"Everyday Use" is also critical to Walker's work in that it is the pivotal story in her first short-story collection, *In Love and Trouble: Stories of Black Women* (1973). As its title indicates, this book placed African American women's voices at the center of the narrative, an unusual position at that time. *The Third Life of Grange Copeland*, Walker's first book of fiction, is told primarily from the point of view of Southern black men, but the stories in Walker's next publication, *In Love and Trouble*, are narrated from the point of view of women. *In Love and Trouble* is linked to *The Third Life of Grange Copeland* because the Copeland women, Margaret and Mem, like the younger protagonists of the short stories, are very much "in trouble." Thus, *In Love and Trouble* represents an important shift in Walker's work: from then on, women will occupy the center of her narratives. In one of her first interviews (with John O'Brien, included in this volume), Walker tells us that she is "preoccupied with the spiritual survival, the survival *whole* of [her] people," and that she is "committed to exploring the oppressions, the insanities, the loyalties, and the triumphs of black women."

Most reviewers of *In Love and Trouble* were aware of the distinctly new emphasis Walker placed on African American women. Barbara Smith, in her review in *Ms.*, was exuberant about Walker's ability to "explore with honesty the texture and terrors of black women's lives."[9] Mel Watkins, in *The New York Times Book Review*, characterized these stories as "perspective minatures, snapshots that capture their subjects at crucial and revealing moments"[10]—qualities seldom found at that time in writings about African American women. Still, few reviewers were then aware of the importance "Everyday Use" would have in Walker's opus, either as a harbinger of the importance of the quilt in her work or as a new beginning in the creation of African American Southern women as subjects in their own right.

Walker's attention to black women's voices in *In Love*

and Trouble is especially significant in that perhaps for the first time in contemporary United States literary history, a writer featured a variety of *Southern* black women's perspectives. In so doing, Walker had to confront the variety of stereotypes which had shaped earlier accounts of black Southern women. Walker was certainly aware of the traditional stereotypes of "the mammy" and "the wench" that had developed during slavery, for these stereotypes continued to have currency in twentieth-century American culture.[11] No doubt, she was also aware of the ways in which these stereotypes had become standard in American literature, a conspicuous example being William Faulkner's portrait of Dilsey in *The Sound and the Fury* (1929). A descendant of the historical representation of slave mammies, Dilsey has little life outside of the terrain of her employers, the Compsons. She has no black context, little family or life of her own, and exists only to enhance her white folks' lives. So incensed was Walker by this character that she called the portrayal of Dilsey, in one of her interviews, an "embarrassment" to black people.[12]

But Walker not only had to contend with American white authors' constructions of Southern black women, she had to revise African American men's representations of these women. She clearly appreciated Jean Toomer's haunting portraits of African American Southern women's sexuality in his masterpiece, *Cane* (1923), for she named her second novel, *Meridian* (1976), after Toomer's "The Blue Meridian" (1933), his prophetic poem about women and men, the earth and survival. Yet Toomer's women are silent, their sense of themselves and their condition interpreted by a male narrator.

Walker did discover a writer who allowed her Southern black women to speak. While writing "The Revenge of Hannah Kemhuff," another story in *In Love and Trouble*, Walker accidently came upon the works of Zora Neale Hurston, another black Southern woman writer, who, in 1937, published *Their Eyes Were Watching God*, a novel which emphasized a Southern black woman's search for her own voice. In one of her later essays, Walker tells us that *"There is no book more important to me than this one* (including Toomer's *Cane*, which comes close, but from what I recognize is a more perilous direction)."[13] Hurston's works were to inspire Walker, not only because of their use of black folk English, which clearly influenced Walker's use of black folk English in *The Color Purple*, but also because of Hurston's abiding respect for Southern black folk. Understanding the importance of Hurston's legacy to American literature, Alice Walker would be a major force in the rediscovery of her maternal ancestor's works, to the extent that today, in significant measure because of her efforts, Hurston is considered a great American writer.[14] Walker's discovery of Hurston and the inspiration she drew from her literary maternal ancestor exemplifies the critical role models play in the development of young writers, as well as the importance of passing on the literary tradition of black people in educational institutions.

Walker's first collection of short stories was not only influenced by past stereotypes of black women in American literature, it was also very much affected by the present within which she was living. "Everyday Use" is, in part, Walker's response to the concept of heritage as articulated by the black movements of the 1960s. In that period, many African Americans, disappointed by the failure of integration, gravitated to the philosophy of cultural nationalism as the means to achieve liberation. In contrast to the veneration of Western ideas and ideals by many integrationists of the 1950s, Black Power ideologues emphasized the African cultural past as the true heritage of African Americans. The acknowledgment and appreciation of that heritage, which had too often been denigrated by African Americans themselves as well as by Euro-Americans, was a major tenet of the revolutionary movements of the period. Many blacks affirmed their African roots by changing their "slave names" to African names, and by wearing Afro hair styles and African clothing. Yet, ideologues of the period also lambasted older African Americans, opposing them to the lofty mythical models of the ancient past. These older men and women, they claimed, had become Uncle Toms and Aunt Jemimas who displayed little awareness of their culture and who, as a result of the slave past, had internalized the white man's view of blacks. So while these 1960s ideologues extolled an unknown ancient history, they denigrated the known and recent past. The tendency to idealize an ancient

African past while ignoring the recent African American past still persists in the Afrocentric movements of the 1990s.

In contrast to that tendency, Walker's "Everyday Use" is dedicated to "your grandmama." And the story is told by a woman many African Americans would recognize as their grandmama, that supposedly backward Southern ancestor the cultural nationalists of the North probably visited during the summers of their youth and probably considered behind the times. Walker stresses those physical qualities which suggest such a person, qualities often demeaned by cultural nationalists. For this grandmama, like the stereotypical mammy of slavery, is "a large big-boned woman with rough, man-working hands," who wears "flannel nightgowns to bed and overalls during the day," and whose "fat keeps [her] hot in zero weather." Nor is this grandmama politically conscious according to the fashion of the day: she never had an education after the second grade, she knows nothing about African names, and she eats pork. In having the grandmama tell this story, Walker gives voice to an entire maternal ancestry often silenced by the political rhetoric of the period. Indeed, Walker tells us in "In Search of Our Mothers' Gardens" that her writing is part of her mother's legacy to her, that many of her stories are based on stories *her* mother told her. Thus, Walker's writing is her way of breaking silences and stereotypes about her grandmothers', mothers', sisters' lives. In effect, her work is a literary continuation of a distinctly oral tradition in which African American women have been and still are pivotal participants.

Other African American women writers have also been aware of the ways in which the cultural nationalist rhetoric attempted to erase the importance of these ancestors. Toni Cade Bambara in her short story "My Man Bovanne," published in the early seventies, also critiques the demeaning of older black women.[15] Bambara's story, however, takes place in the urban North, rather than the rural South, and her character, Hazel, is a decidedly urban woman. In contrast, Walker's story emphasizes the rural Southern roots of African American heritage.

Mrs. Johnson, Walker's grandmama, typifies the elder

protagonists in *In Love and Trouble*. Southern contentions about family, community, the general society, even their conscious understanding of who they *should* be, hem them in. But, denying the passive images of Southern black women accepted by our society, these women actively seek to be themselves; they are often, therefore, in conflict with social restrictions rooted in racist and sexist ideologies and may appear crazed or at least contrary. Walker underlines these internal conflicts by introducing *In Love and Trouble* with quotations from two seemingly unrelated figures: the west African writer Elechi Amadi and the early twentieth-century German poet Rainer Maria Rilke. Both excerpts stress that "everything in nature grows and defends itself in its own way," and "is characteristically and spontaneously itself," against all opposition. In using an excerpt from a West African writer about the restrictions imposed on a young girl, as well as an excerpt from a European writer, Walker challenges the stereotypes of women, especially of older women within black societies, as well as the racism these women must confront within white societies. When Mrs. Johnson yanks the old quilts away from Dee/Wangero, the seemingly educated and politically correct daughter, and gives them to Maggie, the scarred and supposedly backward daughter who would put them to everyday use, she might appear unreasonable or contrary.[16] Yet her act is in keeping with her own knowledge of the meaning of the quilts, the spirit that they embody, and her need to make decisions based upon her own values.

Alice Walker is well aware of the restrictions of the African American Southern past, for she is the eighth child of Georgia sharecroppers. Born in 1944, she grew up during that period when, as she put it, apartheid existed in America.[17] For in the 1940s and 1950s, when segregation was the law of the South, opportunities for economic and social advancement were legally denied to Southern blacks. Walker was fortunate to come to adulthood during the social and political movements of the late fifties and sixties. Of her siblings, only she, and a slightly older sister, Molly, were able even to imagine the possibility of moving beyond the poverty of their parents. It is unlikely that Alice Walker would have been able to go to college—first at Spelman, the African American woman's college in Atlanta, and then at Sarah Lawrence, the white woman's college near New York City—if it had not been for the changes that came about as a result of the Civil Rights Movement. Nor is it likely that she, a Southern black woman from a poor family, would have been able to become the writer that she did without the changes resulting from the ferment of the Black and Women's movements of the 1960s and early 1970s.

While Walker was a participant in these movements, she was also one of their most astute critics. As a Southerner, she was aware of the ways in which black Southern culture was often thought of as backward by predominantly Northern Black Power ideologues, even as they proclaimed their love for black people. She was also acutely aware of the ways in which women were oppressed within the Black Power Movement itself, even as the very culture its participants revered was so often passed on by women. Walker had also visited Africa during her junior year of college and had personally experienced the gap between the Black Power advocates' idealization of Africa and the reality of the African societies she visited.

One of Walker's distinctive qualities as a writer is the way she plays on one idea in different modes, in much the same way that a musical idea in jazz is explored through different instruments. Walker's instruments are literary genres: the poem, the short story, the essay, the novel. Her first publication, a book of poetry called *Once* (1968), criticizes the uses the Black Power Movement made of Africa, particularly the movement's tendency to turn Africans into artifacts, an objection she develops in her third novel, *The Color Purple,* and in her fifth novel, *Possessing the Secret of Joy.* Ironically, the name given to Walker by Africans during her trip there was Wangero, a name she uses for herself in *Once* and for the educated sister in "Everyday Use."

Names are extremely important in African and African American culture as a means of indicating a person's spirit. During the 1960s Walker criticized the tendency among some African Americans to give up the names their parents gave them—names which embodied the history of their recent past—for African names that did not relate to a single person they knew. Hence the grandmama in "Everyday Use" is amazed that Dee would give up her name for the name

13

Wangero. For Dee was the name of her great-grandmother, a woman who had kept her family together against great odds. Wangero might have sounded authentically African but it had no relationship to a person she knew, nor to the personal history that had sustained her.

Walker has always been concerned with the ways in which artifacts of the African American past are celebrated by black political ideologues while the people who created them are not—a theme she develops in many of the short stories in *In Love and Trouble*. Perhaps that volume's most succinct expression of the theme is "Everyday Use." She would continue to explore the same theme in her later work. For example, the grandmama in "Everyday Use" has many qualities in common with Gracie Mae Stills, the blues singer in Walker's short story "1955," published eight years later in the volume *You Can't Keep a Good Woman Down*. Both women appear to be traditional mammy figures, but they are in fact the creators and guardians of the culture. By contrast, the young Celie in *The Color Purple* is in many ways like the scarred sister, Maggie, in "Everyday Use," but, as Thadious Davis notes in an essay included in this volume, Celie, created some ten years later, is able to acquire her own voice.

In "Everyday Use," by contrasting a sister who has the opportunity to go to college with a sister who stays at home, Walker reminds us of the challenges that contemporary African American women face as they discover what it means to be truly educated. The same concern appears in many of her works. For example, in "For My Sister Molly Who in the Fifties," she explores the conflicts that can result from an education that takes a woman away from her cultural source. Like Molly, Dee/Wangero in "Everyday Use" is embarrassed by her folk. She has been to the North, wears an Afro, and knows the correct political rhetoric of the 1960s, but she has little regard for her relatives who have helped to create that heritage. Thus, she does not know how to quilt and can only conceive of her family's quilts as priceless artifacts, as *things*, which she intends to hang on her wall as a means of demonstrating to others that she has "heritage." On the other hand, Maggie, the supposedly uneducated sister, who has been nowhere beyond the supposedly uneducated black South, loves and understands her family and can appreciate its history. She knows how to quilt and would put the precious quilts to "everyday use," which is precisely what, Walker suggests, one needs to do with one's heritage. For Maggie, the quilts are an embodiment of the *spirit* her folk have passed on to her.

It is worth noting that Walker, in interviews as well as in her dedication to *In Search of Our Mothers' Gardens*, refers to herself as scarred, perhaps because of the tragedy she endured at the age of eight when her brother accidently shot her with a BB gun and left her blind in one eye.[18] The two sisters in "Everyday Use," then, are related to different aspects of Walker's own personal experience as an African American woman scarred by the poverty of her origins, and as a African American woman whose awareness of the richness of the culture of her origins causes her to question the meaning of her education in prestigious American colleges.

Because Walker came from a background of poverty and social restriction, she also experienced first hand those values through which the grandmama and Maggie transformed the little they had into much more, so that they might survive. As important, Walker understood that poor people needed beauty in their lives and went to great lengths to create it. Although Walker's mother worked long hours in the fields and as a domestic, she cultivated beautiful gardens, artfully told stories, and created beautiful, functional quilts out of scraps. In creating beauty in the media available to them, Walker's mother and other "ordinary" African American women not usually considered artists were, in face, models of creativity for young African American women who now have the opportunity to become artists.

In Alice Walker's works, from *Once* (1968) to *Possessing the Secret of Joy* (1992), the pieces of the ancestors' quilts continue to be restitched. As the essays in this volume suggest, the figure of this older African American woman who knows the patterns of the past and therefore knows how to stitch together patterns for the future—a perspective first enunciated in "Everyday Use"—is central to our understanding of African American culture as well as that culture we call American. While there are differences between the patterns of African American quilts and those of other American women, as Margot Kelly's essay delineates, there are also the powerful similarities between these apparently disparate cultures, as Elaine Showalter points out. Without question, a significant number of American writings published in the last decade have illuminated ways in which "ordinary" Americans used female folk creations to articulate distinct American cultures. In that same decade, more and more American writings are focussed on women's voices, women as subjects. By emphasizing the power and variety of African American women's voices, Walker forecast the primary focus of an entire generation of African American women writers, who, in the 1970s and 1980s, published more fiction than they ever had, fiction in which they consistently constructed themselves as major actors in the world. Walker's literary works and the wisdom she exhibited in articulating the legacy of African American female creativity symbolized by the quilt helped bring about this significant development in American literature.

☐ *Notes* ■

1. Barbara T. Christian, "Novels for Everyday Use," in *Black Women Novelists, the Development of a Tradition, 1892–1976* (Westport: Greenwood Press, 1980), pp. 180–238.

2. Toni Morrison, *Beloved* (New York: Alfred A. Knopf, 1987).

3. Gloria Naylor, *Mama Day* (New York: Ticknor and Fields, 1988).

4. Margot Anne Kelley, "Quilting Aesthetics in Contemporary African-American Women's Fiction," in *Quilt and Metaphor,* ed. Judy Elsley and Cheryl Torsney (Columbia: University of Missouri Press, forthcoming). It appears for the first time in this volume.

5. Margo Jefferson, "Across the Barricades" *Newsweek* 87, (31 May 1976): 71–72.

6. Claudia Tate, "Interview with Alice Walker," in *Black Women Writers at Work,* ed. Claudia Tate (New York: Continuum, 1983), pp. 175–187.

7. Tate, "Interview with Alice Walker."

8. See Barbara T. Christian, "Novels for Everyday Use," in *Black Women Novelists.*

9. Barbara Smith, "The Souls of Black Women," *Ms.* 2 (February 1974): 42.

10. Mel Watkins, *The New York Times Book Review* 123, #42, Section 1 (17 March 1974): 40–41.

11. See, for example, Barbara T. Christian, "Shadows Up-lifted," in *Black Women Novelists,* pp. 1–34.

12. Alice Walker, "Alice Walker and *The Color Purple*," BBC production, 1986.

13. Alice Walker, "Zora Neale Hurston: A Cautionary Tale," introduction to *I Love Myself When I'm Laughing . . . And Then Again When I Am Looking Mean and Impressive: A Zora Neale Hurston Reader* (Old Westbury, New York: Feminist Press, 1979).

14. See Alice Walker, "In Search of Zora Neale Hurston," *Ms.* 2, no. 11 (March 1975).

15. See Toni Cade, "My Man Bovanne," *Gorilla My Love: Short Stories* (New York: Random House, 1972).

16. See Barbara Christian, "The Contrary Women of Alice Walker," *The Black Scholar* (March–April 1981): 21–30.

17. For a succinct biography of Alice Walker, see Barbara T. Christian, "Alice Walker," *Dictionary of Literary Biography, Vol. 33: Afro-American Fiction Writers After 1955,* ed. Thadious Davis and Trudier Harris (Detroit: Gale Research Company, 1984), pp. 257–270.

18. Alice Walker, dedication to *In Search of Our Mothers' Gardens: Womanist Prose* (New York: Harcourt Brace Jovanovich, 1983). The dedication reads: "To My Daughter Rebecca / Who saw in me / what I considered / a scar / And redefined it / as / a world."

1944	Born Alice Walker on February 9 in Eatonton, Georgia, to Minnie Lou Grant and Willie Lee Walker.
1952	An accident leaves her permanently blind in one eye.
1961	Matriculates at Spelman College, Atlanta, Georgia.
1963	Transfers to Sarah Lawrence College, New York.
1964	Travels to Uganda, Africa, as exchange student.
1965	Receives B.A. degree from Sarah Lawrence College.
1967	Publishes first piece, short story, "To Hell with Dying," and marries Melvyn Levanthal, a white civil rights lawyer.
1967–1968	Consultant to Black Studies Friends of the Children of Mississippi, collecting oral histories of black women.
1968	Publishes *Once: Poems;* has daughter, Rebecca.
1970	Publishes *The Third Life of Grange Copeland.*
1970–1971	Writer-in-Residence at Tougaloo College, Mississippi.
1973	Publishes *In Love and Trouble: Stories of Black Women* and *Revolutionary Petunias and Other Poems,* a National Book Award nominee and the winner of the Lillian Smith Award from the Southern Regional Council.
1974	Publishes *Langston Hughes, American Poet,* a children's book; receives the Rosenthal Award from the National Institute of Arts and Letters for *In Love and Trouble;* and becomes contributing editor to *Ms.*

1976	Publishes *Meridian;* divorced from Melvyn Levanthal.
1977	Appointed Associate Professor at Yale University.
1978	Receives Guggenheim.
1979	Moves to Northern California.
1980	Teaches African American Studies at U. C. Berkeley.
1981	Publishes *You Can't Keep a Good Woman Down: Stories.*
1982	Publishes *The Color Purple,* which is nominated for the National Book Critics Circle Award.
1983	Becomes first black woman to receive The Pulitzer Prize for fiction, for *The Color Purple;* publishes *In Search of Our Mothers' Gardens: Womanist Prose.*
1985	Consultant for movie *The Color Purple,* which is released in December.
1988	Publishes *Living by the Word.*
1992	Publishes *Possessing the Secret of Joy.*

❑ Everyday Use

☐ Everyday Use

for your grandmama

I will wait for her in the yard that Maggie and I made so clean and wavy yesterday afternoon. A yard like this is more comfortable than most people know. It is not just a yard. It is like an extended living room. When the hard clay is swept clean as a floor and the fine sand around the edges lined with tiny, irregular grooves, anyone can come and sit and look up into the elm tree and wait for the breezes that never come inside the house.

Maggie will be nervous until after her sister goes: she will stand hopelessly in corners, homely and ashamed of the burn scars down her arms and legs, eying her sister with a mixture of envy and awe. She thinks her sister has held life always in the palm of one hand, that "no" is a word the world never learned to say to her.

You've no doubt seen those TV shows where the child who has "made it" is confronted, as a surprise, by her own mother and father, tottering in weakly from backstage. (A pleasant surprise, of course: What would they do if parent and child came on the show only to curse out and insult each other?) On TV mother and child embrace and smile into each other's faces. Sometimes the mother and father weep, the child wraps them in her arms and leans across the table to tell how she would not have made it without their help. I have seen these programs.

Sometimes I dream a dream in which Dee and I are suddenly brought together on a TV program of this sort. Out of a dark and soft-seated limousine I am ushered into a bright room filled with many people. There I meet a smiling, gray, sporty man like Johnny Carson who shakes my hand and tells me what a fine girl I have. Then we are on the stage and Dee is embracing me with tears in her eyes. She pins on my dress a large orchid, even though she has told me once that she thinks orchids are tacky flowers.

In real life I am a large, big-boned woman with rough, man-working hands. In the winter I wear flannel nightgowns to bed and overalls during the day. I can kill and clean a hog as mercilessly as a man. My fat keeps me hot in zero weather. I can work outside all day, breaking ice to get water for washing; I can eat pork liver cooked over the open fire minutes after it comes steaming from the hog. One winter I knocked a bull calf straight in the brain between the eyes with a sledge hammer and had the meat hung up to chill before nightfall. But of course all this does not show on television. I am the way my daughter would want me to be: a hundred pounds lighter, my skin like an uncooked barley pancake. My hair glistens in the hot bright lights. Johnny Carson has much to do to keep up with my quick and witty tongue.

But that is a mistake. I know even before I wake up. Who ever knew a Johnson with a quick tongue?

Who can even imagine me looking a strange white man in the eye? It seems to me I have talked to them always with one foot raised in flight, with my head turned in whichever way is farthest from them. Dee, though. She would always look anyone in the eye. Hesitation was no part of her nature.

"How do I look, Mama?" Maggie says, showing just enough of her thin body enveloped in pink skirt and red blouse for me to know she's there, almost hidden by the door.

"Come out into the yard," I say.

Have you ever seen a lame animal, perhaps a dog run over by some careless person rich enough to own a car, sidle up to someone who is ignorant enough to be kind to him? That is the way my Maggie walks. She has been like this, chin on chest, eyes on ground, feet in shuffle, ever since the fire that burned the other house to the ground.

Dee is lighter than Maggie, with nicer hair and a fuller figure. She's a woman now, though sometimes I forget. How long ago was it that the other house burned? Ten, twelve years? Sometimes I can still hear the flames and feel Maggie's arms sticking to me, her hair smoking and her dress falling off her in little black papery flakes. Her eyes seemed stretched open, blazed open by the flames reflected in them. And Dee. I see her standing off under the sweet gum tree she used to dig gum out of; a look of concentration on her face as she watched the last dingy gray board of the house fall in toward the red-hot brick chimney. Why don't you do a dance around the ashes? I'd wanted to ask her. She had hated the house that much.

I used to think she hated Maggie, too. But that

was before we raised the money, the church and me, to send her to Augusta to school. She used to read to us without pity; forcing words, lies, other folks' habits, whole lives upon us two, sitting trapped and ignorant underneath her voice. She washed us in a river of make-believe, burned us with a lot of knowledge we didn't necessarily need to know. Pressed us to her with the serious way she read, to shove us away at just the moment, like dimwits, we seemed about to understand.

Dee wanted nice things. A yellow organdy dress to wear to her graduation from high school; black pumps to match a green suit she'd made from an old suit somebody gave me. She was determined to stare down any disaster in her efforts. Her eyelids would not flicker for minutes at a time. Often I fought off the temptation to shake her. At sixteen she had a style of her own: and knew what style was.

I never had an education myself. After second grade the school was closed down. Don't ask me why: in 1927 colored asked fewer questions than they do now. Sometimes Maggie reads to me. She stumbles along good-naturedly but can't see well. She knows she is not bright. Like good looks and money, quickness passed her by. She will marry John Thomas (who has mossy teeth in an earnest face) and then I'll be free to sit here and I guess just sing church songs to myself. Although I never was a good singer. Never could carry a tune. I was always better at a man's job. I used to love to milk till I was hooked in the side in '49. Cows are soothing and slow and don't bother you, unless you try to milk them the wrong way.

I have deliberately turned my back on the house. It is three rooms, just like the one that burned, except the roof is tin; they don't make shingle roofs any more. There are no real windows, just some holes cut in the sides, like the portholes in a ship, but not round and not square, with rawhide holding the shutters up on the outside. This house is in a pasture, too, like the other one. No doubt when Dee sees it she will want to tear it down. She wrote me once that no matter where we "choose" to live, she will manage to come see us. But she will never bring her friends. Maggie and I thought about this and Maggie asked me, "Mama, when did Dee ever *have* any friends?"

She had a few. Furtive boys in pink shirts hanging about on washday after school. Nervous girls who never laughed. Impressed with her they worshiped the well-turned phrase, the cute shape, the scalding humor that erupted like bubbles in lye. She read to them.

When she was courting Jimmy T she didn't have much time to pay to us, but turned all her faultfinding power on him. He *flew* to marry a cheap city girl from a family of ignorant flashy people. She hardly had time to recompose herself.

When she comes I will meet—but there they are!

Maggie attempts to make a dash for the house, in her shuffling way, but I stay her with my hand. "Come back here," I say. And she stops and tries to dig a well in the sand with her toe.

It is hard to see them clearly through the strong sun. But even the first glimpse of leg out of the car tells me it is Dee. Her feet were always neat-looking, as if God himself had shaped them with a certain style. From the other side of the car comes a short, stocky man. Hair is all over his head a foot long and hanging from his chin like a kinky mule tail. I hear Maggie suck in her breath. "Uhnnnh," is what it sounds like. Like when you see the wriggling end of a snake just in front of your foot on the road. "Uhnnnh."

Dee next. A dress down to the ground, in this hot weather. A dress so loud it hurts my eyes. There are yellows and oranges enough to throw back the light of the sun. I feel my whole face warming from the heat waves it throws out. Earrings gold, too, and hanging down to her shoulders. Bracelets dangling and making noises when she moves her arm up to shake the folds of the dress out of her armpits. The dress is loose and flows, and as she walks closer, I like it. I hear Maggie go "Uhnnnh" again. It is her sister's hair. It stands straight up like the wool on a sheep. It is black as night and around the edges are two long pigtails that rope about like small lizards disappearing behind her ears.

"Wa-su-zo-Tean-o!" she says, coming on in that gliding way the dress makes her move. The short stocky fellow with the hair to his navel is all grinning and he follows up with "Asalamalakim,* my mother and sister!" He moves to hug Maggie but she falls back, right up against the back of my chair. I feel her trembling there and when I look up I see the perspiration falling off her chin.

"Don't get up," says Dee. Since I am stout it takes something of a push. You can see me trying to move a second or two before I make it. She turns, showing white heels through her sandals, and goes back to the car. Out she peeks next with a Polaroid. She stoops

---

*Arabic greeting meaning "Peace be with you" used by members of the Islamic faith.

down quickly and lines up picture after picture of me sitting there in front of the house with Maggie cowering behind me. She never takes a shot without making sure the house is included. When a cow comes nibbling around the edge of the yard she snaps it and me and Maggie *and* the house. Then she puts the Polaroid in the back seat of the car, and comes up and kisses me on the forehead.

Meanwhile Asalamalakim is going through motions with Maggie's hand. Maggie's hand is as limp as a fish, and probably as cold, despite the sweat, and she keeps trying to pull it back. It looks like Asalamalakim wants to shake hands but wants to do it fancy. Or maybe he don't know how people shake hands. Anyhow, he soon gives up on Maggie.

"Well," I say. "Dee."

"No, Mama," she says. "Not 'Dee,' Wangero Leewanika Kemanjo!"

"What happened to 'Dee'?" I wanted to know.

"She's dead," Wangero said. "I couldn't bear it any longer, being named after the people who oppress me."

"You know as well as me you was named after your aunt Dicie," I said. Dicie is my sister. She named Dee. We called her "Big Dee" after Dee was born.

"But who was *she* named after?" asked Wangero.

"I guess after Grandma Dee," I said.

"And who was she named after?" asked Wangero.

"Her mother," I said, and saw Wangero was getting tired. "That's about as far back as I can trace it," I said. Though, in fact, I probably could have carried it back beyond the Civil War through the branches.

"Well," said Asalamalakim, "there you are."

"Uhnnnd," I heard Maggie say.

"There I was not," I said, "before 'Dicie' cropped up in our family, so why should I try to trace it that far back?"

He just stood there grinning, looking down on me like somebody inspecting a Model A car. Every once in a while he and Wangero sent eye signals over my head.

"How do you pronounce this name?" I asked.

"You don't have to call me by it if you don't want to," said Wangero.

"Why shouldn't I?" I asked. "If that's what you want us to call you, we'll call you."

"I know it might sound awkward at first," said Wangero.

"I'll get used to it," I said. "Ream it out again."

Well, soon we got the name out of the way. Asalamalakim had a name twice as long and three times as hard. After I tripped over it two or three times he told me to just call him Hakim-a-barber. I wanted to ask him was he a barber, but I didn't really think he was, so I didn't ask.

"You must belong to those beef-cattle peoples down the road," I said. They said "Asalamalakim" when they met you, too, but they didn't shake hands. Always too busy: feeding the cattle, fixing the fences, putting up salt-lick shelters, throwing down hay. When the white folks poisoned some of the herd the men stayed up all night with rifles in their hands. I walked a mile and a half just to see the sight.

Hakim-a-barber said, "I accept some of their doctrines, but farming and raising cattle is not my style." (They didn't tell me, and I didn't ask, whether Wangero (Dee) had really gone and married him.)

We sat down to eat and right away he said he didn't eat collards and pork was unclean. Wangero, though, went on through the chitlins and corn bread, the greens and everything else. She talked a blue streak over the sweet potatoes. Everything delighted her. Even the fact that we still used the benches her daddy made for the table when we couldn't afford to buy chairs.

"Oh, Mama!" she cried. Then turned to Hakim-a-barber. "I never knew how lovely these benches are. You can feel the rump prints," she said, running her hands underneath her and along the bench. Then she gave a sigh and her hand closed over Grandma Dee's butter dish. "That's it!" she said. "I knew there was something I wanted to ask you if I could have." She jumped up from the table and went over in the corner where the churn stood, the milk in it clabber by now. She looked at the churn and looked at it.

"This churn top is what I need," she said. "Didn't Uncle Buddy whittle it out of a tree you all used to have?"

"Yes," I said.

"Uh huh," she said happily. "And I want the dasher, too."

"Uncle Buddy whittle that, too?" asked the barber.

Dee (Wangero) looked up at me.

"Aunt Dee's first husband whittled the dash," said Maggie so low you almost couldn't hear her. "His name was Henry, but they called him Stash."

"Maggie's brain is like an elephant's," Wangero said, laughing. "I can use the churn top as a centerpiece for the alcove table," she said, sliding a plate over the churn, "and I'll think of something artistic to do with the dasher."

When she finished wrapping the dasher the handle stuck out. I took it for a moment in my hands. You didn't even have to look close to see where hands pushing the dasher up and down to make butter had left a kind of sink in the wood. In fact, there were a lot of small sinks; you could see where thumbs and fingers had sunk into the wood. It was beautiful light yellow wood, from a tree that grew in the yard where Big Dee and Stash had lived.

After dinner Dee (Wangero) went to the trunk at the foot of my bed and started rifling through it. Maggie hung back in the kitchen over the dishpan. Out came Wangero with two quilts. They had been pieced by Grandma Dee and then Big Dee and me had hung them on the quilt frames on the front porch and quilted them. One was in the Lone Star pattern. The other was Walk Around the Mountain. In both of them were scraps of dresses Grandma Dee had worn fifty and more years ago. Bits and pieces of Grandpa Jarrell's Paisley shirts. And one teeny faded blue piece, about the size of a penny matchbox, that was from Great Grandpa Ezra's uniform that he wore in the Civil War.

"Mama," Wangero said sweet as a bird. "Can I have these old quilts?"

I heard something fall in the kitchen, and a minute later the kitchen door slammed.

"Why don't you take one or two of the others?" I asked. "These old things was just done by me and Big Dee from some tops your grandma pieced before she died."

"No," said Wangero. "I don't want those. They are stitched around the borders by machine."

"That'll make them last better," I said.

"That's not the point," said Wangero. "These are all pieces of dresses Grandma used to wear. She did all this stitching by hand. Imagine!" She held the quilts securely in her arms, stroking them.

"Some of the pieces, like those lavender ones, come from old clothes her mother handed down to her," I said, moving up to touch the quilts. Dee (Wangero) moved back just enough so that I couldn't reach the quilts. They already belonged to her.

"Imagine!" she breathed again, clutching them closely to her bosom.

"The truth is," I said, "I promised to give them quilts to Maggie, for when she marries John Thomas."

She gasped like a bee had stung her.

"Maggie can't appreciate these quilts!" she said. "She'd probably be backward enough to put them to everyday use."

"I reckon she would," I said. "God knows I been saving 'em for long enough with nobody using 'em. I hope she will!" I didn't want to bring up how I had offered Dee (Wangero) a quilt when she went away to college. Then she had told me they were old-fashioned, out of style.

"But they're *priceless!*" she was saying now, furiously; for she has a temper. "Maggie would put them on the bed and in five years they'd be in rags. Less than that!"

"She can always make some more," I said. "Maggie knows how to quilt."

Dee (Wangero) looked at me with hatred. "You just will not understand. The point is these quilts, *these* quilts!"

"Well," I said, stumped. "What would *you* do with them?"

"Hang them," she said. As if that was the only thing you *could* do with quilts.

Maggie by now was standing in the door. I could almost hear the sound her feet made as they scraped over each other.

"She can have them, Mama," she said, like somebody used to never winning anything, or having anything reserved for her. "I can 'member Grandma Dee without the quilts."

I looked at her hard. She had filled her bottom lip with checkerberry snuff and it gave her face a kind of dopey, hangdog look. It was Grandma Dee and Big Dee who taught her how to quilt herself. She stood there with her scarred hands hidden in the folds of her skirt. She looked at her sister with something like fear but she wasn't mad at her. This was Maggie's portion. This was the way she knew God to work.

When I looked at her like that something hit me in the top of my head and ran down to the soles of my feet. Just like when I'm in church and the spirit of God touches me and I get happy and shout. I did something I never had done before: hugged Maggie to me, then dragged her on into the room, snatched the quilts out of Miss Wangero's hands and dumped them into Maggie's lap. Maggie just sat there on my bed with her mouth open.

"Take one or two of the others," I said to Dee.

But she turned without a word and went out to Hakim-a-barber.

"You just don't understand," she said, as Maggie and I came out to the car.

"What don't I understand?" I wanted to know.

"Your heritage," she said. And then she turned to Maggie, kissed her, and said, "You ought to try to make something of yourself, too, Maggie. It's really a new day

34

for us. But from the way you and Mama still live you'd never know it."

She put on some sunglasses that hid everything above the tip of her nose and her chin.

Maggie smiled; maybe at the sunglasses. But a real smile, not scared. After we watched the car dust settle I asked Maggie to bring me a dip of snuff. And then the two of us sat there just enjoying, until it was time to go in the house and go to bed.

Background to the Story

In Search of
Our Mothers' Gardens

> I described her own nature and temperament.
> Told how they needed a larger life for their expression. . . .
> I pointed out that in lieu of proper channels, her
> emotions had overflowed into paths that dissipated them.
> I talked, beautifully I thought, about an art that would be
> born, an art that would open the way for women the likes
> of her. I asked her to hope, and build up an inner life
> against the coming of that day. . . . I sang, with a strange
> quiver in my voice, a promise song.
> —JEAN TOOMER, *"Avey," Cane*

The poet speaking to a prostitute who falls asleep while he's talking—

When the poet Jean Toomer walked through the South in the early twenties, he discovered a curious thing: black women whose spirituality was so intense, so deep, so *unconscious*, that they were themselves unaware of the richness they held. They stumbled blindly through their lives: creatures so abused an mutilated in body, so dimmed and confused by pain, that they considered themselves unworthy even of hope. In the self-less abstractions their bodies became to the men who used them, they became more than "sexual objects," more even than mere women: they became "Saints." Instead of being perceived as whole persons, their bodies became shrines: what was thought to be their minds became temples suitable for worship. These crazy Saints stared out at the world, wildly, like lunatics—or quietly, like suicides; and the "God" that was in their gaze was as mute as a great stone.

Who were these Saints? These crazy, loony, pitiful women?

Some of them, without a doubt, were our mothers and grandmothers.

In the still heat of the post-Reconstruction South, this is how they seemed to Jean Toomer: exquisite butterflies trapped in an evil honey, toiling away their lives in an era, a century, that did not acknowledge them, except as "the *mule* of the world." They dreamed dreams that no one knew—not even themselves, in any coherent fashion—and saw visions no one could understand. They wandered or sat about the countryside crooning lullabies to ghosts, and drawing the mother of Christ in charcoal on courthouse walls.

They forced their minds to desert their bodies and their striving spirits sought to rise, like frail whirlwinds from the hard red clay. And when those frail whirlwinds fell, in scattered particles, upon the ground, no one mourned. Instead, men lit candles to celebrate the emptiness that remained, as people do who enter a beautiful but vacant space to resurrect a God.

Our mothers and grandmothers, some of them: moving to music not yet written. And they waited.

They waited for a day when the unknown thing that was in them would be made known; but guessed, somehow in their darkness, that on the day of their revelation they would be long dead. Therefore to Toomer they walked, and even ran, in slow motion. For they were going nowhere immediate, and the future was not yet within their grasp. And men took our mothers and grandmothers, "but got no pleasure from it." So complex was their passion and their calm.

To Toomer, they lay vacant and fallow as autumn fields, with harvest time never in sight: and he saw them enter loveless marriages, without joy; and become prostitutes, without resistance; and become mothers of children, without fulfillment.

For these grandmothers and mothers of ours were not Saints, but Artists; driven to a numb and bleeding madness by the springs of creativity in them for which there was no release. They were Creators, who lived lives of spiritual waste, because they were so rich in spirituality—which is the basis of Art—that the strain of enduring their unused and unwanted talent drove them insane. Throwing away this spirituality was their pathetic attempt to lighten the soul to a weight their work-worn, sexually abused bodies could bear.

What did it mean for a black woman to be an artist in our grandmothers' time? In our great-grandmothers' day? It is a question with an answer cruel enough to stop the blood.

Did you have a genius of a great-great-grandmother who died under some ignorant and depraved white overseer's lash? Or was she required to bake biscuits for a lazy backwater tramp, when she cried out in her soul to paint watercolors of sunsets, or the rain falling on the green and peaceful pasturelands? Or was her body broken and forced to bear children (who were more often than not sold away from her)—eight, ten, fifteen, twenty children—when her one joy was the thought of modeling heroic figures of rebellion, in stone or clay?

How was the creativity of the black woman kept alive, year after year and century after century, when for most of the years black people have been in America, it was a punishable crime for a black person to read or write? And the freedom to paint, to sculpt, to expand the mind with action did not exist. Consider, if you can bear to imagine it, what might have been the result if singing, too, had been forbidden by law. Listen to the voices of Bessie Smith, Billie Holiday, Nina Simone, Roberta Flack, and Aretha Franklin, among others, and imagine those voices muzzled for life. Then you may begin to comprehend the lives of our "crazy," "Sainted" mothers and grandmothers. The agony of the lives of women who might have been Poets, Novelists, Essayists, and Short-Story Writers (over a period of centuries), who died with their real gifts stifled within them.

And, if this were the end of the story, we would have

cause to cry out in my paraphrase of Okot p'Bitek's* great poem:

> O, my clanswomen
> Let us all cry together!
> Come,
> Let us mourn the death of our mother,
> The death of a Queen
> The ash that was produced
> By a great fire!
> O, this homestead is utterly dead
> Close the gates
> With *lacari* thorns,
> For our mother
> The creator of the Stool is lost!
> And all the young women
> Have perished in the wilderness!

But this is not the end of the story, for all the young women—our mothers and grandmothers, *ourselves*—have not perished in the wilderness. And if we ask ourselves why, and search for and find the answer, we will know beyond all efforts to erase it from our minds, just exactly who, and of what, we black American women are.

One example, perhaps the most pathetic, most misunderstood one, can provide a backdrop for our mothers' work: Phillis Wheatley, a slave in the 1700s.

Virginia Woolf, in her book *A Room of One's Own*, wrote that in order for a woman to write fiction she must have two things, certainly: a room of her own (with key and lock) and enough money to support herself.

What then are we to make of Phillis Wheatley, a slave, who owned not even herself? This sickly, frail black girl who required a servant of her own at times—her health was so precarious—and who, had she been white, would have been easily considered the intellectual superior of all the women and most of the men in the society of her day.

---

*One of East Africa's best-known contemporary poets.

Virginia Woolf wrote further, speaking of course not of our Phillis, that "any woman born with a great gift in the sixteenth century [insert "eighteenth century," insert "black woman," insert "born or made a slave"] would certainly have gone crazed, shot herself, or ended her days in some lonely cottage outside the village, half witch, half wizard [insert "Saint"], feared and mocked at. For it needs little skill and psychology to be sure that a highly gifted girl who had tried to use her gift for poetry would have been so thwarted and hindered by contrary instincts [add "chains, guns, the lash, the ownership of one's body by someone else, submission to an alien religion"], that she must have lost her health and sanity to a certainty."

The key words, as they relate to Phillis, are "contrary instincts." For when we read the poetry of Phillis Wheatley—as when we read the novels of Nella Larsen or the oddly false-sounding autobiography of that freest of all black women writers, Zora Hurston—evidence of "contrary instincts" is everywhere. Her loyalties were completely divided, as was, without question, her mind.

But how could this be otherwise? Captured at seven, a slave of wealthy, doting whites who instilled in her the "savagery" of the Africa they "rescued" her from . . . one wonders if she was even able to remember her homeland as she had known it, or as it really was.

Yet, because she did try to use her gift for poetry in a world that made her a slave, she was "so thwarted and hindered by . . . contrary instincts, that she . . . lost her health. . . ." In the last years of her brief life, burdened not only with the need to express her gift but also with a penniless, friendless "freedom" and several small children for whom she was forced to do strenuous work to feed, she lost her health, certainly. Suffering from malnutrition and neglect and who knows what mental agonies, Phillis Wheatley died.

So torn by "contrary instincts" was black, kidnapped, enslaved Phillis that her description of "the Goddess"—as she poetically called the Liberty she did not have—is ironically, cruelly humorous. And, in fact, has held Phillis up to ridicule for more than a century. It is usually read prior to hanging Phillis's memory as that of a fool. She wrote:

The Goddess comes, she moves divinely fair,
Olive and laurel binds her *golden* hair
Wherever shines this native of the skies,
Unnumber'd charms and recent graces rise. [My italics]

It is obvious that Phillis, the slave, combed the "Goddess's" hair every morning; prior, perhaps, to bringing in the milk, or fixing her mistress's lunch. She took her imagery from the one thing she saw elevated above all others.

With the benefit of hindsight we ask, "How could she?"

But at last, Phillis, we understand. No more snickering when your stiff, struggling, ambivalent lines are forced on us. We know now that you were not an idiot or a traitor; only a sickly little black girl, snatched from your home and country and made a slave; a woman who still struggled to sing the song that was your gift, although in a land of barbarians who praised you for your bewildered tongue. It is not so much what you sang, as that you kept alive, in so many of our ancestors, *the notion of song.*

Black women are called, in the folklore that so aptly identifies one's status in society, "the *mule* of the world," because we have been handed the burdens that everyone else—*everyone else*—refused to carry. We have also been called "Matriarchs," "Superwomen," and "Mean and Evil Bitches." Not to mention "Castraters" and "Sapphire's Mama."* When we have pleaded for understanding, our character has been distorted; when we have asked for simple caring, we have been handed empty inspirational appellations, then stuck in the farthest corner. When we have asked for love, we have been given children. In short, even our plainer gifts, our labors of fidelity and love, have been knocked down our throats. To be an artist and a black woman, even today, lowers our status in many respects, rather than raises it: and yet, artists we will be.

Therefore we must fearlessly pull out of ourselves and

---

*Sapphire was a black female character on the radio/television series "Amos and Andy" whose constant berating of her husband was exceeded only by what was inflicted on him by his mother-in-law.

look at and identify with our lives the living creativity some of our great-grandmothers were not allowed to know. I stress *some* of them because it is well known that the majority of our great-grandmothers knew, even without "knowing" it, the reality of their spirituality, even if they didn't recognize it beyond what happened in the singing at church—and they never had any intention of giving it up.

How they did it—those millions of black women who were not Phillis Wheatley, or Lucy Terry or Frances Harper or Zora Hurston or Nella Larsen or Bessie Smith; or Elizabeth Catlett, or Katherine Dunham,* either—brings me to the title of this essay, "In Search of Our Mothers' Gardens," which is a personal account that is yet shared, in its theme and its meaning, by all of us. I found, while thinking about the far-reaching world of the creative black woman, that often the truest answer to a question that really matters can be found very close.

In the late 1920s my mother ran away from home to marry my father. Marriage, if not running away, was expected of seventeen-year-old girls. By the time she was twenty, she had two children and was pregnant with a third. Five children later, I was born. And this is how I came to know my mother: she seemed a large, soft, loving-eyed woman who was rarely impatient in our home. Her quick, violent temper was on view only a few times a year, when she battled with the white landlord who had the misfortune to suggest to her that her children did not need to go to school.

She made all the clothes we wore, even my brothers' overalls. She made all the towels and sheets we used. She spent the summers canning vegetables and fruits. She spent the winter evenings making quilts enough to cover all our beds.

---

*Of the lesser known or not previously identified of these African American women, Lucy Terry was an eighteenth-century poet; Frances Harper a nineteenth-century author, abolitionist and woman's rights activist; Elizabeth Catlett is a contemporary sculptor and Katherine Dunham a contemporary choreographer and dancer.

During the "working" day, she labored beside—not be-hind—my father in the fields. Her day began before sunup, and did not end until late at night. There was never a moment for her to sit down, undisturbed, to unravel her own private thoughts; never a time free from interruption—by work or the noisy inquiries of her many children. And yet, it is to my mother—and all our mothers who were not famous—that I went in search of the secret of what has fed that muzzled and often mutilated, but vibrant, creative spirit that the black woman has inherited, and that pops out in wild and unlikely places to this day.

But when, you will ask, did my overworked mother have time to know or care about feeding the creative spirit?

The answer is so simple that many of us have spent years discovering it. We have constantly looked high, when we should have looked high—and low.

For example: in the Smithsonian Institution in Wash-ington, D.C., there hangs a quilt unlike any other in the world. In fanciful, inspired, and yet simple and identifiable figures, it portrays the story of the Crucifixion. It is considered rare, beyond price. Though it follows no known pattern of quilt-making, and though it is made of bits and pieces of worthless rags, it is obviously the work of a person of powerful imagina-tion and deep spiritual feeling. Below this quilt I saw a note that says it was made by "an anonymous Black woman in Ala-bama, a hundred years ago."

If we could locate this "anonymous" black woman from Alabama, she would turn out to be one of our grandmoth-ers—an artist who left her mark in the only materials she could afford, and in the only medium her position in society allowed her to use.

As Virginia Woolf wrote further, in *A Room of One's Own:*

Yet genius of a sort must have existed among women as it must have existed among the working class. [Change this to "slaves" and "the wives and daughters of sharecroppers."] Now and again an Emily Brontë or a Robert Burns [change this to "a Zora Hurston or a Richard Wright"] blazes out and proves its presence. But certainly it never got itself on to paper. When, however, one reads of a witch being ducked, of a woman possessed by devils [or "Sainthood"], of a wise woman selling herbs [our root workers], or even a very remarkable man who had a mother, then I think we are on the track of a lost novelist, a suppressed poet, of some mute and inglorious Jane Austen. . . . Indeed, I would venture to guess that Anon, who wrote so many poems without signing them, was often a woman.

And so our mothers and grandmothers have, more often than not anonymously, handed on the creative spark, the seed of the flower they themselves never hoped to see; or like a sealed letter they could not plainly read.

And so it is, certainly, with my own mother. Unlike "Ma" Rainey's songs, which retained their creator's name even while blasting forth from Bessie Smith's mouth, no song or poem will bear my mother's name. Yet so many of the stories that I write, that we all write, are my mother's stories. Only recently did I fully realize this: that through years of listening to my mother's stories of her life, I have absorbed not only the stories themselves, but something of the manner in which she spoke, something of the urgency that involves the knowledge that her stories—like her life—must be recorded. It is probably for this reason that so much of what I have written is about characters whose counterparts in real life are so much older than I am.

But the telling of these stories, which came from my mother's lips as naturally as breathing, was not the only way my mother showed herself as an artist. For stories, too, were subject to being distracted, to dying without conclusion. Dinners must be started, and cotton must be gathered before the big rains. The artist that was and is my mother showed itself to me only after many years. This is what I finally noticed:

Like Mem, a character in *The Third Life of Grange Copeland*, my mother adorned with flowers whatever shabby house we were forced to live in. And not just your typical straggly country stand of zinnias, either. She planted ambitious gardens—and still does—with over fifty different varieties of plants that bloom profusely from early March until late November. Before she left home for the fields, she watered her flowers, chopped up the grass, and laid out new beds. When she returned from the fields she might divide clumps of bulbs, dig a cold pit, uproot and replant roses, or prune branches from her taller bushes or trees—until night came and it was too dark to see.

Whatever she planted grew as if by magic, and her fame as a grower of flowers spread over three counties. Because of her creativity with her flowers, even my memories of poverty are seen through a screen of blooms—sunflowers, petunias, roses, dahlias, forsythia, spirea, delphiniums, verbena . . . and on and on.

And I remember people coming to my mother's yard to be given cuttings from her flowers; I hear again the praise showered on her because whatever rocky soil she landed on, she turned into a garden. A garden so brilliant with colors, so original in its design, so magnificent with life and creativity, that to this day people drive by our house in Georgia—perfect strangers and imperfect strangers—and ask to stand or walk among my mother's art.

I notice that it is only when my mother is working in her flowers that she is radiant, almost to the point of being invisible—except as Creator: hand and eye. She is involved in work her soul must have. Ordering the universe in the image of her personal conception of Beauty.

Her face, as she prepares the Art that is her gift, is a legacy of respect she leaves to me, for all that illuminates and cherishes life. She has handed down respect for the possibilities—and the will to grasp them.

For her, so hindered and intruded upon in so many ways, being an artist has still been a daily part of her life. This ability to hold on, even in very simple ways, is work black women have done for a very long time.

This poem is not enough, but it is something, for the woman who literally covered the holes in our walls with sunflowers:

> They were women then
> My mama's generation
> Husky of voice—Stout of
> Step

With fists as well as
Hands
How they battered down
Doors
And ironed
Starched white
Shirts
How they led
Armies
Headragged Generals
Across mined
Fields
Booby-trapped
Kitchens
To discover books
Desks
A place for us
How they knew what we
Must know
Without knowing a page
Of it
Themselves

Guided by my heritage of a love of beauty and a respect for strength—in search of my mother's garden, I found my own.

And perhaps in Africa over two hundred years ago, there was just such a mother; perhaps she painted vivid and daring decorations in oranges and yellows and greens on the walls of her hut; perhaps she sang—in a voice like Roberta Flack's—*sweetly* over the compounds of her village; perhaps she wove the most stunning mats or told the most ingenious stories of all the village storytellers. Perhaps she was herself a poet—though only her daughter's name is signed to the poems that we know.

Perhaps Phillis Wheatley's mother was also an artist.

Perhaps in more than Phillis Wheatley's biological life is her mother's signature made clear.

1974

For My Sister Molly
Who in the Fifties

Once made a fairy rooster from
Mashed potatoes
Whose eyes I forget
But green onions were his tail
And his two legs were carrot sticks
A tomato slice his crown.
Who came home on vacation
When the sun was hot
and cooked
and cleaned
And minded least of all
The children's questions
A million or more
Pouring in on her
Who had been to school
And knew (and told us too) that certain
Words were no longer good
And taught me not to say us for we
No matter what "Sonny said" up the
road.

FOR MY SISTER MOLLY WHO IN THE FIFTIES
Knew Hamlet well and read into the night
And coached me in my songs of Africa

———

From *Revolutionary Petunias and Other Poems* (New York: Harcourt Brace Jovanovich, 1972). Copyright © 1972 by Alice Walker.

A continent I never knew
But learned to love
Because "they" she said could carry
A tune
And spoke in accents never heard
In Eatonton.
Who read from *Prose and Poetry*
And loved to read "Sam McGee from Tennessee"
On nights the fire was burning low
And Christmas wrapped in angel hair
And I for one prayed for snow.

WHO IN THE FIFTIES
Knew all the written things that made
Us laugh and stories by
The hour   Waking up the story buds
Like fruit. Who walked among the flowers
And brought them inside the house
And smelled as good as they
And looked as bright.
Who made dresses, braided
Hair. Moved chairs about
Hung things from walls
Ordered baths
Frowned on wasp bites
And seemed to know the endings
Of all the tales
I had forgot.

*

WHO OFF INTO THE UNIVERSITY
Went exploring   To London and
To Rotterdam
Prague and to Liberia
Bringing back the news to us
Who knew none of it
But followed
crops and weather

52

funerals and
Methodist Homecoming;
easter speeches,
groaning church.

WHO FOUND ANOTHER WORLD
Another life   With gentlefolk
Far less trusting
And moved and moved and changed
Her name
And sounded precise
When she spoke   And frowned away
Our sloppishness.

WHO SAW US SILENT
Cursed with fear   A love burning
Inexpressible
And sent me money not for me
But for "College."
Who saw me grow through letters
The words misspelled   But not
The longing   Stretching
Growth
The tied and twisting
Tongue
Feet no longer bare
Skin no longer burnt against
The cotton.

WHO BECAME SOMEONE OVERHEAD
A light   A thousand watts
Bright and also blinding
And saw my brothers cloddish
And me destined to be
Wayward

My mother remote   My father
A wearisome farmer
With heartbreaking
Nails.

FOR MY SISTER MOLLY WHO IN THE FIFTIES
Found much
Unbearable
Who walked where few had
Understood   And sensed our
Groping after light
And saw some extinguished
And no doubt mourned.

FOR MY SISTER MOLLY WHO IN THE FIFTIES
Left us.
　　　　**

Interview with
Alice Walker

Alice Walker's first collection of poems, *Once,* was published when she was only twenty-four. Her first novel, *The Third Life of Grange Copeland,* appeared two years later. Her second collection of poems, *Revolutionary Petunias,* is due in 1973, and a collection of short stories will be published either in late 1973 or early 1974. All of this suggests how productive Alice Walker has been in so short a time. Along the way she has also managed to publish essays, teach, and raise a family. Yet the most amazing thing is less the ambition she has demonstrated than the maturity she has achieved so early.

The thematic scope of her poetry is the past, both personal and historical. *Once* catalogues her experiences in the civil rights demonstrations of the 1960s and her travels in Africa. The poems are highly personal, recounting first loves and early disappointments. *Revolutionary Petunias* indicates that since her first collection, Walker learned more about both her craft and her subjects. The poems are less marked by abstract observations than by a dependance upon brief anecdotes and precise memories. The language is sharper; the forms, more disciplined. And there is a simplicity of style and imagery which, as Yeats knew, is arrived at only after much labor, but appears spontaneous. More so than the first volume, *Revolutionary Petunias* focuses on specific memories that belong to her family, her small Southern town, and herself.

Walker's most notable accomplishment, however, has been in fiction. *The Third Life of Grange Copeland* traces the life of its hero from his early boyhood through his reckless youth, and finally to his old age. It is a novel of education, in which Walker demonstrates a remarkable ability to show the change and transformation of a character without violating either her characters or human nature. For her subject she chooses a character

From *Interviews with Black Writers,* by John O'Brien (New York: Liveright, 1973), 185–212. Copyright © 1973 by Liveright Publishing Corporation.

who is uneducated, oftentimes inarticulate, deprived, abused by his family, and usually trapped by circumstances which he seems unable to control. In other words, she picks an unlikely character in whom to explore the possibility of growth and change. Most impressive about her fiction is Walker's power as a storyteller. She does not indulge in awkward asides in which characters have revelations, or in extended dialogues where they work out the themes of the novel. Walker depends upon her capacity to render theme in terms of action.

The interview was arranged through the help of Miss Walker's editor, Hiram Haydn. Because of a complicated set of circumstances we were forced to conduct the interview through the mail. I sent a long list of questions which she reshaped and worked together, so that—rather than answering specific questions—she most frequently developed brief essays. Her responses are expansive, illuminating, and painstakingly phrased. Miss Walker lives in Jackson, Mississippi, where she is at work on another novel.

INTERVIEWER: Could you describe your early life and what led you to begin writing?

WALKER: I have always been a solitary person, and since I was eight years old (and the recipient of a disfiguring scar, since corrected, somewhat), I have daydreamed—not of fairytales— but of falling on swords, of putting guns to my heart or head, and of slashing my wrists with a razor. For a long time I thought I was very ugly and disfigured. This made me shy and timid, and I often reacted to insults and slights that were not intended. I discovered the cruelty (legendary) of children, and of relatives, and could not recognize it as the curiosity it was.

I believe, though, that it was from this period—from my solitary, lonely position, the position of an outcast—that I began to really see people and things, to really notice relationships and to learn to be patient enough to care about how they turned out. I no longer felt like the little girl I was. I felt old, and because I felt I was unpleasant to look at, filled with shame. I retreated into solitude, and read stories and began to write poems.

But it was not until my last year in college that I realized, nearly, the consequences of my daydreams. That year I made myself acquainted with every philosopher's position on suicide, because by that time it did not seem frightening or even odd—but only inevitable. Nietzsche and Camus made the most sense, and were neither maudlin nor pious. God's displeasure didn't seem to matter much to them, and I had reached the same conclusion. But in addition to finding such dispassionate commentary from them—although both hinted at the cowardice involved, and that bothered me—I had been to Africa during the summer, and returned to school healthy and brown, and loaded down with sculptures and orange fabric—and pregnant.

I felt at the mercy of everything, including my own body, which I had learned to accept as a kind of casing over what I considered my real self. As long as it functioned properly, I dressed it, pampered it, led it into acceptable arms, and forgot about it. But now it refused to function properly. I was so sick I could not even bear the smell of fresh air. And I had no money, and I was, essentially—as I had been since grade school—alone. I felt there was no way out, and I was not romantic enough to believe in maternal instincts alone as a means of survival; in any case, I did not seem to possess those instincts. But I knew no one who knew about the secret, scary thing abortion was. And so, when all my efforts at finding an abortionist failed, I planned to kill myself, or—as I thought of it then—to "give myself a little rest." I stopped going down the hill to meals because I vomited incessantly, even when nothing came up but yellow, bitter bile. I lay on my bed in a cold sweat, my head spinning.

While I was lying there, I thought of my mother, to whom abortion is a sin; her face appeared framed in the window across from me, her head wreathed in sunflowers and giant elephant-ears (my mother's flowers love her; they grow as tall as she wants); I thought of my father, that suspecting, once-fat, slowly shrinking man, who had not helped me at all since I was twelve years old, when he bought me a pair of ugly saddle-oxfords I refused to wear. I thought of my sisters, who had their own problems (when approached with the problem I had; one sister never replied, the other told me—in forty-five minutes of long-distance carefully enunciated language—that

I was a slut). I thought of the people at my high-school graduation who had managed to collect seventy-five dollars, to send
me to college. I thought of my sister's check for a hundred
dollars that she gave me for finishing high school at the head
of my class: a check I never cashed, because I knew it would
bounce.

I think it was at this point that I allowed myself exactly
two self-pitying tears; I had wasted so much, how dared I? But
I hated myself for crying, so I stopped, comforted by knowing
I would not have to cry—or see anyone else cry—again.

I did not eat or sleep for three days. My mind refused,
at times, to think about my problem at all—it jumped ahead
to the solution. I prayed to—but I don't know Who or What I
prayed to, or even if I did. Perhaps I prayed to God awhile,
and then to the Great Void awhile. When I thought of my family, and when—on the third day—I began to see their faces
around the walls, I realized they would be shocked and hurt
to learn of my death, but I felt they would not care deeply at
all, when they discovered I was pregnant. Essentially, they
would believe I was evil. They would be ashamed of me.

For three days I lay on the bed with a razorblade under
my pillow. My secret was known to three friends only—all in-
experienced (except verbally), and helpless. They came often
to cheer me up, to bring me up-to-date on things as frivolous
as classes. I was touched by their kindness, and loved them.
But each time they left, I took out my razorblade and pressed
it deep into my arm. I practiced a slicing motion. So that when
there was no longer any hope, I would be able to cut my wrists
quickly, and (I hoped) painlessly.

In those three days, I said good-bye to the world (this
seemed a high-flown sentiment, even then, but everything
was beginning to be unreal); I realized how much I loved it,
and how hard it would be not to see the sunrise every morning, the snow, the sky, the trees, the rocks, the faces of people,
all so different (and it was during this period that all things
began to flow together; the face of one of my friends revealed
itself to be the friendly, gentle face of a lion, and I asked her
one day if I could touch her face and stroke her mane. I felt
her face and hair, and she really was a lion; I began to feel the
possibility of someone as worthless as myself attaining wis-

dom). But I found, as I had found on the porch of that building in Liberty County, Georgia—when rocks and bottles bounced off me as I sat looking up at the stars—that I was not afraid of death. In a way, I began looking forward to it. I felt tired. Most of the poems on suicide in *Once* come from my feelings during this period of waiting.

On the last day for miracles, one of my friends telephoned to say someone had given her a telephone number. I called from the school, hoping for nothing, and made an appointment. I went to see the doctor and he put me to sleep. When I woke up, my friend was standing over me holding a red rose. She was a blonde, gray-eyed girl, who loved horses and tennis, and she said nothing as she handed me back my life. That moment is engraved on my mind—her smile, sad and pained and frightfully young—as she tried so hard to stand by me and be my friend. She drove me back to the school and tucked me in. My other friend, brown, a wisp of blue and scarlet, with hair like thunder, brought me food.

That week I wrote without stopping (except to eat and go to the toilet) almost all of the poems in *Once*—with the exception of one or two, perhaps, and these I no longer remember.

I wrote them all in a tiny blue notebook that I can no longer find—the African ones first, because the vitality and color and friendships in Africa rushed over me in dreams the first night I slept. I had not thought about Africa (except to talk about it) since I returned. All the sculptures and weavings I had given away, because they seemed to emit an odor that made me more nauseous than the smell of fresh air. Then I wrote the suicide poems, because I felt I understood the part played in suicide by circumstances and fatigue. I also began to understand how alone woman is, because of her body. Then I wrote the love poems (love real and love imagined), and tried to reconcile myself to all things human. "Johann" is the most extreme example of this need to love even the most unfamiliar, the most fearful. For, actually, when I traveled in Germany I was in a constant state of terror, and no amount of flattery from handsome young German men could shake it. Then I wrote the poems of struggle in the South. The picketing, the marching, all the things that had been buried, because when

I thought about them the pain was a paralysis of intellectual and moral confusion. The anger and humiliation I had suffered was always in conflict with the elation, the exaltation, the *joy* I felt when I could leave each vicious encounter or confrontation whole, and not—like the people before me— spewing obscenities, or throwing bricks. For, during those encounters, I had begun to comprehend what it meant to be lost.

Each morning, the poems finished during the night were stuffed under Muriel Rukeyser's door—her classroom was an old gardener's cottage in the middle of the campus. Then I would hurry back to my room to write some more. I didn't care what she did with the poems. I only knew I wanted someone to read them as if they were new leaves sprouting from an old tree. The same energy that impelled me to write them carried them to her door.

This was the winter of 1965, and my last three months in college. I was twenty-one years old, although *Once* was not published till three years later, when I was twenty-four (Muriel Rukeyser gave the poems to her agent, who gave them to Hiram Haydn—who is still my editor at Harcourt, Brace— who said right away that he wanted them; so I cannot claim to have had a hard time publishing, yet). By the time *Once* was published, it no longer seemed important—I was surprised when it went, almost immediately, into a second printing—that is, the book itself did not seem to me important; only the writing of the poems, which clarified for me how very much I love being alive. It was this feeling of gladness that carried over into my first published short story, "To Hell With Dying," about an old man saved from death countless times by the love of his neighbor's children. I was the children, and the old man.

I have gone into this memory because I think it might be important for other women to share. I don't enjoy contemplating it; I wish it had never happened. But if it had not, I firmly believe I would never have survived to be a writer. I know I would not have survived at all.

Since that time, it seems to me that all of my poems—and I write groups of poems rather than singles—are written when I have successfully pulled myself out of a completely numbing despair, and stand again in the sunlight.

Writing poems is my way of celebrating with the world that I have not committed suicide the evening before.

Langston Hughes wrote in his autobiography that when he was sad, he wrote his best poems. When he was happy, he didn't write anything. This is true of me, where poems are concerned. When I am happy (or neither happy nor sad), I write essays, short stories, and novels. Poems—even happy ones—emerge from an accumulation of sadness.

INTERVIEWER: Can you describe the process of writing a poem? How do you know, for instance, when you have captured what you wanted to?

WALKER: The writing of my poetry is never consciously planned; although I become aware that there are certain emotions I would like to explore. Perhaps my unconscious begins working on poems from these emotions long before I am aware of it. I have learned to wait patiently (sometimes refusing good lines, images, when they come to me, for fear they are not lasting), until a poem is ready to present itself—*all* of itself, if possible. I sometimes feel the urge to write poems way in advance of ever sitting down to write. There is a definite restlessness, a kind of feverish excitement that is tinged with dread. The dread is because after writing each batch of poems I am always convinced that I will never write poems again. I become aware that I am controlled by them, not the other way around. I put off writing as long as I can. Then I lock myself in my study, write lines and lines and lines, then put them away, underneath other papers, without looking at them for a long time. I am afraid that if I read them too soon they will turn into trash; or worse, something so topical and transient as to have no meaning—not even to me—after a few weeks. (This is how my later poetry-writing differs from the way I wrote *Once*.) I also attempt, in this way, to guard against the human tendency to try to make poetry carry the weight of half-truths, of cleverness. I realize that while I am writing poetry, I am so high as to feel invisible, and in that condition it is possible to write anything.

INTERVIEWER: What determines your interests as a writer? Are there preoccupations you have which you are not conscious of until you begin writing?

WALKER: You ask about "preoccupations." I am preoccupied with the spiritual survival, the survival *whole* of my people. But beyond that, I am committed to exploring the oppressions, the insanities, the loyalties, and the triumphs of black women. In *The Third Life of Grange Copeland*, ostensibly about a man and his son, it is the women and how they are treated that colors everything. In my new book *In Love & Trouble: Stories of Black Women*, thirteen women—mad, raging, loving, resentful, hateful, strong, ugly, weak, pitiful, and magnificent, try to live with the loyalty to black men that characterizes all of their lives. For me, black women are the most fascinating creations in the world.

Next to them, I place the old people—male and female—who persist in their beauty in spite of everything. How do they do this, knowing what they do? Having lived what they have lived? It is a mystery, and so it lures me into their lives. My grandfather, at eighty-five, never been out of Georgia, looks at me with the glad eyes of a three-year-old. The pressures on his life have been unspeakable. How can he look at me in this way? "Your eyes are widely open flowers / Only their centers are darkly clenched / To conceal / Mysteries / That lure me to a keener blooming / Then I know / And promise a secret / I must have." All of my "love poems" apply to old, young, man, woman, child, and growing things.

INTERVIEWER: Your novel, *The Third Life of Grange Copeland,* reaffirms an observation I have made about many novels: there is a pervasive optimism in these novels, an indomitable belief in the future, and in man's capacity for survival. I think that this is generally opposed to what one finds in the mainstream of American literature. One can cite Ahab, Gatsby, Jake Barnes, Young Goodman Brown. . . . You seem to be writing out of a vision which conflicts with that of the culture around you. What I may be pointing out, is that you do not seem to see the profound evil present in much of American literature.

WALKER: It is possible that while male writers are more conscious of their own evil (which, after all, has been documented for several centuries—in words and in the ruin of the land, the earth—) than black male writers, who, along with black and white women, have seen themselves as the recipients of that evil, and therefore on the side of Christ, of the oppressed, of the innocent.

The white women writers that I admire: [Kate] Chopin, the Brontës, Simone De Beauvoir, and Doris Lessing, are well aware of their own oppression and search incessantly for a kind of salvation. Their characters can always envision a solution, an evolution to higher consciousness on the part of society, even when society itself cannot. Even when society is in the process of killing them for their vision. Generally, too, they are more tolerant of mystery than is Ahab, who wishes to dominate, rather than be on equal terms with the whale.

If there is one thing African-Americans have retained of their African heritage, it is probably animism: a belief that makes it possible to view all creation as living, as being inhabited by spirit. This belief encourages knowledge perceived intuitively. It does not surprise me, personally, that scientists now are discovering that trees, plants, flowers, have feelings . . . emotions, that they shrink when yelled at; that they faint when an evil person is about who might hurt them.

One thing I try to have in my life and in my fiction is an awareness of and openness to mystery, which, to me, is deeper than any politics, race, or geographical location. In the poems I read, a sense of mystery, a deepening of it, is what I look for—for that is what I respond to. I have been influenced—especially in the poems in *Once*—by Zen epigrams and by Japanese haiku. I think my respect for short forms comes from this. I was delighted to learn that in three or four lines a poet can express mystery, evoke beauty and pleasure, paint a picture—and not dissect or analyze in any way. The insects, the fish, the birds, and the apple blossoms in haiku are still whole. They have not been turned into something else. They are allowed their own majesty, instead of being used to emphasize the majesty of people; usually the majesty of the poets writing.

INTERVIEWER: A part of your vision—which is explored in your novel—is a belief in change, both personal and political. By showing the change in Grange Copeland you suggest the possibility of change in the political and social systems within which he lives.

WALKER: Yes, I believe in change: change personal, and change in society. I have experienced a revolution (unfinished, without question, but one whose new order is everywhere on view) in the South. And I grew up—until I refused to go—in the Methodist Church, which taught me that Paul *will* sometimes change on the way to Damascus, and that Moses—that beloved old man—went through so many changes he made God mad. So Grange Copeland was *expected* to change. He was fortunate enough to be touched by love of something beyond himself. Brownfield did not change, because he was not prepared to give his life for anything, or *to* anything. He was the kind of man who could never understand Jesus (or Ché or King or Malcolm or Medgar) except as the white man's tool. He could find nothing of value within himself and he did not have the courage to imagine a life without the existence of white people to act as a foil. To become what he hated was his inevitable destiny.

A bit more about the "Southern Revolution." When I left Eatonton, Georgia, to go off to Spelman College in Atlanta (where I stayed, uneasily, for two years), I deliberately sat in the front section of the Greyhound bus. A white woman complained to the driver. He—big and red and ugly—ordered me to move. I moved. But in those seconds of moving, everything changed. I was eager to bring an end to the South that permitted my humiliation. During my sophomore year I stood on the grass in front of Trevor-Arnett Library at Atlanta University and I listened to the young leaders of SNCC. John Lewis was there, and so was Julian Bond—thin, well starched and ironed in light-colored jeans, he looked (with his cropped hair that still tried to curl) like a poet (which he was). Everyone was beautiful, because everyone (and I think now of Ruby Doris Robinson who since died) was conquering fear by holding the hands of the persons next to them. In those days, in Atlanta, springtime turned the air green. I've never known this to happen in any other place I've been—not even in Uganda, where green, on hills, plants, trees, begins to dominate the imagination. It was as if the air turned into a kind of water—and the short walk from Spelman to Morehouse was like walking through a green sea. Then, of course, the cherry trees—cut down, now, I think—that were always blooming away while we—young and bursting with fear and determination to change our world—thought, beyond our fervid singing, of death. It is not surprising, considering the intertwined thoughts of beauty and death, that the majority of the people in and around SNCC at that time were lovers of Camus.

Random memories of that period: myself, moving like someone headed for the guillotine, with (as my marching mate) a beautiful girl who spoke French and came to Spelman from Tuskegee, Alabama ("Chic Freedom's Reflection" in *Once*), whose sense of style was unfaltering, in the worst of circumstances. She was the only really black-skinned girl at Spelman who would turn up dressed in stark white from head to toe—because she knew, instinctively, that white made an already beautiful black girl look like the answer to everybody's prayer: myself, marching about in front of a restaurant, seeing—inside—the tables set up with clean napkins and glasses of water. The owner standing in front of us barring the door. A Jewish man who went mad on the spot, and fell to the floor: myself, dressed in a pink faille dress, with my African roommate, my first real girl friend, walking up the broad white steps of a broad white church. And men (white) in blue suits and bow-ties materializing on the steps above with axehandles in their hands (see: "The Welcome Table" in *In Love and Trouble*). We turned and left. It was a bright, sunny day. Myself, sitting on a porch in Liberty County, Georgia, at night, after picketing the jailhouse (where a local black schoolteacher was held) and holding in my arms the bleeding head of a little girl—where is she now?—maybe eight or ten years old, but small, who had been cut by a broken bottle held by one of the mob in front of us. In this memory there is a white girl I grew to respect because she never flinched and never closed her eyes, no matter what the mob—where are they now?—threw. Later, in New York, she tried to get me to experiment with LSD with her, and the only reason I never did was because on the night we planned to try it I had a bad cold. I believe the reason she never closed her eyes was because she couldn't believe what she was seeing. We tried to keep in touch—but, because I had never had very much (not even a house that didn't leak), I was always conscious of the need to be secure. Because she came from an eleven-room house in the suburbs of Philadelphia and, I assume, never had worried about material security, our deepest feelings began to miss each other. I identified her as someone who could afford to play poor for awhile (her poverty interrupted occasionally by trips abroad), and she probably identified me as one of those inflexible black women black men constantly complain about: the kind who interrupt lighthearted romance by saying, "Yes, well . . . but what are the children going to eat?"

The point is that less than ten years after all these things I walk about Georgia (and Mississippi)—eating, sleeping, loving, singing, burying the dead—the way men and women are supposed to do, in a place that is the only "home" they've ever known. There is only one "for coloreds" sign left in Eatonton, and it is on a black man's barber shop. He is merely outdated. Booster, if you read this, *change* your sign!

INTERVIEWER: I wonder how clear it was to you what you were going to do in your novel before you started? Did you know, for instance, that Grange Copeland was capable of change?

WALKER: I see the work that I have done already as a foundation. That being so, I suppose I knew when I started *The Third Life of Grange Copeland* that it would have to cover several generations, and nearly a century of growth and upheaval. It begins around 1900 and ends in the sixties. But my first draft (which was never used, not even one line, in the final version) began with Ruth as a civil-rights lawyer in Georgia going to rescue her father, Brownfield Copeland, from a drunken accident, and to have a confrontation with him. In that version she is married—also to a lawyer—and they are both committed to insuring freedom for black people in the South. In Georgia, specifically. There was lots of love-making and courage in that version. But it was too recent, too superficial—everything seemed a product of the immediate present. And I believe nothing ever is.

So, I brought in the grandfather. Because all along I wanted to explore the relationship between parents and children: specifically between daughters and their father (this is most interesting, I've always felt; for example, in "The Child Who Favored Daughter" in *In Love and Trouble,* the father cuts off the breasts of his daughter because she falls in love with a white boy; why this, unless there is sexual jealousy?), and I wanted to learn, myself, how it happens that the hatred a child can have for a parent becomes inflexible. *And* I wanted to explore the relationship between men and women, and why women are always condemned for doing what men do as an expression of their masculinity. Why are women so easily "tramps" and "traitors" when men are heroes for engaging in the same activity? Why do women stand for this?

My new novel will be about several women who came of age during the sixties and were active (or not active) in the Movement in the South. I am exploring their backgrounds, familial and sibling connections, their marriages, affairs, and political persuasions, as they grow toward a fuller realization (and recognition) of themselves.

Since I put together my course on black women writers, which was taught first at Wellesley College and later at the University of Massachusetts, I have felt the need for real critical and biographical work on these writers. As a beginning, I am writing a long personal essay on my own discovery of these writers (designed, primarily, for lectures), and I hope soon to visit the birthplace and home of Zora Neale Hurston, Eatonville, Florida. I am so involved with my own writing that I don't think there will be time for me to attempt the long, scholarly involvement that all these writers require. I am hopeful, however, that as their books are reissued and used in classrooms across the country, someone will do this. If no one does (or if no one does it to my satisfaction), I feel it is my duty (such is the fervor of love) to do it myself.

INTERVIEWER: Have women writers, then, influenced your writing more than male? Which writers do you think have had the most direct influence upon you?

WALKER: I read all of the Russian writers I could find, in my sophomore year in college. I read them as if they were a delicious cake. I couldn't get enough: Tolstoi (especially his short stories, and the novels, *The Kruetzer Sonata* and *Resurrec-*

tion—which taught me the importance of diving through politics and social forecasts to dig into the essential spirit of individual persons—because otherwise, characters, no matter what political or current social issue they stand for, will not live), and Dostoevsky, who found his truths where everyone else seemed afraid to look, and Turgenev, Gorky and Gogol—who made me think that Russia must have something floating about in the air that writers breathe from the time they are born. The only thing that began to bother me, many years later, was that I could find almost nothing written by a Russian woman writer.

Unless poetry has mystery, many meanings, and some ambiguities (necessary for mystery) I am not interested in it. Outside of Bashō and Shiki and other Japanese haiku poets, I read and was impressed by the poetry of Li Po, the Chinese poet, Emily Dickinson, e.e. cummings (deeply) and Robert Graves—especially his poems in *Man Does, Woman Is;* which is surely a pure male-chauvinist title, but I did not think about that then. I liked Graves because he took it as given that passionate love between man and woman does not last forever. He enjoyed the moment, and didn't bother about the future. My poem, "The Man in the Yellow Terry," is very much influenced by Graves.

I also loved Ovid and Catullus. During the whole period of discovering haiku and the sensual poems of Ovid, the poems of e.e. cummings and William Carlos Williams, my feet did not touch the ground. I ate, I slept, I studied other things (like European history) without ever doing more than giving it serious thought. It could not change me from one moment to the next, as poetry could.

I wish I had been familiar with the poems of Gwendolyn Brooks when I was in college. I stumbled on them later. If there was ever a *born* poet, I think it is Brooks. Her natural way of looking at anything, of commenting on anything, comes out as a vision, in language that is peculiar to her. It is clear that she is a poet from the way your whole spiritual past begins to float around in your throat when you are reading, just as it is clear from the first line of *Cane* that Jean Toomer is a poet, blessed with a soul that is surprised by nothing. It is not unusual to weep when reading Brooks, just as when read-

ing Toomer's "Song of the Sun" it is not unusual to comprehend—in a flash—what a dozen books on black people's
history fail to illuminate. I have embarrassed my classes occasionally by standing in front of them in tears as Toomer's
poem about "some genius from the South" flew through my
body like a swarm of golden butterflies on their way toward a
destructive sun. Like DuBois, Toomer was capable of compre-
hending the black soul. It is not "soul," which *can* become a
cliché, but rather something to be illuminated rather than
explained.

The poetry of Arna Bontemps has strange effects on me
too. He is a great poet, even if he is not recognized as such
until after his death. Or is never acknowledged. The passion
and compassion in his poem, "A Black Man Talks of Reaping,"
shook the room I was sitting in the first time I read it. The
ceiling began to revolve and a breeze—all the way from Alabama—blew through the room. A tide of spiritual good health
tingled the bottom of my toes. I changed. Became someone
the same, but different. I understood, at last, what the trans-
ference of energy was.

It is impossible to list all of the influences on one's
work. How can you even remember the indelible impression
upon you of a certain look on your mother's face? But random
influences are these: music; which is the art I most envy.

Then there's travel—which really made me love the
world, its vastness, and variety. How moved I was to know that
there is no center of the universe. Entebbe, Uganda or Brati-
slava, Czechoslovakia exist no matter what we are doing here.
Some writers—Camara Laye, or the man who wrote *One
Hundred Years of Solitude* (Gabriel García Márquez)—have
illumined this fact brilliantly in their fiction, which brings me
to African writers I *hope* to be influenced by: Okot p'Bitck has
written my favorite modern poem, "Song of Lawino." I am also
crazy about *The Concubine* by Elechi Amadi (a perfect story,
I think), *The Radiance of the King,* by Camara Laye, and
Maru, by Bessie Head. These writers do not seem afraid of
fantasy, of myth and mystery. Their work deepens one's com-
prehension of life by going beyond the bounds of realism. They
are like musicians: at one with their cultures and their historical subconscious.

Flannery O'Connor has also influenced my work. To me, she is the best of the white southern writers, including Faulkner. For one thing, she practiced economy. She also knew that the question of race was really just the first question on a long list. This is hard for just about everybody to accept, we've been trying to answer it for so long.

I did not read *Cane* until 1967, but it has been reverberating in me to an astonishing degree. *I love it passionately; could not possibly exist without it. Cane* and *Their Eyes Were Watching God* are probably my favorite books by black American writers. Jean Toomer has a very feminine sensibility (or phrased another way, he is both feminine and masculine in his perceptions), unlike most black male writers. He loved women.

Like Toomer, Zora Neale Hurston was never afraid to let her characters be themselves, funny talk and all. She was incapable of being embarrassed by anything black people did, and so was able to write about everything with freedom and fluency. My feeling is that Zora Neale Hurston is probably one of the most misunderstood, least appreciated writers of this century. Which is a pity. She is great. A writer of courage, and incredible humor, with poetry in every line.

When I started teaching my course in black women writers at Wellesley (the first one, I think, ever), I was worried that Zora's use of black English of the twenties would throw some of the students off. It didn't. They loved it. They said it was like reading Thomas Hardy, only better. In that same course I taught Nella Larsen, Frances Watkins Harper (poetry and novel), Dorothy West, Ann Petry, Paule Marshall,* etc. Also Kate Chopin and Virginia Woolf—not because they were black, obviously, but because they were women and wrote, as the black women did, on the condition of humankind from the perspective of women. It is interesting to read Woolf's *A Room of One's Own* while reading the poetry of Phillis Wheatley, to read Larsen's *Quicksand* along with [Kate Chopin's]

---

* Of the last three named African American women writers of the twentieth century, Dorothy West is best known for *The Living Is Easy* (1947), Petry for *The Street* (1946), and Marshall for *Brown Girl, Brownstones* (1959).

The Awakening. The deep-throated voice of Sojourner Truth*
tends to drift across the room while you're reading. If you're
not a feminist already, you become one.

INTERVIEWER: Why do you think that the black woman writer
has been so ignored in America? Does she have even more
difficulty than the black male writer, who perhaps has just
begun to gain recognition?

WALKER: There are two reasons why the black woman writer
is not taken as seriously as the black male writer. One is that
she's a woman. Critics seem unusually ill-equipped to intelli-
gently discuss and analyze the works of black women. Generally, they do not even make the attempt; they prefer, rather, to
talk about the lives of black women writers, not about what
they write. And, since black women writers are not—it would
seem—very likable—until recently they were the least willing
worshipers of male supremacy—comments about them tend
to be cruel.

In Nathan Huggins's very readable book, *Harlem Renaissance,* he hardly refers to Zora Neale Hurston's work, except negatively. He quotes from Wallace Thurman's novel,
Infants of the Spring, at length, giving us the words of a character, "Sweetie Mae Carr," who is allegedly based on Zora
Neale Hurston. "Sweetie Mae" is a writer noted more "for her
ribald wit and personal effervescence than for any actual literary work. She was a great favorite among those whites who
went in for Negro prodigies." Mr. Huggins goes on for several
pages, never quoting Zora Neale Hurston herself, but rather
the opinions of others about her character. He does say that
she was "a master of dialect," but adds that "her greatest
weakness was carelessness or indifference to her art."

Having taught Zora Neale Hurston, and of course, having read her work myself, I am stunned. Personally, I do not
care if Zora Hurston was fond of her white women friends.
When she was a child in Florida, working for nickels and
dimes, two white women helped her escape. Perhaps this

---

*Born Isabella Baumfree, a preacher and abolitionist who raised funds for the
Union during the Civil War, Truth is known for her speech to the Seneca Falls
Convention, "Ain't I a Woman?"

explains it. But even if it doesn't, so what? Her work, far from being done carelessly, is done (especially in *Their Eyes Were Watching God*) almost too perfectly. She took the trouble to capture the beauty of rural black expression. She saw poetry where other writers merely saw failure to cope with English. She was so at ease with her blackness it never occurred to her that she should act one way among blacks and another among whites (as her more sophisticated black critics apparently did).

It seems to me that black writing has suffered, because even black critics have assumed that a book that deals with the relationships between members of a black family—or between a man and a woman—is less important than one that has white people as a primary antagonist. The consequence of this is that many of our books by "major" writers (always male) tell us little about the culture, history, or future, imagination, fantasies, etc. of black people, and a lot about isolated (often improbable) or limited encounters with a nonspecific white world. Where is the book, by an American black person (aside from *Cane*), that equals Elechi Amadi's *The Concubine*, for example? A book that exposes the *subconscious* of a people, because the people's dreams, imaginings, rituals, legends, etc. are known to be important, are known to contain the accumulated collective reality of the people themselves. Or, in *The Radiance of the King*, the white person is shown to be the outsider he is, because the culture he enters into in Africa *itself* expells him. Without malice, but as nature expells what does not suit. The white man is mysterious, a force to be reckoned with, but he is not glorified to such an extent that the Africans turn their attention away from themselves and their own imagination and culture. Which is what often happens with "protest literature." The superficial becomes—for a time—the deepest reality, and replaces the still waters of the collective subconscious.

When my own novel was published, a leading black monthly admitted (the editor did) that the book itself was never read; but the magazine ran an item stating that a *white* reviewer had praised the book (which was, in itself, an indication that the book was no good—such went the logic) and then hinted that the reviewer had liked my book because of my life-style. When I wrote to the editor to complain, he wrote me a small sermon on the importance of my "image," of what is "good" for others to see. Needless to say, what others "see" of me is the least of my worries, and I assume that "others" are intelligent enough to recover from whatever shocks my presence might cause.

Women writers are supposed to be intimidated by male disapprobation. What they write is not important enough to be read. How they live, however, their "image," they owe to the race. Read the reason Zora Neale Hurston gave for giving up her writing. See what "image" the Negro press gave her, innocent as she was. I no longer read articles or reviews unless they are totally about the work. I trust that someday a generation of men and women will arise who will forgive me for such wrong as I do not agree I do, and will read my work because it is a true account of my feelings, my perception, and my imagination, and because it will reveal something to them of their own selves. They will also be free to toss it—and me—out of a high window. They can do what they like.

INTERVIEWER: Have you felt a great deal of coercion to write the kind of fiction and poetry that black writers are "supposed" to write? Does this ever interfere with what you *want* to write?

WALKER: When I take the time to try to figure out what I am doing in my writing, where it is headed, and so on, I almost never can come up with anything. This is because it seems to me that my poetry is quite different from my novels (*The Third Life of Grange Copeland* and the one I am working on now); for example, *Once* is what I think of as a "happy" book, full of the spirit of an optimist who loves the world and all the sensations of caring in it; it doesn't matter that it began in sadness; *The Third Life of Grange Copeland*, though sometimes humorous and celebrative of life, is a grave book in which the characters see the world as almost entirely menacing. The optimism that closes the book makes it different from most of my short stories, and the political and personal content of my essays makes them different—again—from everything else. So I would not, as some critics have done, categorize my work as "gothic." I would not categorize it at all. Eudora Welty, in explaining why she rebels against being labeled "gothic," says that to her "gothic" conjures up the supernatural, and

73

that she feels what she writes has "something to do with real life." I agree with her.

I like those of my short stories that show the plastic, shaping, almost painting quality of words. In "Roselily" and "The Child Who Favored Daughter" the prose is poetry, or, prose and poetry run together to add a new dimension to the language. But the most that I would say about where I am trying to go is this: I am trying to arrive at that place where black music already is; to arrive at that unselfconscious sense of collective oneness; that naturalness, that (even when anguished) grace.

The writer—like the musician or painter—must be free to explore, otherwise she or he will never discover what is needed (by everyone) to be known. This means, very often, finding oneself considered "unacceptable" by masses of people who think that the writer's obligation is not to explore or to challenge, but to second the masses' motions, whatever they are. Yet the gift of loneliness is sometimes a radical vision of society or one's people that has not previously been taken into account. Toomer was, I think, a lonely, wandering man, accustomed to being tolerated and misunderstood—a man who made choices many abhorred—and yet, *Cane* is a great reward; though Toomer himself probably never realized it.

The same is true of Zora Neale Hurston. She is probably more honest in her fieldwork and her fiction than she is in her autobiography, because she was hesitant to reveal how different she really was. It is interesting to contemplate what would have been the result and impact on black women— since 1937—if they had read and taken to heart *Their Eyes Were Watching God*. Would they still be as dependent on material things—fine cars, furs, big houses, pots and jars of face creams—as they are today? Or would they, learning from Janie that materialism is the drag-rope of the soul, become a nation of women immune (to the extent that is possible in a blatantly consumerist society like ours) to the accumulation of things, and aware, to their core, that love, fulfillment as women, peace of mind, should logically come before, not after, selling one's soul for a golden stool on which to sit. Sit and be bored.

Hurston's book, though seemingly apolitical, is in fact, one of the most radical novels (without being a tract) we have.

INTERVIEWER: Christianity is implicitly criticized in your work. Is that because it has historically been both racist and anti-feminist?

WALKER: Although I am constantly involved, internally, with religious questions—and I seem to have spent all of my life rebelling against the church and other people's interpretations of what religion is—the truth is probably that I don't believe there is a God, although I would like to believe it. Certainly I don't believe there is a God beyond nature. The world is God. Man is God. So is a leaf or a snake. . . . So, when Grange Copeland refuses to pray at the end of the book, he is refusing to be a hypocrite. All his life he has hated the church and taken every opportunity to ridicule it. He has taught his granddaughter, Ruth, this same humorous contempt. He does, however, appreciate the humanity of man-womankind as a God worth embracing. To him, the greatest value a person can attain is full humanity, which is a state of oneness with all things, and a willingness to die (or to live) so that the best that has been produced can continue to live in someone else. He "rocked himself in his own arms to a final sleep" because he understood that man is alone—in his life as in his death—without any God but himself (and the world).

Like many, I waver in my convictions about God, from time to time. In my poetry I seem to be for; in my fiction, against.

I am intrigued by the religion of the black Muslims. By what conversion means to black women, specifically, and what the religion itself means in terms of the black American past: our history, our "race memories" our absorption of Christianity, our *changing* of Christianity to fit our needs. What will the new rituals mean? How will this new religion imprint itself on the collective consciousness of the converts? Can women be free in such a religion? Is such a religion, in fact, an anachronism? So far I have dealt with this interest in two stories, "Roselily," about a young woman who marries a young Muslim because he offers her respect and security, and

"Everyday Use" a story that shows respect for the "militance" and progressive agricultural programs of the Muslims, but at the same time shows skepticism about a young man who claims attachment to the Muslims because he admires the rhetoric. It allows him to acknowledge his contempt for whites, which is all he believes the group is about.

In other stories, I am interested in Christianity as an imperialist tool used against Africa ("Diary of an African Nun") and in Voodoo used as a weapon against oppression ("The Revenge of Hannah Kemhuff"). I see all of these as religious questions.

INTERVIEWER: Could you tell me about the genesis of your title poem "Revolutionary Petunias"? Why was "Sammy Lou" chosen as the heroine of the poem?

WALKER: The poem "Revolutionary Petunias" did not have a name when I sat down to write it. I wanted to create a person who engaged in a final struggle with her oppressor, and won, but who, in every other way, was "incorrect." Sammy Lou in the poem is everything she should not be: her name is Sammy Lou, for example; she is a farmer's wife; she works in the fields. She goes to church. The walls of her house contain no signs of her blackness—though that in itself reveals it; anyone walking into that empty house would know Sammy Lou is black. She is so incredibly "incorrect" that she is only amused when the various poets and folksingers rush to immortalize her heroism in verse and song. She did not think of her killing of her oppressor in that way. She thought—and I picture her as tall, lean, black, with short, badly straightened hair and crooked teeth—that killing is never heroic. Her reaction, after killing this cracker-person, would be to look up at the sky and not pray or ask forgiveness but to say—as if talking to an old friend—"Lord, you know my heart. I never wanted to have to kill nobody. But I couldn't hold out to the last, like Job. I had done took more than I could stand."

Sammy Lou is so "incorrect" she names her children after Presidents and their wives: she names one of them after the founder of the Methodist church. To her, this does not mean a limitation of her blackness, it means she feels she is so black she can absorb—and change—all things, since everybody knows that a black-skinned Jackie Kennedy still bears resemblance only to her own great aunt, Sadie Mae Johnson.

But the most "incorrect" thing about Sammy Lou is that she loves flowers. Even on her way to the electric chair she reminds her children to water them. This is crucial, for I have heard it said by one of our cultural visionaries that whenever you hear a black person talking about the beauties of nature, that person is not a black person at all, but a Negro. This is meant as a put-down, and it is. It puts down all of the black folks in Georgia, Alabama, Mississippi, Texas, Louisianna—in fact, it covers just about everybody's Mama. Sammy Lou, of course, is so "incorrect" she does not even know how ridiculous she is for loving to see flowers blooming around her unbearably ugly gray house. To be "correct" she should consider it her duty to let ugliness reign. Which is what "incorrect" people like Sammy Lou refuse to do.

Actually, the poem was to claim (as Toomer claimed the people he wrote about in *Cane* who, as you know, were all as "incorrect" as possible) the most incorrect black person I could, and to honor her as my own—on a level with, if not above the most venerated saints of the black revolution. It seems our fate to be incorrect (look where we live, for example), and in our incorrectness, stand.

Although Sammy Lou is more a rebel than a revolutionary (since you need more than one for a revolution) I named the poem "Revolutionary Petunias" because she is not—when you view her kind of person historically—isolated. She is part of an ongoing revolution. Any black revolution, instead of calling her "incorrect," will have to honor her single act of rebellion.

Another reason I named it "Revolutionary Petunias" is that I like petunias and like to raise them because you just put them in any kind of soil and they bloom their heads off—exactly, it seemed to me, like black people tend to do. (Look at the blues and jazz musicians, the blind singers from places like Turnip, Mississippi, the poets and writers and all-around blooming people you know, who—from all visible evidence—achieved their blooming by eating the air for bread and drinking muddy water for hope.) Then I thought too, of the petunias my mother gave me when my daughter was born, and of the story (almost a parable) she told me about them. Thirty-seven years ago, my mother and father were coming home from somewhere in their wagon—my mother was pregnant with one of my older brothers at the time—and they passed a deserted house where one lavender petunia was left, just blooming away in the yard (probably to keep itself company)—and my mother said Stop! let me go and get that petunia bush. And my father, grumbling, stopped, and she got it, and they went home, and she set it out in a big stump in the yard. It never wilted, just bloomed and bloomed. Every time the family moved (say twelve times) she took her petunia—and thirty-seven years later she brought me a piece of that same petunia bush. It had never died. Each winter it lay dormant and dead-looking, but each spring it came back, more lively than before.

What underscored the importance of this story for me is this: modern petunias do not live forever. They die each winter and the next spring you have to buy new ones.

In a way, the whole book is a celebration of people who will not cram themselves into any ideological or racial mold. They are all shouting Stop! I want to go get that petunia!

Because of this they are made to suffer. They are told that they do not belong, that they are not wanted, that their art is not needed, that nobody who is "correct" could love what they love. Their answer is resistance, without much commentary; just a steady knowing that they stand at a point where—with one slip of the character—they might be lost, and the bloom they are after wither in the winter of self-contempt. They do not measure themselves against black people or white people; if anything, they learn to walk and talk in the presence of DuBois, Hurston, Hughes, Toomer, Attaway,* Wright, and others—and when they bite into their pillows at night these spirits comfort them. They are aware that the visions that created them were all toward a future where all people—and flowers too—can bloom. They require that in the midst of the bloodiest battles or revolution this thought not be forgotten.

When I married my husband there was a law that said

---

*William Attaway, twentieth-century African American novelist best known for *Blood on the Forge* (1941).

I could not. When we moved to Mississippi three years after the lynching of Cheney, Schwerner and Goodman,* it was a punishable crime for a black person and a white person of opposite sex to inhabit the same house. But I felt then—as I do now—that in order to be able to live at all in America I must be unafraid to live anywhere in it, and I must be able to live in the fashion and with whom I choose. Otherwise, I'd just as soon leave. If society (black or white) says, Then you must be isolated, an outcast—then I will be a hermit. Friends and relatives may desert me, but the dead—Douglass, DuBois, Hansberry,** Toomer, and the rest—are a captive audience. . . . These feelings went into two poems, "Be Nobody's Darling," and "While Love Is Unfashionable."

INTERVIEWER: There is one poem in *Revolutionary Petunias* which particularly interests me—"For My Sister Molly Who in the Fifties." Can you tell me about what went into the structuring of this rather long poem, and perhaps something about the background of it?

WALKER: "For My Sister Molly Who in the Fifties" is a pretty real poem. It really is about one of my sisters, a brilliant, studious girl who became one of those Negro Wonders—who collected scholarships like trading stamps and wandered all over the world. (Our home town didn't even have a high school when she came along.) When she came to visit us in Georgia it was—at first—like having Christmas with us all during her vacation. She loved to read and tell stories; she taught me African songs and dances; she cooked fanciful dishes that looked like anything but plain old sharecropper food. I loved her so much it came as a great shock—and a shock I don't expect to recover from—to learn she was ashamed of us. We were so poor, so dusty, and sunburnt. We talked wrong. We didn't know how to dress, or use the right eating utensils. And so, she drifted away, and I did not understand it. Only later, I realized that sometimes (perhaps), it becomes too painful to

---

*Civil rights workers slain in Mississippi in 1964.

**Lorraine Hansberry, African American playwright, best known for *A Raisin in the Sun* (1959).

bear: seeing your home and family—shabby and seemingly without hope—through the eyes of your new friends and strangers. She had felt—for her own mental health—that the gap that separated us from the rest of the world was too wide for her to keep trying to bridge. She understood how delicate she was.

I started out writing this poem in great anger; hurt, really. I thought I could write a magnificently vicious poem. Yet, even from the first draft, it did not turn out that way. Which is one of the great things about poetry. What you really feel, underneath everything else, will present itself. Your job is not to twist that feeling. So that although being with her now is too painful with memories for either of us to be comfortable, I still retain (as I hope she does) in memories beyond the bad ones, my picture of a sister I loved, "Who walked among the flowers and brought them inside the house, who smelled as good as they, and looked as bright."

This poem (and my sister received the first draft, which is hers alone, and the way I wish her to relate to the poem) went through fifty drafts (at least) and I worked on it, off and on, for five years. This has never happened before or since. I do not know what to say about the way it is constructed other than to say that as I wrote it the lines and words went, on the paper, to a place comparable to where they lived in my head.

I suppose, actually, that my tremendous response to the poems of W. C. Williams, cummings and Bashō convinced me that poetry is more like music—in my case, improvisational jazz, where each person blows the note that she hears—than like a cathedral, with every stone in a specific, predetermined place. Whether lines are long or short depends on what the poem itself requires. Like people, some poems are fat and some are thin. Personally, I prefer the short thin ones, which are always like painting the eye in a tiger (as Muriel Rukeyser once explained it). You wait until the energy and vision are just right, then you write the poem. If you try to write it before it is ready to be written you find yourself adding stripes instead of eyes. Too many stripes and the tiger herself disappears. You will paint a photograph (which is what is wrong with "Burial") instead of creating a new way of seeing.

The poems that fail will always haunt you. I am

haunted by "Ballad of the Brown Girl" and "Johann" in *Once*, and I expect to be haunted by "Nothing Is Right" in *Revolutionary Petunias*. The first two are dishonest, and the third is trite.

The poem "The Girl Who Died #2" was written after I learned of the suicide of a student at the college I attended. I learned, from the dead girl's rather guilty-sounding "brothers and sisters" that she had been hounded constantly because she was so "incorrect" she thought she could be a black hippie. To top that, they tried to make her feel like a traitor because she refused to limit her interest to black men. Anyway, she was a beautiful girl. I was shown a photograph of her by one of her few black friends. She was a little brown-skinned girl from Texas, away from home for the first time, trying to live a life she could live with. She tried to kill herself two or three times before, but I guess the brothers and sisters didn't think it "correct" to respond with love or attention, since everybody knows it is "incorrect" to even think of suicide if you are a black person. And, of course, black people do not commit suicide. Only colored people and Negroes commit suicide. (See "The Old Warrior Terror": Warriors, you know, always die on the battlefield.) I said, when I saw the photograph, that I wished I had been there for her to talk to. When the school invited me to join their Board of Trustees, it was her face that convinced me. I know nothing about Boards and never really trusted them; but I can listen to problems pretty well. . . . I believe in listening—to a person, the sea, the wind, the trees, but especially to young black women whose rocky road I am still traveling.

❑ Critical Essays

An Essay
on Alice Walker

From whatever vantage point one investigates the work of Alice Walker—poet, novelist, short story writer, critic, essayist, and apologist for black women—it is clear that the special identifying mark of her writing is her concern for the lives of black women. In the two books of poetry, two novels, one short story collection, and many essays and reviews she has produced since she began publishing in 1966, her main preoccupation has been the souls of black women. Walker herself, writing about herself as writer, has declared herself committed to "exploring the oppressions, the insanities, the loyalties, and the triumphs of black women."[1] In her first four published works—*Once,* her earliest book of poetry; *Revolutionary Petunias,* also poetry; *The Third Life of Grange Copeland,* her first novel; *In Love and Trouble,* a collection of thirteen stories—and her latest novel, *Meridian*—there are more than twenty-five characters from the slave woman to a revolutionary woman of the sixties. Within each of these roles Walker has examined the external realities facing these women as well as the internal world of each woman.

We might begin to understand Alice Walker, the apologist and spokeswoman for black women, by understanding the motivation for Walker's preoccupation with her subject. Obviously there is simply a personal identification. She says in her interview with John O'Brien, "I believe in listening—to a person, the sea, the wind, the trees, but especially to young black

From *Sturdy Black Bridges: Visions of Black Women in Literature,* ed. Roseann P. Bell, Bettye J. Parker, and Beverley Guy-Sheftall (Garden City, N.Y.: Anchor/Doubleday, 1979), pp. 133–149.

women whose rocky road I am still traveling." Moreover her sense of personal identification with black women includes a sense of sharing in their peculiar oppression. In some length she describes her own attempts at suicide when she discovered herself pregnant in her last year of college and at the mercy of everything, especially her own body. Throughout the interview with this writer in 1973,[2] Ms. Walker spoke of her own awareness of and experiences with brutality and violence in the lives of black women, many of whom she had known as a girl growing up in Eatonton, Georgia, some in her own family. The recurrent theme running throughout that interview and in much of her other pieces on women is her belief that "Black women . . . are the most oppressed people in the world."

In one of her earliest essays, "The Civil Rights Movement: What Good Was It?" she herself recalls "being young and well-hidden among the slums,"[3] knowing that her dreams of being an author or scientist were unattainable for a black child growing up in the poorest section of rural Georgia, that no one would encourage a black girl from the backwoods to become an artist or writer. In the same essay she recounts an episode in her mother's life that underscores her sensitivity to the peculiar oppression of black women. She saw her mother, a woman of heavy body and swollen feet, a maid in the houses of white women for forty years, having raised eight children in Eatonton, Georgia, turn to the stories of white men and women on television soap operas to satisfy her yearnings for a better life:

> My mother, a truly great woman who raised eight children of her own and half a dozen of the neighbors' without a single complaint—was convinced that she did not exist compared to "them." She subordinated her soul to theirs and became a faithful and timid supporter of the "Beautiful White People." Once she asked me in a moment of vicarious pride and despair, if I didn't think that "they" were "jest naturally smarter, prettier, better."[4]

Walker understands that what W.E.B. Du Bois called double consciousness, "this sense of always looking at one's self through the eyes of others, of measuring one's soul by the tape

86

of a world that looks on in amused contempt and pity,"[5] creates its own particular kind of disfigurement in the lives of black women, and that, far more than the external facts and figures of oppression, the true terror is within; the mutilation of the spirit *and* the body. Though Walker does not neglect to deal with the external *realities* of poverty, exploitation, and discrimination, her stories, novels, and poems most often focus on the intimate reaches of the inner lives of her characters; the landscape of her stories is the spiritual realm where the soul yearns for what it does not have.[6]

In the O'Brien interview Ms. Walker makes a statement about Elechi Amadi's *The Concubine,* a Nigerian novel, and in that statement there is an important revelation about Walker's own writings. She sees Amadi as unique among black writers because through his book he exposes the subconscious of a people; that is, he has written about the dreams, rituals, legends, and imaginings which contain the "accumulated collective reality of the people themselves."[7] It would be possible to apply that same description to Walker's writings about black women, particularly the stories in *In Love and Trouble,* through which we can see a conscious effort by Walker to explore the imaginings, dreams, and rituals of the subconscious of black women which contains their accumulated collective reality. We begin this analysis of Walker's writings with a discussion of her personal identification with the lives of black women because it is that internal personal sharing that has put Walker in touch with this selective reality. Speaking of her short story "The Revenge of Hannah Kemhuff," Walker says:

> In that story I gathered up the historical and psychological threads of the life some of my ancestors lived, and in the writing of it I felt joy and strength and my own continuity. I had that wonderful feeling writers get sometimes, not very often, of being *with* a great many people, ancient spirits, all very happy to see me consulting and acknowledging them, and eager to let me know, through the joy of their presence that indeed I am not alone.[8]

One vital link to those "historical and psychological threads" of her ancestors' lives is the stories passed on to her by her mother, stories which Walker absorbed through years of listening to her mother tell them. The oral stories are often the basis for her own stories, as are the lives and stories of people she grew up with in Eatonton, Georgia. Once when questioned about the violence and pain in the lives of so many of her women, she recounted an incident from her childhood which was the basis for the story of Mem in Walker's novel *The Third Life of Grange Copeland*. When she was thirteen, a friend's father killed his wife, and Walker, a curious child, saw the mother's body laid out on a slab in the funeral home:

> . . . there she was, hard working, large, overweight. Black, somebody's cook, lying on the slab with half her head shot off, and on her feet were those shoes that I describe—hole in the bottom, and she had stuffed paper in them . . . we used to have, every week, just such a murder as these (in my home town), and it was almost always the wife and sometimes the children.[9]

The true empathy Alice Walker has for the oppressed woman comes through in all her writings—stories, essays, poems, novels. Even in a very brief review of a book of poetry [in *Ms.*, June 1974] by a woman who calls herself "Ai," Ms. Walker exhibits, almost with conscious design, her instinctive concern for the experiences of women. The choice of "Ai" as a pen name appeals to Ms. Walker because of the images of women it suggests:

> And one is glad she chose "Ai" as her name because it is like a cry. If I close my eyes and say the word (the sound) to myself, it is to see a woman raising an ax, to see a woman crying out in childbirth or abortion, to see a woman surrendering a man who is oblivious to the sound of her true—as opposed to given—name.

Raising an ax, crying out in childbirth or abortion, surrendering to a man who is oblivious to her real name—these are the kinds of images which most often appear in Ms. Walker's own writing and have prompted critic Carolyn Fowler to say that

Walker has the true gift of revealing the authentic "Heart of Woman" in her stories.

What particularly distinguishes Alice Walker in her role as apologist [10] and chronicler for black women is her evolutionary treatment of black women; that is, she sees the experiences of black women as a series of movements from women totally victimized by society and by the men in their lives to the growing developing women whose consciousness allows them to have control over their lives.

In historical terms the women of the first cycle belong to the eighteenth and nineteenth centuries and the early decades of the twentieth century. Although only one of Walker's characters is a slave, the institution of slavery set up the conditions and environment for the period immediately following, extending from the end of the Reconstruction Era to the first two decades of the twentieth century. Borrowing the term first used by novelist Zora Neale Hurston, the black women of this period are "the mules of the world," carrying the burdens heaped upon them by society and by the family, the victims of both racial and sexual oppression. Walker calls them her "suspended" women: a concept she develops in an important historical essay entitled "In Search of Our Mothers' Gardens: The Creativity of Black Women in the South," published in *Ms.* magazine in May 1974. Walker has explained this state of suspension as caused by pressures in society which made it impossible for the black women of this era to move forward:

> They were suspended in a time in history where the options for Black women were severely limited. . . . And they either kill themselves or they are used up by the man, or by the children, or by . . . whatever the pressures against them. And they cannot go anywhere. I mean, you can't, you just can't move, until there is room for you to move *into*. And that's the way I see many of the women I have created in fiction. They are closer to my mother's generation than to mine. They had few choices. [11]

Suspended in time and place by a century, an era that only acknowledged them as laborers, these women were simply defeated in one way or another by the external circumstances of their lives. For such women—the great-grandmothers of the black women of contemporary times—pain, violence, poverty, and oppression were the essential content of their lives. Writer June Jordan calls them "black-eyed Susans—flowers of the blood-soaked American soil."

If these were the pressures and obstacles against the ordinary black woman who existed in the eighteenth and nineteenth centuries, what, then, did it mean for a black woman to be an artist, or want to be an artist in such times? Walker poses the question: "How was the creativity of the Black woman kept alive, year after year, century after century, when for the most of the years Black people have been in America, it was a punishable crime for a Black person to read or write?"[12] If the freedom to read and write, to paint, to sculpt, to experience one's creativity in any way did not exist, what became of the black woman artist? Walker says it is a question with an answer "cruel enough to stop the blood."

> For these grandmothers and mothers of ours were not Saints, but Artists; driven to a numb and bleeding madness by the springs of creativity in them for which there was no release. They were Creators, who lived lives of spiritual waste, because they were so rich in spirituality—which is the basis of Art—that the strain of enduring their unused and unwanted talent drove them insane. Throwing away this spirituality was their pathetic attempt to lighten the soul to a weight their work-worn, sexually abused bodies could bear.

Of course, in spite of these many circumstances in which the art of the black woman was denied or stifled, some evidences of the creative genius of the black women of that age still remain. Walker cites the poetry of Phillis Wheatley, the quilt-making of so many anonymous black women of the South, the wise woman selling herbs and roots, as well as the brilliant and original gardens designed and cultivated by her own mother, as evidence that the creative spirit was nourished somehow and showed itself in wild and unlikely places. Through Ms. Walker is the first writer to define and develop the concept of the black women of the post-Reconstruction period as "suspended," as artists "hindered and thwarted by contrary instincts," the suspended black woman is a recurrent theme in the writers who deal with black women. Many of the black women characters in women writers from Frances Harper to Toni Morrison, as well as the women of Jean Toomer's *Cane,* are suspended women, artists without an outlet for their art or simply women of deep spirituality who "stumble blindly through their lives . . . abused and mutilated in body . . . dimmed and confused by pain, unaware of the richness of their gifts but nonetheless suffering as their gifts are denied."

So we have part one of Walker's personal construct of the black woman's history—the woman suspended, artist thwarted and hindered in her desires to create, living through two centuries when her main role was to be a cheap source of cheap labor in the American society. This is the construct developed mainly in Walker's interviews and essays: How, then, does this construct fit in the fiction of Alice Walker?

Most of Walker's women characters belong to the first part of the cycle—the suspended woman. Three women from her first novel, *The Third Life of Grange Copeland,* and seven of the thirteen women from her short story collection *In Love and Trouble* are women who are cruelly exploited, spirits and bodies mutilated, relegated to the most narrow and confining lives, sometimes driven to madness. They are the contemporary counterparts of the crazy, pitiful women Jean Toomer saw in the South in the early 1920s.

In "Roselily," the opening story of *In Love and Trouble,* the main character, Roselily—young, black, poor, trapped in the southern backwoods, unmarried, the mother of three children, each by a different man—is about to give herself in marriage to a Muslim man. His religion requires a set of customs and beliefs that control women and subordinate them to men. She will have to wear her hair covered, sit apart from the men in church; her required place will be in the home. There will be more babies regardless of her wishes. She also senses another kind of oppression, dictated not by his religion, but by his condescension. He is annoyed by country black folk, their way of doing things, the country wedding. Roselily knows that in his eyes her three illegitimate children, not all by the same man, add to her lowliness. He makes her feel "ignorant, wrong, backward." But he offers her a chance that she must take. A chance for her children. A chance for her to be "respectable," "reclaimed," "renewed." And it is a chance she cannot afford to miss because marriage is perhaps her only way out of brutal poverty.

The excerpt from Elechi Amadi's *The Concubine,* a prefatory piece to *In Love and Trouble,* is a particularly interesting one for the light it throws on Roselily's situation. This excerpt depicts a woman named Ahurole who is given to unprovoked sobbing and fits of melancholia. An intelligent woman, Ahurole is generally cheerful and normal, so her parents blame her fits on the influence of an unlucky and troublesome personal spirit. At the end of the excerpt, it is revealed that "Ahurole was engaged to Ekwueme when she was *eight days old."* Walker sees Roselily, like Ahurole, as a woman trapped and cut down by archaic conventions, by superstition, by traditions that in every way cut women off from the right to life. Their personal and inner rebellion against the restrictions of their lives is reduced to the level of an unlucky spirit.

Roselily, too, has no way to explain her troubled and rebellious spirit. She has married off well, she will give her children a better life; but she is disturbed by what she senses will be an iron shackle around her life and her self. All of the fleeting images that inadvertently break through her consciousness are premonitions of what is to come: *quicksand, flowers choked to death, cotton being weighed, ropes, chains, handcuffs, cemeteries, a cornered rat.* The very robe and veil she is wearing are emblems of servitude that she yearns to be free of.

Mrs. Jerome Franklin Washington III, a beautician, another of Walker's suspended women, not unlike Roselily, is caught in a marriage that destroys her little by little. When she discovers how very little she means to her husband, she burns herself up.

Ms. Washington (we know her in this story only through her husband's name) is an unlovely, unloved woman: big, awkward, with rough skin, greasy, hard pressed hair. She is married, because of a small inheritance, to a quiet, "cute," dapper young schoolteacher whom she adores. She buys him clothes and cars, lavishly spending money on him, money she has earned in her beauty shop by standing many hours on her feet. It is not long before he is beating her and ridiculing her coarseness; for he considers himself one of the elite, the "black bourgeoisie," and his wife is so obviously, in spite of her heard-earned money, a woman of no learning, no elegance. In short, she is devoid of any black middle-class pretensions. Even her pretensions are clearly indicative of her lower class. She tells her customers as she does hair behind dark glasses, "'One thing my husband does not do, he don't beat me.'" She discovers Jerome's infidelity is his dedication to some sort of revolutionary cadre. He has hidden it from her no doubt because her is ignorant, but it is a revolution financed by her money and her devotion to him. She sets fire to their marriage bed, and she herself is caught in the blaze.

The physical and psychic brutality that are part of the lives of several other women in Walker's *In Love and Trouble* are almost always associated with poverty. Rannie Toomer, in "Strong Horse Tea," for example, struggling to get a doctor for her dying child, is handicapped by poverty and ignorance as well as by the racism of the southern rural area she lives in. No "real" doctor will come to see about her child, so she gives into the "witche's" medicine of Aunt Sarah and goes out in the rain to catch horse urine, which is the "strong horse tea" the old rootworker has requested. Her child dies while she is out filling up her shoes with the tea. In his death, all of the elements seem to have conspired—the earth, the "nigger" magic of Aunt Sarah, the public and private racism of the South. One wonders what desperate hysteria allowed Rannie Toomer to stomach the taste and smell of horse urine.

In "The Child Who Favored Daughter," the father presides over the destruction of three women in his family: his own wife, whom he drives to suicide after beating and crippling her; his sister, named Daughter, whose suicide is the result of the punishment her family exacts after she has an affair with a white man; and his own daughter, whom he mutilates because she will not renounce her white lover. To understand the violence of this man toward these three women in his family, author Walker makes us know that it is the result of an immense chaos within—the components of which are his impotent rage against the white world which abuses him, his vulnerable love for his child and his sister, both of whom chose white lovers. He is so threatened by that inner chaos that the very act of violence is a form of control, a way of imposing order on his own world. By killing his daughter, he has at once shut out the image of Daughter which haunts him, he has murdered his own incest, and he has eliminated the last woman who has the power to hurt him. His brutality toward women foreshadows other Walker characters—Grange and Brownfield in *The Third Life of Grange Copeland,* the farmer who cripples his wife in "Really Doesn't Crime Pay," Hannah Kemhuff's husband ("The Revenge of Hannah Kemhuff"), and Ruth's father in "A Sudden Trip Home in the Spring."

It is Walker's own documentation and analysis of the historical struggles of the black women that authenticates the terrible and chilling violence of these stories. These are stories about several generations of black women whose lives were severely limited by sexual and racial oppression. First slaves, then sharecroppers, then part of the vast army of the urban poor, their lives were lived out in slow motion, going nowhere, a future not yet within their grasp.

Such were the women Jean Toomer discovered in *Cane,* and the similarity between Toomer's women and the women of Walker's first cycle (the suspended woman) is striking:

> To Toomer they lay vacant and fallow as Autumn fields, with harvest time never in sight: and he saw them enter loveless marriages, without joy; and become prostitutes without resistance; and become mothers of children, without fulfillment.[13]

Both Toomer and Walker have explored the tragedies in the lives of Black women—the tragedy of poverty, abuse from men who are themselves abused, the physical deterioration—but there is greater depth in Walker's exploration because not only does she comprehend the past lives of these women but she has also questioned their fates and dared to see through to a time when black women would no longer live in suspension, when there would be a place for them to move into.

In the second cycle of Walker's personal construct of the history of black women are the women who belong to the decades of the forties and fifties, those decades when black people (then "Negroes") wanted most to be part of the mainstream of American life even though assimilation required total denial of one's ethnicity. Several literary critics have labeled this period in black literature a period of "mainstreaming" because of the indications in literature that writers such as Willard Motley and Frank Yerby and even one novel of Zora Neale Hurston were "raceless." And what of the black women during this period, particularly the woman who had some chance at education? Walker writes of her as a woman pushed and pulled by the larger world outside of her, urged to assimilate (to be "raceless") in order to overcome her background. In Walker's historical construct, these black women were, ironically, victims of what were ostensibly greater opportunities:

> I have this theory that Black women in the '50s, in the '40s—the late '40s and early '50s—got away from their roots much more than they will probably ever do again, because that was the time of greatest striving to get into White Society, and to erase all of the backgrounds of poverty. It was a time when you could be the Exception, could be the One, and my sister was The One. But I think she's not unique—so many, many, many Black families have a daughter or sister who was the one who escaped because, you see, that was what was set up for her; she was going to be the one who escaped, and the rest of us weren't supposed to escape, because we had given our One.[14]

The women in this cycle are also victims, not of physical violence, but of a kind of psychic violence that alienates them from their roots, cutting them off from real contact.

The woman named Molly from Walker's poem "For My Sister Molly Who in the Fifties" is the eldest sister in a poor rural family in Eatonton; she is, in fact, Alice Walker's sister and Walker is the child narrator of the poem mourning the loss of her talented and devoted "Molly." When Molly first comes home on vacation from college, she is very close to her brothers and sisters, teaching them what she has learned, reading to them about faraway places like Africa. The young narrator is enraptured by Molly, spellbound by the bright colorful sister who changes her drab life into beauty:

95

WHO IN THE FIFTIES
Knew all the written things that made
Us laugh and stories by
The hour   Waking up the story buds
Like fruit. Who walked among the flowers
And brought them inside the house
And smelled as good as they
And looked as bright.
Who made dresses, braided
Hair. Moved chairs about
Hung things from walls
Ordered baths
Frowned on wasp bites
And seemed to know the endings
Of all the tales
I had forgot.

As a writer especially concerned with the need for black people to acknowledge and respect their roots, Walker is sensitive to these women who are divorced from their heritage. As she describes them, the Chosen Ones were always the bright and talented ones in the family. They were the ones selected to go to college if the family could afford to send only one; they were meant to have the better life, the chance at success. And they learned early the important lesson that to be chosen required them to feel shame for their background, and to strive to be as different and removed as possible from those not chosen. But being a child, the narrator does not realize or suspect the growing signs of Molly's remoteness. Molly goes off to the university, travels abroad, becoming distant and cold and frowning upon the lives of the simple folks she comes from:

WHO FOUND ANOTHER WORLD
Another life   With gentlefolk
Far less trusting
And moved and moved and changed
Her name
And sounded precise

When she spoke   And frowned away
Our sloppishness.

From her superior position she can only see the negatives—
the silent, fearful, barefoot, tongue-tied, ignorant brothers and
sisters. She finds the past, her backward family, unbearable,
and though she may have sensed their groping after life, she
finally leaves the family for good. She has, of course, been
leaving all along with her disapproval of their ways, her precise
speech, her preference for another world. The tone of the last
two lines suggests the finality about her leaving, as though
Molly has become too alienated from her family to ever return:

FOR MY SISTER MOLLY WHO IN THE FIFTIES
Left us.

The women of the second cycle are destroyed spiritu-
ally rather than physically, and yet there is still some movement forward, some hope that did not exist for the earlier
generation of American black women. The women in this cycle
are more aware of their condition and they have greater potential for shaping their lives, although they are still thwarted because they feel themselves coming to life before the necessary
changes have been made in the political environment—before
there is space for them to move into. The sense of "twoness"
that Du Bois spoke of in *The Souls of Black Folk* is perhaps
most evident in the lives of these women; they are the most
aware of and burdened by the "double consciousness" that
makes one measure one's soul by the tape of the other world.

In June of 1973 in an interview with this writer,
Ms. Walker made one of the first statements about the direction and development of her black women characters into a
third cycle:

> My women, in the future, will not burn themselves up—that's
> what I mean by coming to the end of a cycle, and understand-
> ing something to the end . . . now I am ready to look at women
> who have made the room larger for others to move in. . . . I
> think one reason I never stay away from the Southern Move-

ment is because I realize how deeply political changes affect the choices and life-styles of people. The Movement of the Sixties, Black Power, the Muslims, the Panthers . . . have changed the options of Black people generally and of Black women in particular. So that my women characters won't all end the way they have been, because Black women now offer varied, live models of how it is possible to live. We have made a new place to move. . . .

The women of the third cycle are, for the most part, women of the late sixties, although there are some older women in Walker's fiction who exhibit the qualities of the developing, emergent model. Greatly influenced by the political events of the sixties and the changes resulting from the freedom movement, they are women coming just to the edge of a new awareness and making the first tentative steps into an uncharted region. And although they are more fully conscious of their political and psychological oppression and more capable of creating new options for themselves, they must undergo a harsh initiation before they are ready to occupy and claim any new territory. Alice Walker, herself a real-life prototype of the emergent black woman, speaks of having been called to life by the civil rights movement of the sixties, as being called from the shadows of a world in which black people existed as statistics, problems, beasts of burden, a life that resembled death; for one was not aware of the possibilities within one's self or of possibilities in the larger world outside of the narrow restraints of the world black people inhabited before the struggles of the sixties. When Walker and other civil rights activists like Fannie Lou Hamer began the fight for their lives, they were beaten, jailed, and, in Fannie Lou Hamer's case, widowed and made homeless, but they never lost the energy and courage for revolt.[15] In the same way Walker's own characters, through suffering and struggle, lay the groundwork for a new type of woman to emerge.

The process of cyclical movement in the lives of Walker's black women is first evident in her first novel, *The Third Life of Grange Copeland.* The girl, Ruth, is the daughter of Mem Copeland and the granddaughter of Margaret Copeland—two women whose lives were lived out under the most extreme forms of oppression. Under the pressure of poverty and alienation from her husband, Margaret kills herself and her child; and Mem, wife of Brownfield Copeland, is brutally murdered by her husband in one of his drunken rages. Ruth is brought up by her grandfather, Grange, who in his "third life" attempts to salvage some of his own wasted life by protecting Ruth. Ruth emerges into a young woman at the same time as the civil rights movement, and there is just a glimpse at the end of the novel of how that movement will affect Ruth's life. We see her becoming aware, by watching the civil rights activists—both women and men—that it is possible to struggle against the abuses of oppression. Raised in the sixties, Ruth is the natural inheritor of the changes in a new order, struggling to be, this marking the transition of the women in her family from death to life.

Besides political activism, a fundamental activity the women in the third cycle engage in is the search for meaning in their roots and traditions. As they struggle to reclaim their past and to re-examine their relationship to the black community, there is a consequent reconciliation between themselves and black men.

In Sarah Davis, the main character of Walker's short story "A Sudden Trip Home in the Spring,"[16] we have another witness to the end of the old cycles of confusion and despair. Her search begins when she returns home to the South from a northern white college to bury her father. She is an artist, but because of her alienation from her father, whom she blames for her mother's death, she is unable to paint the faces of black men, seeing in them only defeat. It is important for her, therefore, to answer the questions she is pondering: What is the duty of the child toward the parents after they are dead? What is the necessity of keeping alive in herself a sense of continuity with the past and a sense of community with her family? Through a series of events surrounding her father's funeral, Sarah rediscovers the courage and grace of her grandfather and re-establishes the vital link between her and her brother. Her resolve at the end of the story to do a sculpture of her grandfather ("I shall soon know how to make my grandpa up in stone") signifies the return to her roots and her own personal sense of liberation. This story, more than any other, indicates the contrast between the women of the second cycle who were determined to escape their roots in order to make it in a white world and the emergent women of the third cycle who demonstrate a sense of freedom by the drive to re-establish those vital links to their past.

In Walker's second novel, *Meridian,* the cyclical process is clearly defined in the life of the main character, Meridian Hill, who evolves from a woman trapped by racial and sexual oppression to a revolutionary figure, effecting action and strategy to bring freedom to herself and other poor disenfranchised blacks in the South. Again, as with other third-cycle women who are depicted in the short story collection, the characters in the two novels—*Grange Copeland* and *Meridian*—follow certain patterns: They begin existence in a numb state, deadened, insensible to a life beyond poverty and degradation; they are awakened to life by a powerful political force; in discovering and expanding their creativity, there is a consequent effort to reintegrate themselves into their culture in order to rediscover its value. Historically, the second novel, dealing with a woman who came of age during the sixties, brings Walker's women characters into the first few years of the seventies.

Mary Helen Washington asked to add the following post-script to this reprinting of her earlier essay. She is currently a professor of English at the University of Maryland–College Park. She has edited the collections *Black-Eyed Susans/Midnight Birds* (1990), *Invented Lives* (1987), and *Memory of Kin* (1991).

A Postscript to My 1979 Essay on Alice Walker

Looking back at this 1979 essay on Alice Walker I see how much my thinking about Walker's fiction has changed in the nearly fifteen years since that essay was published. The language of that essay suggests a belief in meaningful and positive change, faith in the possibility of progress, a kind of certainty that was created partly by the heightened hope of the Civil Rights and Black Power movements of the fifties and sixties and partly by the post–World War II climate of inevitable peace, progress, and prosperity. Alice Walker and I, both children of the war years, came of age during the years of intense civil rights activism. Walker's rather rigid schema that organizes the lives of her women characters into three cycles—the suspended woman, the assimilated woman, and the emergent woman—is rooted in the belief that political change would bring about personal and psychological emancipations. Precisely because of what seemed to me its clear-eyed optimism, its powerful representation of the possibility of change, "A Sudden Trip Home in the Spring" seemed ideal as the closing story of my 1975 anthology, *Black-Eyed Susans: Classic Stories By and About Black Women*. The ending of that story, in which a young woman is granted "permission" for her art through her relationship with a wise, militant-preacher older brother and a patriarchal grandfather did not strike me then as contradictory but as recuperative. And I did not question Walker's easy resolution of the young woman's alienation from both her family and her art: "Sarah rediscovers the courage and grace of her grandfather and re-establishes the vital link between her and her brother." Now, in 1993, where I once read optimism and faith, I now read a much more disturbing subtext in which the female artist, disconnected from any community of women, negotiates a temporary truce by her accommodation to male power.

One of the most interesting and glaring omissions of my earlier Walker essay is Walker's statement in the 1973 interview (which took place in her home in Jackson, Mississippi) of the way she sees the story "Everyday Use" as a reflection of her own struggles as an artist, an admission that suggests that female conflicts over art are not so easily resolved as they are in "A Sudden Trip Home . . ." In "Everyday Use" (published in 1973) all three women characters are artists: Mama, as the narrator, tells her own story; Maggie is the quiltmaker, the creator of art for "everyday use"; Dee, the photographer and collector of art, has designed her jewelry, dress, and hair so deliberately and self-consciously that she appears in the story as a self-creation. Walker says in the interview that she thinks of these three characters as herself split into three parts:

> . . . I really see that story as almost about one person, the old woman and two daughters being one person. The one who

stays and sustains—this is the older woman—who has on the one hand a daughter who is the same way, who stays and abides and loves, plus the part of them—*this autonomous person,* the part of them that also wants to go out into the world to see change and be changed. . . . I do in fact have an African name that was given to me, and I love it and use it when I want to, and I love my Kenyan gowns and my Ugandan gowns—the whole bit—it's a part of me. But, on the other hand, my parents and grandparents were part of it, and they take precedence.[17]

Walker is most closely aligned in the story with the "bad daughter," Dee, "this autonomous person," the one who goes out in the world and returns with African clothes and an African name. Like Dee, Walker leaves the community, appropriating the oral tradition in order to turn it into a written artifact, which will no longer be available for "everyday use" by its originators. Everywhere in the story the fears and self-doubt of the woman artist are revealed. The narrator-mother remains hostile to Dee and partial to the homely daughter, Maggie, setting up the opposition between the two daughters that Walker says mirrors her own internal struggles. The male triumvirate of "A Sudden Trip Home" has been replaced by these three women, but this female community does not generate reconciliation.

Susan Willis points out in *Specifying: Black Women Writing the American Experience* that when the black writer takes the materials of folk culture and subjects them to fiction, a system of meaning and telling that originates in the dominant culture, she is engaged in "an enterprise fraught with contradiction."[18] The oppositions in "Everyday Use," between mother and daughters and sisters, between art for everyday use and art for art's sake, between insider and outsider, certainly capture that sense of contradiction and conflict. The story ends with Mama choosing Maggie and rejecting Dee, but Dee, who represents Walker herself as the artist who returns home, at least imaginatively, in order to collect the material for her art, certainly cannot be repressed. In this story, as in her essays, Walker shows that the quiltmaker, who has female precursors and female guidance, has an easier relationship with her art than the "deviant" female who finds herself outside of acceptable boundaries. Unlike quiltmaking and garden making and even blues singing, which are a part of women's traditions, the writing of fiction is still done under the shadow of men, without female authority. The self-assurance of "A Sudden Trip Home in the Spring" is acquired through an alliance with that male authority. "Everyday Use" tells a different, more threatening tale of the woman writer's fears, of the difficulty of reconciling home and art, particularly when the distance from home has been enlarged by education, by life among the "gentlefolk," and by literary recognition.

☐ Notes ■

1. John O'Brien, ed., *Interviews with Black Writers* (New York: Liverwright, 1973), p. 192. Reprinted in this volume.

2. Interview with Mary Helen Washington, Jackson, Mississippi, June 17, 1973. I traveled to Jackson in June of 1973 in order to meet, talk with, and interview Ms. Walker.

3. Alice Walker, "The Civil Rights Movement: What Good Was It?," *American Scholar* (Winter 1970–71), p. 551.

4. "The Civil Rights Movement," p. 552.

5. W.E.B. Du Bois, *Souls of Black Folk* (New York: Blue Heron Press, 1953), pp. 16–17.

6. Carolyn Fowler, "Solid at the Core," *Freedomways* 14 (First Quarter, 1974), p. 60.

7. O'Brien, *Interview*, p. 202.

8. Reid Lecture at Barnard College, November 11, 1975 ["Saving the Life That Is Your Own," repr. in *Our Mothers' Gardens*].

9. Interview with Mary Helen Washington.

10. Apologist is used here to mean one who speaks or writes in defense of a cause or a position.

11. Interview with Mary Helen Washington.

12. "In Search of Our Mothers' Gardens," *Ms.* (May 1974), p. 66. Reprinted in this volume.

13. "Our Mothers' Gardens," p. 66.

14. Interview with Mary Helen Washington.

15. The identification of Hamer as a model for the emergent woman is developed in Walker's review of a biography of Hamer by

June Jordan. The review appeared in *The New York Times Book Review,* April 29, 1973.

16. In Mary Helen Washington, ed., *Black-Eyed Susans: Classic Stories By and About Black Women* (Garden City, N.Y.: Doubleday and Company, 1975).

17. Mary Helen Washington, "Interview with Alice Walker," June 1973, in *Black-Eyed Susans/Midnight Birds* (Garden City, N.Y.: Doubleday, 1991), 286.

18. Susan Willis, *Specifying: Black Women Writing the American Experience* (Madison: University of Wisconsin Press, 1987), 69–70.

□ THADIOUS M. DAVIS ■

Alice Walker's
Celebration of Self
in Southern Generations

Perhaps Alice Walker alone of her generation of black women Southern writers persistently identifies herself and her concerns with her native region—the deep South of Georgia and Mississippi. "No one," she has concluded, "could wish for a more advantageous heritage than that bequeathed to the black writer in the South: a compassion for the earth, a trust in humanity beyond our knowledge of evil, an abiding love of justice. We inherit a great responsibility . . . for we must give voice to centuries not only of silent bitterness and hate but also of neighborly kindness and sustaining love" ("Black Writer" 26). Her heritage is complex; nevertheless, like Louisiana native Ernest Gaines, Walker grounds her fiction and poetry primarily in the experiences of the South and Southern blacks. Her three volumes of poetry, three novels, and two collections of stories, all depend upon what black life is, has been, and can be in a specified landscape that becomes emblematic of American life.

While Walker's paradigm communities are nearly always black, rural, and Southern, they become viable emblems by means of her creation of familial and social generations that underscore her concerns with familial identity, continuity and rupture, and with social roles, order and change. In shaping her fiction and much of her poetry according to patterns of

From *Women Writers of the Contemporary South,* ed. Peggy Whitman Prenshaw (Jackson: University Press of Mississippi, 1984), pp. 39–53.

generations, she has established a concrete means of portraying who her people are and what their lives mean.

Though her dominant themes (spiritual survival and individual identity, as well as freedom, power, and community) link her to the literary heritages of both Southern and black writers, her structures and forms address most clearly the uniqueness of her particular vision within these traditions. Walker weds her intellectual themes to the life experiences of "just plain folk" who are also black and mainly poor; she has said of them, "their experience as ordinary human beings" is "valuable," and should not be "misrepresented, distorted, or lost" ("Saving the Life" 158). In her literary works, she stresses her own history and by extension the cultural history of Southern blacks and American blacks. "It is," Walker asserts in the novel *Meridian*, "the song of the people, transformed by the experiences of each generation, that holds them together, and if any part of it is lost the people suffer and are without soul" (205–206). Her own works are, in a sense, "the song of the people" celebrating and preserving each generation.

Walker's heritage and history provide a vehicle for understanding the modern world in which her characters live. "Because I'm black and I'm a woman and because I was brought up poor and because I'm a Southerner, . . . the way I see the world is quite different from the way many people see it," she has observed to Krista Brewer: "I could not help but have a radical vision of society . . . the way I see things can help people see what needs to be changed" ("Writing to Survive" 13). Her vision, however, is a disturbing one to share. Walker relies upon sexual violence and physical abuse to portray breaches in black generations. Typically, she brings to her work a terrible observance of black self-hatred and destruction. While Walker does not negate the impact of a deleterious past, she rarely incorporates white characters as perpetrators of crimes against blacks. Her works simply presume, as she states, that "all history is current; all injustice continues on some level" ("One Child" 129). Her images of people destroyed or destroying others originate in a vision of cultural reality expressed matter-of-factly, such as in the poem from *Revolutionary Petunias* "You Had to Go to Funerals": "At six and seven / The face in the gray box / Is nearly always your daddy's / Old schoolmate / Mowed down before his / Time." Walker's racial memory of a tangible, harsh reality succeeds in focusing experience, holding it fixed, and illuminating some aspects of brutality that might well be overlooked or obscured.

Walker's fiction expresses the outrage that she feels about the injustices of society; "I think," she has stated, "that growing up in the South, I have a very keen sense of injustice—a very prompt response to it" ("Writing to Survive" 14). It may well be that some of the brutal depictions of life in her writings are ways of responding to both particular and general injustices suffered by blacks throughout their history in the United States. Gloria Steinem, for instance, has concluded after interviewing Walker that "the rage and the imaginings of righteous murders that are in her writing are also in her. You just have to know her long enough to see the anger flash" ("Do You Know" 93). There are hidden layers in Walker's handling of injustice, so that it is not so easy to follow the logic behind it in her fiction. She herself has confessed, "It's true that I fantasize revenge for injustices, big and small. . . . I imagine how wonderful it must feel to kill the white man who oppresses you. . . . Lately . . . I've come to believe that you have some help when you fight. If a country or a person oppresses folks, it or he will pay for it. That happens more often than not. Years after the Indians died in the Trail of Tears, Andrew Jackson, who had been President at the time, had to be wrapped like a mummy to keep the flesh on his bones" ("Do You Know" 93). Her fictional use of rage, however, is more often than not contained within a family environment and directed toward self or kin, rather than toward outsiders.

One scene in *Meridian* delineates the everyday quality of familial rage in Walker's fiction. A woman who believes that her family and community, as well as the racial barriers and social order of the South, have all combined to rob her of a full life irons into her children's and husband's clothes her frustrations and her creativity. Instead of loving her family openly or accusing anyone explicitly, she uses her ordinary domestic chore to enclose her children in "the starch of her anger," as Walker labels it. This character, Mrs. Hill, includes her children in her victimization, and in the process she excludes them from any meaningful, close relationship with her. The result is a tension- and guilt-ridden existence, both for Mrs. Hill and for her family. The scene suggests how personal outrage and anger stemming from social and historical forces (particularly ignorance, discrimination, racism, exploitation, and sexism) become warped and distorted in Walker's world.

In fact, Walker has discussed her writing, and need to write, in terms that articulate her deflection of rage and her reconciliation with it. After the birth of her daughter, she put her frustrations and her energy into her work: "Write I did, night and day, *something*, and it was not even a choice, . . . but a necessity. When I didn't write I thought of making bombs and throwing them. . . . Writing saved me from the sin and *inconvenience* of violence—as it saves most writers who live in 'interesting' oppressive times and are not afflicted by personal immunity" ("One Child" 127). She does not have to add that her writing absorbed the violence, especially emotional violence, in the lives of her characters. Walker's recollection and the scene from *Meridian* add a situational context to the prevalent violence and excessive pain found in all of her fiction, but they do not fully address the motivational context for the choice of family as the expressive vehicle.

Walker creates a multiplicity of permanently maimed and damaged souls within the family structure who feel no pressure for responsible living or assume exemption from the demands of responsibility. There may be occasions of optimism or hope; for example, when Sarah, a Southern black art student in "A Sudden Trip Home in the Spring," returns from New York for her father's funeral, she comes, with the help of her brother, to understand her father's life after years of resenting his flaws, and she resolves to learn how to make her grandfather's face in stone. But more pervasive in Walker's fiction is despair: women who commit suicide, such as the wife in "Her Sweet Jerome," who sets fire to herself and her marriage bed; men who maim or kill, such as the father in "The Child Who Favored Daughter," who cuts off his daughter's breasts; people who allow themselves to become animals, such as Brownfield in *The Third Life of Grange Copeland*, who, accepting a "nothingness" in himself, shoots his wife in the face while his children watch; and people who simply give

108

up on life, such as Myrna in "Really Doesn't Crime Pay?" who spends her days softening her hands and thwarting her husband's desire for a child.

Walker assumes that by revealing negative actions and violent encounters, she may be able to repair the damage done by unreflective people who are unable to recognize that their actions have more than personal consequences, that they may rend bonds between generations and thus affect all members of a family, community, race, or society. In her depictions of abuse and violence, Walker takes the risk of misrepresenting the very people whom she seeks to change. Yet her unrelenting portraits of human weaknesses convey her message that art should "make us better"; "if [it] doesn't . . . then what on earth is it for?" ("Do You Know" 94). Her message, postulated in her novels, is that the breaches and violations must be mended for health and continuity, for "survival *whole*," as her character Grange Copeland declares.

Reparation or redemption may be undertaken by a single individual in whom Walker vests the responsibility for survival, because it is the action of a single individual that has caused the breakdown of experience or identity in private lives, and ultimately in the public or social life of the group. Individual characters acting alone become repositories of decent behavior, as well as harbingers that the messages embedded in the lives of generations of blacks will not be lost. One example is Elethia, a young woman who masterminds the retrieval of "Uncle Albert," a mummified black man who is all teeth, smiles, and servitude as a decoration in the window of a "whites only" restaurant, despite the reality of his having been a rebellious slave whose teeth were knocked out for his efforts to remain human. Elethia knows that Uncle Albert's denigration to a subservient happy waiter cannot be allowed. She and her cohorts break the plate glass, reclaim the mummy, burn it, and save the ashes. She aims to rid the world of all false, stereotypical images of blacks, especially men, and to recover the past, rectify its misrepresentations, and preserve the truth for future generations. Elethia realizes that the work will not end with rescuing Uncle Albert, but that it will extend over her lifetime. Walker's individual Elethias understand that breaches may have occurred between succeeding generations, but that progress in the present and toward the future depends upon reconstruction of the bridges that, as Carolyn Rodgers says in her poem "It Is Deep," one generation has "crossed over on." Although "Elethia" is not one of Walker's most successful stories, it adheres to her belief that the world, her reality, is filled with connections, oftentimes unsuspected connections, which she as an artist can illuminate.

Walker believes that as a writer she must work toward a larger perspective, which she describes as "connections made, or at least attempted, where none existed before, the straining to encompass in one's glance at the varied world the common thread, the unifying theme through immense diversity, a fearlessness of growth, of search, of look, that enlarges the private and the public world" ("Saving the Life" 152). For her, one way of structuring "the common thread" is by means of generations; she values the strength and purpose black generations have given to her writing, but she refuses to reduce their meanings to platitudes or to ignore the complexities of their lives.

"It is not," Walker stresses, "my child who has purged my face from history and herstory and left mystory . . . a mystery; my child loves my face . . . as I have loved my own parents' faces . . . and have refused to let them be denied, or myself to let them go" ("One Child" 139). Repeatedly, she uses the image of her mother's face "radiant," "ordering the universe in her personal conception of beauty. Her face . . . is a legacy . . . she leaves to me" ("In Search" 64). Walker treasures and preserves in her works not merely her parents' faces and her own, but those of her grandparents and great-grandparents and all her blood and social relatives as well. For instance, in the poem from *Goodnight Willie Lee* entitled "talking to my grandmother who died poor (while hearing Richard Nixon declare 'I am not a crook')," she concludes: "i must train myself to want / not one bit more / than i need to keep me alive / working / and recognizing beauty / in your so nearly undefeated face" (47). It is in her grandmother's "so nearly undefeated face" that Walker reads at what cost her people have survived.

Her conception of the black writer and herself is inextricably linked to survival. She has said, "Only recently did I fully realize . . . that through the years of listening to my mother's stories of her life, I have absorbed not only the stories themselves, but something of the manner in which she spoke, something of the urgency that involves the knowledge that her stories like her life must be recorded" ("In Search" 64). Derived partly from the urge to retain her parents' faces and their stories, her sense of black writers is that they are involved in a moral and physical struggle "the result of which," as she points out, "is expected to be some kind of larger freedom" ("Saving the Life" 152). Walker attributes this search for freedom to a black literary tradition based upon slave narratives which foster the belief in escape from the body along with freedom for the soul. Indeed, while the oral tradition, essential to even the most literary of slave narratives, such as Frederick Douglass's, is a prominent part of Walker's writing, its strength as a mode of telling in her work may be more immediately linked to her mother's voice. "Do you actually speak with your mother's voice?" Mary Helen Washington has asked Walker. The response is forthright: "Just as you have certain physical characteristics of your mother's—her laughter or her toes or her grade of hair—you also internalize certain emotional characteristics that are like hers. That is part of the legacy. They are internalized, merged with your own, transformed through the stories. When you're compelled to write her stories, it's because you recognize and prize those qualities of her in yourself" ("Her Mother's Gifts" 38).

Because of her conception of art and the artist, as well as her recognition of the value of her mother's stories and her family's faces, Walker displays an enormous sympathy for the older generation of Southern women ("Headragged Generals") and men ("billy club scar[ed]"), whose lives were sacrificed. As she has revealed in "The Women" from *Revolutionary Petunias:* "They were women then / My mama's generation / . . . How they battered down / Doors / . . . To discover books / Desks / A place for us / How they knew what we / Must know /Without knowing a page / Of it / Themselves." The poem celebrates the generation that preceded Walker's own, those men and women who opened doors through which they themselves would never pass and who were unafraid to attempt personal and social change in order to restructure subsequent generations. Walker acknowledges their achievement, but also their adversities.

Her older men, in particular, have experienced troubled, difficult lives, such as those of Grange Copeland, and Albert in *The Color Purple*. These men have been abusive in their youths, but they come to an essential understanding of their own lives and their families' as they learn to be reflective, responsible, and expressive individuals. Although they may seem to reflect her anti-male bias, they are more significant as portrayals of Walker's truth-telling from a particular perspective that is conscious of their weaknesses—weaknesses that they distort into violence against other blacks, especially women and children—and conscious, too, of their potential for regeneration. Walker's men to whom sexuality is no longer an issue are redeemed by learning to love and assume responsibility for their actions. In presenting these men, Walker first depicts what has come to be the stereotypes of blacks, essentially those set destructive patterns of emotional and psychological responses of black men to black life, their women, children, friends, whites, and themselves. Then she loosens the confines of the stereotype and attempts to penetrate the nexus of feelings that make these lives valuable in themselves and for others.

Much of the redemption, nevertheless, is only potential as Walker portrays it. The nameless husband in *The Color Purple* becomes "Albert" in his later years, because, like Grange Copeland in Walker's first novel, he discovers reflection which makes him a defined person who can accept the responsibility for his mistakes and the suffering he has caused, especially his abusive treatment of his wife whom he had denigrated ("You a woman . . . you nothing at all," 176). Despite his contemplative demeanor at the end of the novel, Albert remains in the realm of potential. His apparent psychological return to roots, though inadequately motivated, is primarily a portent of a healing process.

Walker names this dealing a "wholeness" in her essay "Beyond the Peacock: The Reconstruction of Flannery O'Connor," in which she, like her characters, returns to her roots in order to regenerate herself and to comprehend the pervasive impact of social environment. Her attitude is clear in the poem from *Once,* "South: The Name of Home," which opens: "when I am here again / the years of ease between / fall away / The smell of one / magnolia / sends my heart running / through the swamps. / the earth is red / here— / the trees bent, weeping / what secrets will not / the ravished land / reveal / of its abuse." It is an environment that is not without a history of pain, but it nonetheless connects generations of blacks to one another, to a "wholeness" of self, and to "the old unalterable roots," as in "Burial": "Today I bring my own child here; / to this place where my father's / grandmother rests undisturbed beneath the Georgia sun / . . . Forgetful of geographical resolutions as birds / the farflung young fly South to bury / the old dead." One key to "wholeness," even if it is rarely achieved, is the development of self-perception by means of generational ties to the land.

The achievements and dreams that emerge from the connected experience of generations are expressions of freedom and beauty, of power and community. The primary dream, usually voiced in terms of the creation of art, is that of freedom to be one's own self, specifically to be one's own black self and to claim, as do Walker's blues singers Shug Avery in *The Color Purple* and Gracie Mae Still in "Nineteen Fifty-Five," one's own life for one's self and for future generations.

Walker transforms the individual, so much a part of the special characteristics used to define the white South, into a person who is black and most often female. In the one-page story "Petunias" from *You Can't Keep a Good Woman Down,* she individualizes an unnamed woman with a history and a sense of herself. The woman writes in her diary just before her death in an explosion of a bomb her son intends for the revolution: "my daddy's grandmama was a slave on the Tearslee Plantation. They dug up her grave when I started agitating in the Movement. One morning I found her dust dumped over my verbena bed, a splinery leg bone had fell among my petunias." This woman and others in Walker's canon are the stereotyped, the maimed, the distorted blacks who still rise, as Maya Angelou entitles one of her works, "Still I Rise." These characters become redeemed as individuals with an indelible sense of self. But that act of rising out of the depths of degradation or depression is accomplished by means of the person's

coming to terms with the truth of his or her community, with
his or her social and historical place among others who have
suffered, grieved, laughed, and lusted, but who miraculously
have held on to dignity and selfhood. Characters, such as
Sammy Lou, a woman on her way to the electric chair for
killing her husband's murderer, pass on a powerful legacy of
individual identity; Sammy Lou leaves her children the instructions: "Always respect the word of God," and "Don't yall
forget to *water* my purple petunias."

Walker operates within this legacy. She keeps before
her the vision of her own mother, who cultivated magnificent
flower gardens, despite her work from sunup to dark either in
the fields or as a domestic for less than twenty dollars a week.
Walker refers to her mother's gardens as her "art," "her ability
to hold on, even in simple ways" ("In Search" 64). That garden is her recurrent metaphor for both art and beauty, endurance and survival; it is essentially, too, Walker's articulation of
the process by which individuals find selfhood through examining the experiences of others who have preceded them.
As she has stated, "Guided by my heritage of a love of beauty
and a respect for strength, in search of my mother's garden, I
found my own" ("In Search" 64). In fact, her very first novel,
The Third Life of Grange Copeland, directly involves the gardens of the character Mem as emblems of her tenacious will
to survive in beauty and in love.

In celebrating her people (characters, mediums, models, and family), Walker demonstrates a deeply-rooted consciousness of her role as an artist in a socially and politically
complex world. "To acknowledge ancestors means," she states,
"we are aware that we did not make ourselves. . . . The grace
with which we embrace life, in spite of the pain, the sorrows,
is always a measure of what has gone before" (*RP* Preface 1).
By acknowledging ancestors, she acknowledges that she is
part of a black tradition of artists, particularly that strain stemming from Southern slave narrators, folk tellers of tales, and
literary artists. These include Zora Neale Hurston, one of her
major influences, and Margaret Walker, her fellow poet and
novelist who in the 1940s paid tribute to blacks in "For My
People" and in the process celebrated her roots "deep in
Southern life" and her "grandmothers . . . strong . . . full of

114

memories."[1] Similarly, Alice Walker derives meaning from the historical experiences of her foremothers, because she insists, "nothing is ever a product of the immediate present" (O'Brien, *Interviews* 197).

She takes into account the dynamics of collective identity along with the demands that social codes place upon the group, and she considers the structure of personal identity with its unreflected social relations, especially family. She shapes her fiction so that both collective and personal identities become keys to character, theme, and plot. At the same time, she structures the experience of identity in terms of social and familial generations that have the potential to transform black life.

In her first novel, *The Third Life of Grange Copeland,* three generations of Copelands converge to create Ruth's identity, and three generations form the stages or lives of the patriarch and title character, Grange Copeland. When any one member of the Copeland family or of a particular social generation of blacks (from 1920 to 1960) ignores the dynamics of family structures or forgets the historical perspective that the structures are maintained through necessity and love, he or she loses the capacity for primary identifications with race, family, and community, and loses as well the major basis for defining one's self and one's humanity. The most detailed illustration presented in the novel is Brownfield, the son of Grange and a member of the middle generation in the work.

Brownfield Copeland becomes one of "the living dead, one of the many who had lost their souls in the American wilderness" (*TL* 138). He reduces his murder of his wife to a simple theorem: "*He liked plump women. . . . Ergo,* he had murdered his wife because she had become skinny" (161). Because of his twisted logic, Brownfield "could forget [his wife's] basic reality, convert it into comparisons. She had been like good pie, or good whiskey, but there had never been a self to her" (162). Not only by means of the murder itself, but also by the process of his reasoning about it, he strips himself of his humanity when he negates his culpability with the negation of his wife's existence as a human being.

Brownfield's physical death sadly, though appropriately in Walker's construction, comes at the hands of his father

Grange and over the future of his daughter Ruth. But his spiritual death occurs much earlier "as he lay thrashing about, knowing the rigidity of his belief in misery, knowing he could never renew or change himself, for this changelessness was now all he had, he could not clarify what was the duty of love" (227). He compounds one of the greatest sins in Walker's works, the refusal or inability to change, with his dismissal of meaning in family bonds. Ironically, his death makes possible the completion of change in his daughter's life that had been fostered by his father, who late in his life understood the necessity of moving beyond the perverted emotions constricting the lives of the Copelands.

In *Meridian*, Walker's second novel, the heroine divests herself of immediate blood relations—her child and her parents—in order to align herself completely with the larger racial and social generations of blacks. Meridian Hill insists that although seemingly alone in the world, she has created a fusion with her generation of activist blacks and older generations of oppressed blacks. The form of the work, developed in flashbacks, follows a pattern of Meridian's casting off the demands made by authority and responsibility within the conventional family and traditional institutions. Unlike Brownfield's rejection of responsibility, the rupture in this novel is ultimately positive, despite its being the most radical and mysterious instance of change and acceptance in Walker's fiction. It is positive because the novel creates a new basis for defining Meridian's self and for accepting responsibility for one's actions. In fact, the controlling metaphor is resurrection and rebirth, an acting out of the renewal impossible for Brownfield. By the end of the novel, Meridian's personal identity has become a collective identity. "There is water in the world for us / brought by our friends," she writes in one of her two poems, "though the rock of mother and god / vanishes into sand / and we, cast out alone / to heal / and re-create ourselves" (*M* 219). In spite of her painful private experiences, Meridian is born anew into a pluralistic cultural self, a "we" that is and must be self-less and without ordinary prerequisites for personal identity. And significantly, because she exemplifies Walker's recurrent statement of women as leaders and models, Meridian leaves her male disciple Truman Held to follow her and to await the arrival of others from their social group.

Truman's search, structurally a duplication of Meridian's, is part of personal change that is more necessary for men than for women in Walker's fiction and that becomes social change through the consequences of actions taken by individuals who must face constraints, as well as opportunities, in their lives, but must also know why they act and what the consequences will be. Truman resolves to live the life of an ascetic so that he might one day be worthy to join Meridian and others "at the river," where they "will watch the evening sun go down. And in the darkness maybe [they] will know the truth" (227). The search for truth leads Truman, like Meridian, to a commitment to the social generation of blacks to which he belongs. He follows Meridian's rationale for his action: "i want to put an end to guilt / i want to put an end to shame / whatever you have done my sister / (my brother) / know i wish to forgive you / love you" (219). By so doing, Truman accepts his personal duty toward all blacks, discovers his own meaning, and commits his life in love to both present and future generations.

Perhaps Walker's third novel most effectively conveys her messages and evidences her heritage as a black Southern writer. In *The Color Purple*, which won the Pulitzer Prize for fiction in 1983, she takes a perspectivistic or "emic" approach to character delineation and cultural reality. She sees and portrays a world from the inside outward; she uses the eyes of Celie, a surnameless, male-dominated, and abused woman, who records her experiences in letters. Celie is not a "new" character in Walker's fiction; she is similar to one of the sisters in "Everyday Use," the bride in "Roselily," and the daughter in "The Child Who Favored Daughter," but unlike these other silent, suffering women characters, Celie writes her story in her own voice. She tells her life as only she has known it: a girl, merely, a child, raped by her stepfather whom she believes is her natural father, that same girl bearing his two children only to have them stolen by him and to be told that they are dead; the denial and suppression of that girl's actual background and history, as well as her letters from her sister.

In Celie's epistles, Walker makes her strongest effort so far to confront the patterns in a specified world and to order and articulate the codes creating those patterns. In effect, she uses the uncovered patterns to connect, assimilate, and structure the content of one human being's world and relationship to that world. Celie writes letters—her story, history—to God and to her sister Nettie. She writes out of desperation and in order to preserve some core of her existence. In love and hope, she writes to save herself, just as Walker has said of her own writing: "I have written to stay alive . . . I've written to survive"; "writing poetry is my way of celebrating with the world that I have not committed suicide the evening before" ("Writing to Survive" 12, *Interviews* 197). Celie writes from the heart, and grows stronger, more defined, more fluent, while simultaneously her intensively private, almost cryptic style develops into a still personal, subjective style, but one which encompasses much more of the lives surrounding her.

While social interactions and institutions typically define human reality, these do not ultimately define Celie's. She is isolated and alone, despite the numbers of family members and others impinging upon her world. Slowly and cautiously, she builds a reality that is different, one based upon her singular position and the abstractions she herself conceives in the course of her everyday life. Her inner life is unperverted by the abuse and violence she suffers. Only when she has formulated the outlines of her private identity in writing does her interaction with others become a significant factor in making sense of social codes in the public world. When she reaches her conclusions, she has rejected most of the available social models for personal identity; she is neither Shug Avery, the hard-living blues singer who gives and takes what she wants in being herself, nor is she Nettie, her sister who can experience the wider world outside the social environment of her childhood. Yet, Celie passionately loves both of these women, and has tried at different stages to emulate them. Celie's own subjective probings lead her to confirm her individual interpretation of herself and of her situational contexts. Nonetheless, she does arrive, as invariably a Walker bearer of responsibility must, at her place in the spectrum of life, her relationship to others, and her own continuity.

Celie affirms herself: "I'm pore, I'm black, I may be ugly and can't cook, a voice say to everything listening. But I'm here" (*CP* 176). Her words echo those of Langston Hughes's folk philosopher, Jesse B. Semple (Simple): "I'm still here. . . . I've been underfed, underpaid. . . . I've been abused, confused, misused. . . . I done had everything from flat feet to a flat head. . . . but I am still here. . . . I'm still here."[2] Celie's verbal connection to Hughes's black everyman and the black oral tradition extends her affirmation of self, so that it becomes racial, as well as personal, and is an actualization, rather than the potentiality that most often appears in Walker's work. Celie *is*, or in her own black folk English, she *be's* her own black, nappy-haired, ordinary self in all the power and pain that combine in her writing to reveal the girl, the female becoming totally a woman-person who survives and belies the weak, passive exterior her family and community presume to be her whole self. Her act of writing and affirming is magnificent. It is an achievement deserving of celebration, and perhaps not coincidentally, it is Walker's first "happy ending," not only for her character Celie, but for most of her fictional family as well.

Celie's progeny will make the present and future generations. Her two children—Adam, who takes the African name "Omatangu" and marries an African woman, and Olivia, who promises to be a sister to her brother's bride Tashi—exist without the blight affecting their mother and their aunt, even though their lives as children of missionaries in Africa have not been without the problems of colonialization and oppression. Adam's and Olivia's return to America, to the South, and to Celie at the end of the novel may be contrived, but it signals the continuity of generations, the return (ironically perhaps) to the "old, unalterable roots." Their return is cause for a larger hope for the race, and for celebration within the family and community, because they have survived "whole," literally since they miraculously survive a shipwreck and symbolically since they have acquired definite life-affirming attitudes.

Near the end of the novel, Celie's stepson comments on a Fourth of July barbecue, and in the process provides a commentary on the letters Celie has written and the novel Walker has produced; he says, "White folks busy celebrating they independence from England. . . . Us can spend the day celebrating each other" (CP 243). *The Color Purple,* with its reiteration of "purple" as the motif symbolizing the miracle of color and life apparent in all of Walker's works, is a celebration of "each other," individual selves inextricably linked in social and familial generations. In the celebration is an inexplicable strength, which Walker attributes to her own optimism, "based," she states, "on what I saw of the courage and magnificence of people in Mississippi and in Georgia. . . . I saw that the human spirit can be so much more incredible and beautiful than most people ever dream . . . that people who have very little, . . . who have been treated abominably by society, can still do incredible things . . . no only *do* things, but can be great human beings" ("Writing to Survive" 14–15).

Despite her concentration on the brutal treatment of black women and the unmitigated abuse of children, Walker believes in the beauty and the power of the individual, and ultimately of the group. And because she does, she is willing to gamble on ways of articulating her unique vision. She is not always successful; the experimental stories of *You Can't Keep a Good Woman Down* are an example, as are the unconvincing letters from Celie's sister Nettie in Africa. However, even in the less effective works, Walker validates the necessity of struggling out of external constrictions to find meaning in one's own life. It seems quite appropriate that both her dedication and statement at the end of *The Color Purple* reaffirm and invoke the spirits of people who fill her head and her work with their voices and their presence, with the selves that come to *be* within the pages of her writing.

Certainly, in the composition of much of her work so far, Alice Walker must have felt as she did while writing "The Revenge of Hannah Kemhuff," a work inspired by one of her mother's own stories: "I gathered up the historical and psychological threads of the life my ancestors lived, and in the writing . . . I felt joy and strength and my own continuity. I had that wonderful feeling that writers get sometimes . . . of being with a great many people, ancient spirits, all very happy to see me consulting and acknowledging them, and eager to let me know through the joy of their presence, that indeed, I am not alone" ("Saving the Life" 157). Perhaps this consoling vision of interconnections is one reason why Alice Walker can capture the deep layers of affirmative and destructive feelings in human beings who must live and make their lives known, and why she can compel readers to heed their messages.

☐ *Notes* ■

1. See Margaret Walker, "Sorrow's Home," "Lineage," in *For My People* (New Haven: Yale University Press, 1942), 12, 25.
2. See Langston Hughes, "Final Fear," in *Simple Speaks His Mind* (New York: Simon and Schuster, 1950), 112–113.

☐ *Works Cited* ■

Brewer, Krista. "Writing to Survive: An Interview with Alice Walker." *Southern Exposure* 9 (Summer 1981): 12–15.

O'Brien, John. "Interview with Alice Walker." In *Interviews with Black Writers*, ed. John O'Brien. New York: Liveright, 1973. Reprinted in this volume.

Steinem, Gloria. "Do You Know This Woman? She Knows You: A Profile of Alice Walker." *Ms.* 10 (June 1982): 35-37, 89-94.

Walker, Alice. "The Black Writer and the Southern Experience." *New South* 25 (Fall 1970): 23-26.

———. "In Search of Our Mothers' Gardens: The Creativity of Black Women in the South." *Southern Exposure* 4 (Winter 1977): 64-70, 105. Reprinted in this volume.

———. "One Child of One's Own: A Meaningful Digression Within the Work(s)." In *The Writer on Her Work*, ed. Janet Sternberg. New York: Norton, 1980.

———. "Saving the Life That Is Your Own: The Importance of Models in the Artist's Life." In *The Third Woman: Minority Women Writers of the United States*, ed. Dexter Fisher. Boston: Houghton Mifflin, 1980.

Washington, Mary Helen. "Alice Walker: Her Mother's Gifts." *Ms.* 10 (June 1982): 38.

☐ BARBARA T. CHRISTIAN ■

Alice Walker: The Black Woman Artist as Wayward

I find my own
small person
a standing self
against the world
an equality of wills
I finally understand[1]

Alice Walker has produced a significant body of work since 1968, when *Once*, her first volume of poetry, was published. Prolific, albeit a young writer, she is already acclaimed by many to be one of America's finest novelists, having captured both the American Book Award and the coveted Pulitzer in 1983.

Her substantial body of writing, though it varies, is characterized by specific recurrent motifs. Most obvious is Walker's attention to the Black woman as creator, and to how her attempt to be whole relates to the health of her community. This theme is certainly focal to Walker's two collections of short stories, *In Love and Trouble* and *You Can't Keep a Good Woman Down*, to her classic essay, *In Search of Our Mothers' Gardens*, and to *Meridian* and *The Color Purple*, her second and third novels. And it reverberates in her personal

From *Black Women Writers (1950–1980): A Critical Evaluation*, ed. Mari Evans (Garden City, N.Y.: Anchor/Doubleday, 1984), pp. 457–477.

efforts to help rescue the works of Zora Neale Hurston from a threatening oblivion. Increasingly, as indicated by her last collection of poems, *Good Night Willie Lee,* Walker's work is Black women-centered.

Another recurrent motif in Walker's work is her insistence on probing the relationship between struggle and change, a probing that encompasses the pain of Black people's lives, against which the writer protests but which she will not ignore. Paradoxically such pain sometimes results in growth, precisely because of the nature of the struggle that must be borne, if there is to be change. Presented primarily through three generations of one family in Walker's first novel, *The Third Life of Grange Copeland,* the struggle to change takes on overt societal dimensions in *Meridian,* her second novel. Characteristically this theme is presented in her poetry, fiction, and essays, as a spiritual legacy of Black people in the South.

One might also characterize Walker's work as organically spare rather than elaborate, ascetic rather than lush, a process of stripping off layers, honing down to the core. This pattern, impressionistic in *Once,* is refined in her subsequent volumes of poetry and clearly marks the structure of her fiction and essays. There is a concentrated distillation of language which, ironically, allows her to expand rather than constrict. Few contemporary American writers have examined so many facets of sex and race, love and societal changes, as has Walker, without abandoning the personal grace that distinguishes her voice.

These elements—the focus on the struggle of Black people, especially Black women, to claim their own lives, and the contention that this struggle emanates from a deepening of self-knowledge and love—are characteristics of Walker's work. Yet it seems they are not really the essential quality that distinguishes her work, for these characteristics might be said to apply to any number of contemporary Black women writers—e.g., Toni Morrison, Paule Marshall, June Jordan. Walker's peculiar sound, the specific mode through which her deepening of self-knowledge and self-love comes, seems to have much to do with her contrariness, her willingness at all turns to challenge the fashionable belief of the day, to reexamine it in the light of her own experiences and of dearly won principles which she has previously challenged and absorbed. There is a sense in which the "forbidden" in the society is consistently approached by Walker as a possible route to truth. At the core of this contrariness is an unwavering honesty about what she sees. Thus in *Once*, her first volume of poems, the then twenty-three-year-old Walker wrote, during the heyday of Afro-Americans' romanticizing of their motherland, about her stay in Africa, in images that were not always complimentary. In her poem "Karamojans" Walker demystified Africa:

> A tall man
> Without clothes
> Beautiful
> Like a statue
> Up close
> His eyes
> Are running
> Sores[2]

Such a perception was, at that time, practically blasphemy among a progressive element of Black thinkers and activists. Yet, seemingly impervious to the risk of rebuke, the young Walker challenged the idealistic view of Africa as an image, a beautiful artifact to be used by Afro-Americans in their pursuit of racial pride. The poet does not flinch from what she sees—does not romanticize or inflate it ("His eyes / Are running / Sores.") Yet her words acknowledge that she knows the ideal African image as others project it: "Beautiful / Like a statue." It is the "Up close" that sets up the tension in the lines between appearance and reality, mystification and the real, and provides Walker's peculiar sound, her insistence on honesty as if there were no other way to be. The lines, then, do not scream at the reader or harp on the distinction between the image and the man she sees. The lines *are* that distinction. They embody the tension, stripping its dimensions down to the essentials. "Karamojans" ends:

> The Karamojans
> Never civilized

A proud people
I think there
Are
A hundred left (22)

So much for the concept of pride without question.

At the cutting edge of much of Walker's early work is an intense examination of those ideas advocated by the most visible of recent Afro-American spokespersons. In 1970, at the height of cultural nationalism, the substance of most Black literary activity was focused on the rebellious urban Black in confrontation with white society. In that year Walker's first novel, *The Third Life of Grange Copeland,* was published. By tracing the history of the Copeland family through three generations, Walker demonstrated the relationship between the racist sharecropping system and the violence that the men, women, and children of that family inflict on each other. The novel is most emphatically located in the rural South, rather than the Northern urban ghetto; its characters are Southern peasants rather than Northern lumpen, reminding us that much of Afro-American population is still under the yoke of a feudal sharecropping system. And the novel is written more from the angle of the tentative survival of a Black family than from an overt confrontation between Black and white.

Also, Walker's first novel, like Marshall's *The Chosen Place, the Timeless People* (1969) and Morrison's *The Bluest Eye* (1970), seemed out of step with the end-of-the-decade work of such writers as Amiri Baraka, or Ishmael Reed— Black writers on opposing sides of the spectrum—in that the struggle her major characters wage against racism is located in, sometimes veiled by, a network of family and community. The impact of racism is felt primarily through the characters' mistaken definitions of themselves as men and women. Grange Copeland first hates himself because he is powerless, as opposed to powerful, the definition of maleness for him. His reaction is to prove his power by inflicting violence on the women around him. His brief sojourn in the North where he feels invisible, a step below powerlessness, causes him to hate whites as his oppressors. That, however, for Walker, does not precipitate meaningful struggle. It is only when he learns to

126

love himself, through his commitment to his granddaughter, Ruth, that Grange Copeland is able to confront the white racist system. And in so doing, he must also destroy his son, the fruit of his initial self-hatred.

The Third Life of Grange Copeland, then, is based on the principle that societal change is invariably linked to personal change, that the struggle must be inner- as well as outer-directed. Walker's insistence on locating the motivation for struggle within the self led her to examine the definition of nigger, that oft-used word in the literature of the late sixties. Her definition, however, is not generalized but precise: a nigger is a Black person who believes he or she is incapable of being responsible for his or her actions, that the white folks are to blame for everything, including his or her behavior. As Grange says to his son, Brownfield, in their one meaningful exchange in the novel: "'. . . when they get you thinking they're to blame for everything they have you thinking they're some kind of gods. . . . Shit, nobody's as powerful as we make them out to be. We got our own souls, don't we?'"[3]

The question lingering at the end of this novel— whether the psychological impact of oppression is so great that it precludes one's overcoming of it—is also a major undercurrent of the literature of this period. There is a tension in the militant literature of the late sixties between a need to *assert* the love of Black people for Black people and an anger that Black people have somehow allowed themselves to be oppressed. The ambivalence caused by a desire for self-love and an expression of shame is seldom clearly articulated in the literature but implied in the militant Black writer's exhortation to their people to stop being niggers and start becoming Black men and women. What Walker did, in her first novel, was to give voice to this tension and to graph the development of one man in his journey toward its resolution.

Grange Copeland's journey toward this resolution is not, however, an idea that Walker imposes on the novel. A characteristic of hers is her attempt to use the essence of a complex dilemma organically in the composing of her work. So the structure of *The Third Life of Grange Copeland* is based on the dramatic tension between the pervasive racism of the society and the need for her characters, if they are to hold on to self-love, to accept responsibility for their own lives. The novel is divided into two parts, the first analyzing the degeneration of Grange's and then his son Brownfield's respective families, the second focusing on the regeneration of the Copelands, as Grange, against all odds, takes responsibility for Brownfield's daughter, Ruth. Within these two larger pieces, Walker created a quilt of recurring motifs which are arranged, examined, and rearranged so that the reader might understand the complex nature of the tension between the power of oppressive societal forces and the possibility for change. Walker's use of recurring economical patterns, much like a quilting process, gives the novel much of its force and uniqueness. Her insistence on critically examining the idea of the time led her not only to analysis but also to a synthesis that increasingly marks her work.

Walker is drawn to the integral and economical process of quilt making as a model for her own craft. For through it, one can create out of seemingly disparate everyday materials patterns of clarity, imagination, and beauty. Two of her works especially emphasize the idea of this process: her classic essay *In Search of Our Mothers' Gardens* and her short story "Everyday Use." Each piece complements the other and articulates the precise meaning of the quilt as idea and process for this writer.

In *In Search of Our Mothers' Gardens,* Walker directly asks the question that every writer must: From whence do I, as a writer, come? What is my tradition? In pursuing the question she focuses most intensely on her female heritage, in itself a point of departure from the route most writers have taken. Walker traces the images of Black women in the literature as well as those few of them who were able to be writers. However, as significant as the tracing of that literary history is, Walker's major insight in the essay is her illumination of the creative legacy of "ordinary" Black women of the South, a focus which complements but finally transcends literary history. In her insistence on honesty, on examining the roots of *her own* creativity, she invokes not so much the literature of Black women, which was probably unknown to her as a budding child writer, but the creativity known to her of her mother, her grandmother, the women around her.

What did some slave women or Black women of this century do with the creativity that might have, in a less restrictive society, expressed itself in paint, words, clay? Walker reflects on a truth so obvious it is seldom acknowledged: they used the few media left them by a society that labeled them lowly, menial. Some, like Walker's mother, expressed it in the growing of magnificent gardens; some in cooking; others in quilts of imagination and passion like the one Walker saw at the Smithsonian Institution. Walker's description of that quilt's impact on her brings together essential elements of her more recent work: the theme of the Black woman's creativity—her transformation despite opposition of the bits and pieces allowed her by society into a work of functional beauty.

But Walker does not merely acknowledge quilts (or the art Black women created out of "low" media) as high art, a tendency now fostered by many women who have discovered the works of their maternal ancestors. She is also impressed by their *functional* beauty and by the process that produced them. Her short story "Everyday Use" is in some ways a conclusion in fiction to her essay. Just as she juxtaposed the history of Black women writers with the creative legacy of ordinary Black women, so she complemented her own essay, a search for the roots of her own creativity, with a story that embodies the idea itself.

In "Everyday Use," Walker again scrutinizes a popular premise of the times. The story, which is dedicated to "your grandmama," is about the use and misuse of the concept of heritage. The mother of two daughters, one selfish and stylish, the other scarred and caring, passes on to us its true definition. Dee, the sister who has always despised the backward ways of her Southern rural family, comes back to visit her old home. She has returned to her Black roots because now they are fashionable. So she glibly delights in the artifacts of her heritage: the rough benches her father made, the handmade butter churn which she intends to use for a decorative centerpiece, the quilts made by her grandma Dee after whom she was named—the *things* that have been passed on. Ironically, in keeping with the times, Dee has changed her name to Wangero, denying the existence of her namesake, even as she covets the quilts she made.

On the other hand, her sister Maggie is not aware of the word *heritage*. But she loves her grandma and cherishes her memory in the quilts she made. Maggie has accepted the *spirit* that was passed on to her. The contrast between the two sisters is aptly summarized in Dee's focal line in the story: "'Maggie can't appreciate these quilts!' she [Dee] said. 'She'd probably be backward enough to put them to everyday use.'" Which her mother counters with: "'She can always make some more. Maggie knows how to quilt.'"

The mother affirms the functional nature of their heritage and insists that it must continually be renewed rather than fixed in the past. The mother's succinct phrasing of the meaning of *heritage* is underscored by Dee's lack of knowledge about the bits and pieces that make up these quilts, the process of quilting that Maggie knows. For Maggie appreciates the people who made them while Dee can only possess the "priceless" products. Dee's final words, ironically, exemplify her misuse of the concept of heritage, of what is passed on:

"'What don't I understand?' I wanted to know.

"'Your heritage,' she said. And then she turned to Maggie, kissed her and said, 'You ought to try to make something of yourself, too, Maggie. It's a new day for us. But from the way you and mama still live you'd never know it.'"

In critically analyzing the uses of the concept of heritage, Walker arrives at important distinctions. As an abstraction rather than a living idea, its misuse can subordinate people to artifact, can elevate culture above the community. And because she uses, as the artifact, quilts which were made by Southern Black women, she focuses attention on those supposedly backward folk who never heard the word heritage but fashioned a functional tradition out of little matter and much spirit.

In "Everyday Use," the mother, seemingly in a fit of contrariness, snatches the beautiful quilts out of the hands of the "Black" Wangero and gives them to the "backward" Maggie. This story is one of eleven in Walker's first collection of short stories, *In Love and Trouble*. Though written over a period of some five years, the volume is unified by two of Walker's most persistent characteristics: her use of a Southern Black woman character as protagonist, and that character's insistence on challenging convention, on being herself, sometimes in spite of herself.

Walker sets the tone for this volume by introducing the stories with two excerpts, one from *The Concubine*, a novel by the contemporary West African writer Elechi Amadi, the other from *Letters to a Young Poet* by the early-twentieth-century German poet Rainer Maria Rilke. The first excerpt emphasizes the rigidity of West African convention in relation to women. Such convention results in a young girl's contrariness, which her society explains away by saying she is unduly influenced by *agwu*, her personal spirit. The second excerpt from Rilke summarizes a philosophy of life that permeates the work of Alice Walker:

> People have (with the help of conventions) oriented all their solutions towards the easy and towards the easiest of the easy; but it is clear that we must hold to what is difficult; everything in nature grows and defines itself in its own way, and is characteristically and spontaneously itself, seeks at all costs to be so against all opposition.[4]

The protagonists in this volume embody this philosophy. They seek at all costs to be characteristically and spontaneously themselves. But because the conventions which gravely affect relationships between male and female, Black and white, young and old, are so rigid, the heroines of *In Love and Trouble* seem backward, contrary, mad. Depending on their degree of freedom within the society, they express their *agwu* in dream, word, or act.

Roselily, the poor mother of illegitimate children, can express her *agwu* only through dreaming, during her wedding to a Northern Black Muslim. Though her marriage is seen by most as a triumphant delivery from her poor backward condition, she sees that, as a woman, whether single or married, Christian or Muslim, she is confined. She can only dream that "She wants to live for once. But doesn't quite know what that means. Wonders if she ever has done it. If she ever will."[5]

In contrast to Roselily, Myrna, the protagonist of "Really, Doesn't Crime Pay" is the wife of a middle-class Southern Black man. Still, she too is trapped by her husband and society's view of woman, though her confinement is not within a black veil but in the decorative mythology of the Southern Lady. However, unlike Roselily, Myrna does more than dream, she writes. In a series of journal entries, she tells us how the restrictions imposed upon her creativity lead her to attempt to noisily murder her husband, an act certainly perceived by her society as madness.

Most of the young heroines in this volume struggle through dream or word against age-old as well as new manifestations of societal conventions imposed upon them. In contrast, the older women act. Like the mother in "Everyday Use," the old woman in "The Welcome Table" totally ignores convention when she enters the white church from which she is barred. The contrary act of this backward woman challenges all the conventions—"God, mother, country, earth, church. It involved all that and well they knew it."[6]

Again, through juxtaposing the restrictions imposed on her protagonists with their subsequent responses, Walker illuminates the tension as she did in *The Third Life of Grange Copeland* between convention and the struggle to be whole. Only this time, the focus is very much on the unique vortex of restrictions imposed on Black women by their community and white society. Her protagonists' dreams, words, acts, often explained away by society as the expressions of a contrary nature, a troubled *agwu,* are the price all beings, against opposition, would pay to be spontaneously and characteristically themselves. In *In Love and Trouble,* Walker emphasized the impact of sexism as well as racism on Black communities. Her insistence on honesty, on the validity of her own experience as well as the experience of other Southern Black women, ran counter to the popular notion of the early seventies that racism was the only evil that affected Black women. Her first collection of short stories specifically demonstrated the interconnectedness of American sexism and racism, for they are both based on the notion of dominance and on unnatural hierarchical distinctions.

Walker does not choose Southern Black women to be her major protagonists only because she is one, but also, I believe, because she has discovered in the tradition and history they collectively experience an understanding of oppression which has elicited from them a willingness to reject convention and to hold to what is difficult. Meridian, her most developed character, is a person who allows "an idea—no matter where it came from—to penetrate her life." The idea that penetrates Meridian's life, the idea of nonviolent resistance, is really rooted in a question: when is it necessary, when is it right, to kill? And the intensity with which Meridian pursues that question is due to her view of herself as a mother, a creator rather than a destroyer of life. The source to which she goes for the answer to that question is her people, especially the heritage that has been passed on to her by her maternal ancestors. She is thrilled by the fact that Black women were "always imitating Harriet Tubman escaping to become something unheard of. Outrageous." And that "even in more conventional things black women struck out for the unknown."[7] Like Walker in *In Search of Our Mothers' Gardens,* Meridian seeks her identity through the legacy passed on to her by Southern Black women.

Yet Walker does not rest easy even with this idea, an idea which glorifies the Black woman. For in *Meridian* she scrutinizes that tradition which is based on the monumental myth of Black motherhood, a myth based on the true stories of sacrifice Black mothers performed for their children. But the myth is also restrictive, for it imposes a stereotype of Black women, a stereotype of strength which denies them choice, and hardly admits of the many who were destroyed. In her characterization of Margaret and Mem Copeland in *The Third Life of Grange Copeland* Walker acknowledges the abused Black women who, unlike Faulkner's Dilsey, did not endure. She goes a step further in *Meridian.* Meridian's quest for wholeness and her involvement in the Civil Rights Movement is initiated by her feelings of inadequacy in living up to the standards of Black motherhood. Meridian gives up her son because she believes she will poison his growth with the thorns of guilt and she has her tubes tied after a painful abortion. In this novel, then, Walker probes the idea of Black motherhood, as she develops a character who so elevates it that she at first believes she can not properly fulfill it. Again, Walker approaches the forbidden as a possible route to another truth.

Not only did Walker challenge the monument of Black

motherhood in *Meridian,* she also entered the fray about the efficacy of motherhood in which American feminists were then, as they are now, engaged. As many radical feminists blamed motherhood for the waste in women's lives and saw it as a dead end for a woman, Walker insisted on a deeper analysis: she did not present motherhood in itself as restrictive. It is so because of the little value society places on children, especially Black children, on mothers, especially Black mothers, on life itself. In the novel, Walker acknowledges that a mother in this society is often "buried alive, walled away from her own life, brick by brick."[8] Yet the novel is based on Meridian's insistence on the sacredness of life. Throughout her quest she is surrounded by children whose lives she tries to preserve. In seeking the children she can no longer have she takes responsibility for the life of all the people. Her aborted motherhood yields to her a perspective on life—that of "expanding her mind with action." In keeping with this principle, Walker tells us in her essay "*One* Child of One's Own":

> It is not my child who has purged my face from history and herstory and left mystory just that, a mystery; my child loves my face and would have it on every page, if she could, as I have loved my own parents' faces above all others, and refused to let them be denied, or myself to let them go.[9]

In fact, *Meridian* is based on this idea, the sacredness and continuity of life—and on another, that it might be necessary to take life in order to preserve it and make it possible for future generations. Perhaps the most difficult paradox that Walker has examined to date is the relationship between violence and revolution, a relationship that so many take for granted that such scrutiny seems outlandish. Like her heroine, Meridian, who holds on to the idea of nonviolent resistance after it has been discarded as a viable means to change, Walker persists in struggling with this age-old dilemma—that of death giving life. What the novel *Meridian* suggests is that unless such a struggle is taken on by those who would change society, their revolution will not be integral. For they may destroy that which they abhor only to resurrect it in themselves. Meridian discovers, only through personal struggle in conjunction with her involvement with the everyday lives of her people,

> that the respect she owed her life was to continue, against whatever obstacles, to live it, and not to give up any particle of it without a fight to the death, preferably *not* her own. And that this existence extended beyond herself to those around her because, in fact, the years in America had created them One Life.[10]

But though the concept of One Life motivates Meridian in her quest toward physical and spiritual health, the societal evils which subordinate one class to another, one race to another, one sex to another, fragment and ultimately threaten life. So that the novel *Meridian*, like *The Third Life of Grange Copeland*, is built on the tension between the African concept of animism, "that spirit inhabits all life," and the societal forces that inhibit the growth of the living toward their natural state of freedom.

Because of her analysis of sexism in the novel as well as in *In Love and Trouble*, Walker is often labeled a feminist writer. Yet she also challenges this definition as it is formulated by most white American feminists. In "*One* Child of One's Own" (1978), Walker insists on the twin "afflictions" of her life. That white feminists as well as some Black people deny the Black woman her womanhood—that they define issues in terms of Blacks on one hand, women (meaning white women) on the other. They miss the obvious fact—that Black people come in both sexes. Walker put it strongly:

> It occurred to me that perhaps white women feminists, no less than white women generally, cannot imagine that black women have vaginas. Or if they can, where imagination leads them is too far to go.
>
> Perhaps it is the black women's children, whom the white woman—having more to offer her own children, and certainly not having to offer them slavery or a slave heritage or poverty or hatred, generally speaking: segregated schools, slum neighborhoods, the worst of everything—resents. For they must always make her feel guilty. She fears knowing that black

135

women want the best for their children just as she does. But she also knows black children are to have less in this world so that her children, white children, will have more. (In some countries, all.)

Better then to deny that the black woman has a vagina. Is capable of motherhood. Is a woman.[11]

And Walker *also* writes of the unwillingness of many Black women to acknowledge or address the problems of sexism that affect them because they feel they must protect Black men. To this she asserts that if Black women turn away from the women's movement, they turn away from women moving all over the world, not just in America. They betray their own tradition, which includes women such as Sojourner Truth and Ida B. Wells, and abandon their responsibility to their own people as well as to women everywhere.

In refusing to elevate sex above race, on insisting on the Black woman's responsibility to herself and to other women of color, Walker aligns herself neither with prevailing white feminist groups nor with Blacks who refuse to acknowledge male dominance in the world. Because her analysis does not yield to easy generalizations and nice packaged clichés, she continues to resist the trends of the times without discarding the truths upon which they are based.

Walker's second collection of short stories, *You Can't Keep a Good Woman Down* (1981), delves even more emphatically into the "twin afflictions" of Black women's lives. Like *In Love and Trouble,* this book probes the extent to which Black women have the freedom to pursue their selfhood within the confines of a sexist and racist society. However, these two collections, published eight years apart, demonstrate a clear progression of theme. While the protagonists of *In Love and Trouble* wage their struggle in spite of themselves, the heroines of *You Can't Keep a Good Woman Down* consciously insist upon their right to challenge any societal chains that bind them. The titles of the two collections succinctly indicate the shift in tone, the first emphasizing trouble, the second the self-assertiveness of the Black woman so bodaciously celebrated in the blues tradition. The name of a famous blues song, "You Can't Keep a Good Woman Down," is dedicated to those who "*insist* on the value and beauty of the authentic."[12] Walker's intention in this volume is clearly a celebration of the Black woman's insistence on living. From whence does this insistence come, Walker asks? How does it fare in these contemporary times?

The stories in this collection are blatantly topical ·in their subject matter, as Walker focuses on societal attitudes and mores that women have, in the last decade, challenged— pornography and male sexual fantasies in "Porn," and "Coming Apart," abortion in "The Abortion," sadomasochism in "A Letter of the Times," interracial rape in "Luna Advancing." And the forms Walker invents to illuminate these issues are as unconventional as her subject matter. Many of the stories are process rather than product. Feminist thinkers of the seventies asserted a link between process (the unraveling of thought and feeling) and the way women have perceived the world. In keeping with this theory, Walker often gives us the story as it comes into being, rather than delivering the product, classic and clean. The author then not only breaks the rules by writing about "womanist" issues (Walker defines a womanist as a "black feminist"), she also employs a womanist process. For many of these stories reflect the present, when the process of confusion, resistance to the established order, and the discovery of a freeing order is, especially for women, a prerequisite for growth.

Such a story is "Luna Advancing," in which a young Southern Black woman's development is reflected through her growing understanding of the complexity of interracial rape. At the beginning of the story, practically everything she tells us is tinged with an air of taking things for granted. She lightly assumes that Black people are superior. This generalization, however, is tested when Luna, a white friend of hers, tells her that during the "movement," she was raped by a Black man they both know. Our narrator naturally is opposed to rape; yet she had not believed Black men actually raped white women. And she knows what happens if a Black man is even accused of such an act. Her earlier sense of clarity is shattered. Doubts, questions, push her to unravel her own feelings: "Who knows what the black woman thinks of rape? Who has asked her? Who *cares*?"[13]

Again Walker writes about a forbidden topic and again she resists an easy solution. For although she speaks from the point of view of sisterhood with all women she also insists, as she did in "*One* Child of One's Own," that all women must understand that sexism and racism in America are critically related. Like all her previous fiction, this blatantly contemporary story is rooted in and illuminated by history, in this instance, the work of the great antilynching crusader Ida B. Wells. The dialogue between our narrator and this nineteenth-century Black womanist focuses on the convoluted connection between rape and lynchings, sex and race, that continue to this day. As a result, "Luna Advancing" cannot end conclusively. There are two endings, Afterthoughts, Discarded Notes, and a Postscript as the narrator and writer mesh. Walker shows us her writing process, which cannot be neatly resolved since the questions she posed cannot be satisfactorily answered. The many endings prod the reader, insisting on the complexity of the issue and the characters.

> Dear God,
>   Me and Sophie work on the quilt. Got it frame up on the porch. Shug Avery donate her old yellow dress for scrap, and I work in a piece every chance I get. It's a nice pattern call Sister's Choice.[14]

The form of *The Color Purple* (1982), Walker's most recent novel, is a further development in the womanist process she is evolving. The entire novel is written in a series of letters. Along with diaries, letters were the dominant mode of expression allowed women in the West. Feminist historians find letters to be a principal source of information, of facts about the everyday lives of women *and* their own perceptions about their lives, that is of both "objective" and "subjective" information. In using the epistolary style, Walker is able to have her major character, Celie, express the impact of oppression on her spirit as well as her growing internal strength and final victory.

Like Walker's other two novels, this work spans generations of one poor rural Southern Black family, interweaving the personal with the flow of history; and, like her essays and fiction, the image of quilting is central to its concept and form. But in *The Color Purple,* the emphases are the oppression Black women experience in their relationships with Black men (fathers, brothers, husbands, lovers) and the sisterhood they must share with each other in order to liberate themselves. As an image for these themes, two sisters, Celie and Nettie, are the novel's focal characters. Their letters, Celie's to God, Nettie's to Celie, and finally Celie's to Nettie, are the novel's form.

Again, Walker approaches the forbidden in content as well as form. Just as the novel's form is radical, so are its themes, for she focuses on incest in a Black family and portrays a Black lesbian relationship as natural and freeing. The novel begins with Celie, a fourteen-year-old who is sexually abused by her presumed father and who manages to save her sister Nettie from the same fate. Celie is so cut off from everyone and her experience is so horrifying, even to herself, that she can only write it in letters to God. Her letters take us through her awful pregnancies, her children being taken away from her, and the abuses of a loveless marriage. She liberates herself, that is, she comes to value herself, through the sensuous love bond she shares with Shug, her husband's mistress, her appreciation of her sister-in-law Sophie's resistant spirit, and the letters from her sister Nettie which her husband had hidden from her for many years. We feel Celie's transformation intensely since she tells her story in her own rural idiomatic language, a discrete Black speech. Few writers since Zora Neale Hurston have so successfully expressed the essence of the folk's speech as Walker does in *The Color Purple.*

In contrast to Celie's letters, Nettie's letters to Celie from Africa, where she is a missionary, are written in standard English. These letters not only provide a contrast in style, they expand the novel's scope. The comparison-contrast between male-female relationships in Africa and the Black South suggest that sexism for Black women in America does not derive from racism, though it is qualitatively affected by it. And Nettie's community of missionaries graphically demonstrates

Afro-Americans' knowledge of their ancestral link to Africa, which, contrary to American myth, predates the Black Power Movement of the 1960s.

Though different in form and language, *The Color Purple* is inextricably linked to Walker's previous works. In *In Search of Our Mothers' Gardens,* Walker speaks about three types of Black women: the physically and psychologically abused Black women (Mem and Margaret Copeland in *The Third Life of Grange Copeland*), the Black woman who is torn by contrary instincts (Meridian in her youth and college years), and the new Black woman who re-creates herself out of the creative legacy of her maternal ancestors. Meridian begins that journey of transformation. But it is Celie, even more than her predecessor, who completes Walker's cycle. For Celie is a "Mem" who survives and liberates herself through her sisters' strength and wisdom, qualities which are, like the color purple, derived from nature. To be free is the natural state of the living. And Celie's attainment of freedom affects not only others of her sisters, but her brothers as well.

Both Walker's prose and her poetry probe the continuum between the inner self and the outer world. Her volumes of poetry, like her fiction and essays, focus on the self as part of a community of changers, whether it is the Civil Rights Movement in *Once,* the struggle toward liberation in *Revolutionary Petunias,* the community of women who would be free in *Good Night Willie Lee.* Yet her poems are distinguished from her prose in that they are a graph of that self which is specifically Alice Walker. They are perhaps even more than her prose rooted in her desire to resist the easiest of the easy. In her poetry, Walker the wayward child challenges not only the world but herself. And in exposing herself, she challenges us to accept her as she is. Perhaps it is the stripping of bark from herself that enables us to feel that sound of the genuine in her scrutiny of easy positions advocated by progressive Blacks or women.

Her first volume, *Once,* includes a section, "Mornings/ of an Impossible Love," in which Walker scrutinizes herself not through her reflections on the outer world as she does in the other sections, but through self-exposure. In the poem

140

"Johann," Walker expresses feelings forbidden by the world of the 1960s. [15]

In "So We've Come at Last to Freud," she arrogantly insists on the validity of her own emotions as opposed to prescriptives:

> Don't label my love with slogans;
> My father can't be blamed
> > for my affection
>
> Or lack of it.
> Ask him
> He won't understand you
> > (61)

She resists her own attempt at self-pity in "Suicide":

> Thirdly if it is the thought
> of rest that
> fascinates
> laziness should be admitted
> in the clearest terms
> > (74)

Yet in "The Ballad of the Brown Girl," she acknowledges the pain of loss, the anguish of a forbidden love.

As these excerpts show, Walker refuses to embellish or camouflage her emotions with erudite metaphor or phrase. Instead she communicates them through her emphasis on single-word lines, her selection of the essential word, not only for content but for cadence. The result is a graceful directness that is not easily arrived at.

The overriding theme of *Once,* its feel of unwavering honesty in evoking the forbidden, either in political stances or in love, persists in *Revolutionary Petunias.* Walker, however, expands from the almost quixotic texture of her first volume to philosophical though intensely personal probings in her second. For *Revolutionary Petunias* examines the relationship between the nature of love and that of revolution. In these poems she celebrates the openness to the genuine in people,

an essential quality, for her, in those who would be revolutionaries. And she castigates the false conventions constructed by
many so-called revolutionaries. As a result, those who are
committed to more life rather than less are often outcasts and
seem to walk forbidden paths.

The volume is arranged in five sections, each one evoking a particular stage in the movement forward. In the first
section, "In These Dissenting Times," Walker asserts that
while many label their ancestors as backward, true revolutionaries understand that the common folk who precede them are
the source of their strength. She reminds us that we "are not
the first to suffer, rebel fight love and die. The grace with
which we embrace life, in spite of the pain, the sorrows, is
always a measure of what has gone before."[16]

The second section, "Revolutionary Petunias, The Living Through," is about those who know that the need for
beauty is essential to a desire for revolution, that the most rebellious of folk are those who feel so intensely the potential
beauty of life that they would struggle to that end without
ceasing. Yet because the narrow-minded scream that "poems
of / love and flowers are / a luxury the Revolution / cannot
afford," those so human as to be committed to beauty and love
are often seen as "incorrect." Walker warns that in living
through it one must "Expect nothing / Live frugally on surprise . . . wish for nothing larger / than your own small heart /
Or greater than a star" (30). And in words that reverberate
throughout her works, she exposes herself as one who must
question, feel, pursue the mysteries of life. The title of the
poem "Reassurance" affirms for us her need to sustain herself
in her persistent questionings.

> I must love the questions
> themselves
> as Rilke said
> like locked rooms
> full of treasure
> to which my blind
> and groping key
> does not yet fit
> (33)

Flowing out of the second section, the third, "Crucifix-ion," further underscores the sufferings of those who would see the urge to revolution as emanating from a love for people rather than empty prescriptive forms. In it the ideologues drive out the lovers, "forcing . . . the very sun / to mangled perfection / for your cause." And many like the "girl who would not lie; and was not born 'correct,'" or those who "wove a life / of stunning contradiction" are driven mad or die.

Yet some endured. The fourth section, "Mysteries . . . the Living Beyond," affirms the eventual triumph of those who would change the world because:

> . . . the purpose of being
> here, wherever we are, is to increase
> the durability and the occasions of
> love among and between peoples.
>   June Jordan
>   (51)

Love poems dominate this section, though always there is Walker's resistance to preordained form:

> In me there is a rage to defy
> the order of the stars
> despite their pretty patterns
>   (61)

And in "New Face," Walker combines the philosophical urge to penetrate the mysteries of life with the personal renewal which for her is love. From this renewal comes her energy to dig deeper, push further.

A single poem, "The Nature of This Flower Is to Bloom," is the last movement in this five-part collection, as Walker combines through capitalized short phrases ("Rebel-lious. Living. / Against the Elemental crush") the major ele-ments of *Revolutionary Petunias*. In choosing a flower as the symbol for revolution, she suggests that beauty, love, and revo-lution exist in a necessary relationship. And in selecting the petunia as the specific flower, she emphasizes the qualities of color, exuberance, and commonness rather than blandness, rigidity, or delicacy.

In completing the volume with this succinct and graceful poem, Walker also reiterates her own stylistic tendencies. Most of her poems are so cohesive they can hardly be divided into parts. I have found it almost impossible to separate out a few lines from any of her poems without quoting it fully, so seamless are they in construction. This quality is even more pronounced in her most recent volume of poetry, *Good Night Willie Lee, I'll See You in the Morning.* As in Walker's collections, though there are a few long poems, most are compact. In general, the voice in her poem is so finely distilled that each line, each word is so necessary it cannot be omitted, replaced, or separated out.

Like *Revolutionary Petunias, Good Night Willie Lee* is concerned with the relationship between love and change, only now the emphasis is even more on personal change, on change in the nature of relationships between women and men. This volume is very much about the demystification of love itself; yet it is also about the past, especially the pain left over from the "Crucifixion" of *Revolutionary Petunias.*

Good Night Willie Lee, I'll See You in the Morning is a five-part journey from night into morning, the name of each movement being an indication of the route this writer takes in her urge to understand love, without its illusions or veils. In the first movement, "Confession," Walker focuses on a love that declines into suffering. In letting go of it, she must go through the process of "stripping bark from herself" and must go deeper to an understanding of her past in "Early Losses, a Requiem." Having finally let the past rest in peace, she can then move to "Facing the Way," and finally to a "Forgiveness" that frees her.

The first poem of "Confession" is entitled "Did This Happen to Your Mother? Did Your Sister Throw Up a Lot?," while the last poem of this section ends "Other / women have already done this / sort of suffering for you / or so I thought." [17] Between these two points, Walker confesses that "I Love a man who is not worth / my love" and that "Love has made me sick" (2). She sees that her lover is afraid "he may fail me . . .

it is this fear / that now devours / desire" (8). She is astute enough to understand that his fear of love caused him to hold "his soul / so tightly / it shrank / to fit his hand" (5). In tracing the decline of love she understands the pull of pain: "At first I did not fight it / I *loved* the suffering / It was being alive!" "I savored my grief like chilled wine" (15).

From this immersion in self-pity, she is saved by a woman, a friend who reminds her that other women have already done this for her and brings her back to herself. The steps of this first movement are particularly instructive for the rest of this volume, since Walker does not pretend, as so much feminist poetry does, that she is above passion, or the need or the desire for sharing love with a man. What she does is to communicate the peaks and pitfalls of such an experience, pointing always to the absolute necessity for self-love. Only through self-love can the self who can love be preserved. And for Walker, self-love comes from "Stripping Bark from Myself." In one of the finest poems of this volume, Walker chants her song of independence. Her wayward lines are a response to a worldwide challenge:

> because women are expected to keep silent about
> their close escapes I will not keep silent
>
> No I am finished with living
> for what my mother believes
> for what my brother and father defend
> for what my lover elevates
> for what my sister, blushing, denies or rushes
> to embrace

for she has discovered some part of her self:

> Besides
>
> my struggle was always against
> an inner darkness: I carry with myself
> the only known keys
> to my death . . .

So she is

> . . . happy to fight
> all outside murderers
> as I see I must
> (23–24)

Such stripping of bark from herself enables her to face the way, to ask questions about her own commitment to revolution, whether she can give up the comforts of life, especially "the art that transcends time," "whose sale would patch a roof / heat the cold rooms of children, replace an eye / feed a life" (44–45). And it is the stripping of bark from herself that helps her to understand that:

> the healing
> of all our wounds
> is forgiveness
> that permits a promise
> of our return
> at the end
>   (53)

It is telling, I believe, that Walker's discovery of the healing power of forgiveness comes from her mother's last greeting to her father at his burial. In this volume so permeated by the relationship of woman to man, her mother heads the list of a long line of women—some writers, like Zora Neale Hurston, others personal friends of Alice Walker—who pass unto her the knowledge they have garnered on the essence of love. Such knowledge helps Walker to demystify love and enables her to write about the tension between the giving of herself and the desire to remain herself.

In her dedication to the volume she edited of Zora Neale Hurston's work, Walker says of her literary ancestor: "Implicit in Hurston's determination to 'make it' in a career was her need to express 'the folk' and herself. Someone who knew her has said: 'Zora would have been Zora even if she'd been an Eskimo.' That is what it means to be yourself; it is surely what it means to be an artist."[18] These words, it seems to me, apply as well to Alice Walker.

☐ *Notes* ∎

1. Alice Walker, "On Stripping Bark from Myself," *Good Night Willie Lee, I'll See You in the Morning* (New York: Dial, 1979), p. 23. Subsequent page references are to this edition.

2. Alice Walker, "Karamojans," *Once* (New York: Harcourt Brace Jovanovich, 1978), p. 20. Subsequent page references are to this edition.

3. Alice Walker, *The Third Life of Grange Copeland* (New York: Harcourt Brace Jovanovich, 1970), p. 207.

4. Walker, *In Love and Trouble* (New York: Harcourt Brace Jovanovich, 1973), epigraph.

5. Walker, "Roselily," *In Love and Trouble,* p. 8.

6. Walker, "The Welcome Table," *In Love and Trouble,* p. 84.

7. Alice Walker, *Meridian* (New York: Harcourt Brace Jovanovich, 1976), pp. 105–106.

8. *Meridian,* p. 41.

9. Alice Walker, "*One* Child of One's Own: A Meaningful Digression Within the Work(s)," *The Writer on Her Work,* ed. Janet Sternburg (New York: W. W. Norton, 1980), p. 139.

10. Walker, *Meridian,* p. 204.

11. Walker, "*One* Child of One's Own," pp. 131–32.

12. Alice Walker, *You Can't Keep a Good Woman Down* (New York: Harcourt Brace Jovanovich, 1981), dedication.

13. *You Can't Keep a Good Woman Down,* p. 71.

14. Alice Walker, *The Color Purple* (New York: Harcourt Brace Jovanovich, 1982), p. 53.

15. Alice Walker, *Once,* p. 65.

16. Alice Walker, "Fundamental Difference," *Revolutionary Petunias* (New York: Harcourt Brace Jovanovich, 1973), p. 1. Subsequent page references are to this edition.

17. Walker, "At First," *Good Night Willie Lee, I'll See You in the Morning,* p. 15.

18. Alice Walker, ed., *I Love Myself: A Zora Neale Hurston Reader* (Old Westbury, N.Y.: Feminist Press, 1979), p. 3.

HOUSTON A. BAKER, JR. and
CHARLOTTE PIERCE-BAKER ■

Patches: Quilts and Community in Alice Walker's "Everyday Use"

> During the Depression and really hard time,
> people often paid their debts with quilts, and
> sometimes their tithe to the church too.
> —THE QUILTERS

A patch is a fragment. It is a vestige of wholeness that stands as a sign of loss and a challenge to creative design. As a remainder or remnant, the patch may symbolize rupture and impoverishment; it may be defined by the faded glory of the already gone. But as a fragment, it is also rife with explosive potential of the yet-to-be-discovered. Like woman, it is a liminal element between wholes.

Weaving, shaping, sculpting, or quilting in order to create a kaleidoscopic and momentary array is tantamount to providing an improvisational response to chaos. Such activity represents a nonce response to ceaseless scattering; it constitutes survival strategy and motion in the face of dispersal. A patchwork quilt, laboriously and affectionately crafted from bits of worn overalls, shredded uniforms, tattered petticoats,

From *The Southern Review* 21 (Summer 1985): 706–720. Photographs ©
1994 by Roland L. Freeman.

153

and outgrown dresses stands as a signal instance of a patterned wholeness in the African diaspora.

Traditional African cultures were scattered by the European slave trade throughout the commercial time and space of the New World. The transmutation of quilting, a European, feminine tradition, into a black women's folk art, represents an innovative fusion of African cloth manufacture, piecing, and appliqué with awesome New World experiences—and expediencies. The product that resulted was, in many ways, a double patch. The hands that pieced the master's rigidly patterned quilts by day were often the hands that crafted a more functional design in slave cabins by night. The quilts of Afro-America offer a *sui generis* context (a weaving together) of experiences and a storied, vernacular representation of lives conducted in the margins, ever beyond an easy and acceptable wholeness. In many ways, the quilts of Afro-America resemble the work of all those dismembered gods who transmute fragments and remainders into the light and breath of a new creation. And the sorority of quiltmakers, fragment weavers, holy patchers, possesses a sacred wisdom that it hands down from generation to generation of those who refuse the center for the ludic and unconfined spaces of the margins.

Those positioned outside the sorority and enamored of wholeness often fail to comprehend the dignity inherent in the quiltmakers' employment of remnants and conversion of fragments into items of everyday use. Just as the mysteries of, say, the blues remain hidden from those in happy circumstances, so the semantic intricacies of quiltmaking remain incomprehensible to the individualistic sensibility invested in myths of a postindustrial society. All of the dark, southern energy that manifests itself in the conversion of a sagging cabin—a shack really—into a "happy home" by stringing a broom wire between two nails in the wall and making the joint jump, or that shows itself in the "crazy quilt" patched from crumbs and remainders, seems but a vestige of outmoded and best-forgotten customs.

To relinquish such energy, however, is to lose an enduring resourcefulness that has ensured a distinctive aesthetic tradition and a unique code of everyday, improvisational use in America. The tradition-bearers of the type of Afro-

American energy we have in mind have always included ample numbers of southern, black women who have transmuted fragments of New World displacement into a quilted eloquence scarcely appreciated by traditional spokespersons for wholeness. To wit: even the perspicacious and vigilant lion of abolitionism Frederick Douglass responded as follows to Monroe A. Majors' request for inclusions in his book *Noted Negro Women:*

> We have many estimable women of our variety but not many famous ones. It is not well to claim too much for ourselves before the public. Such extravagance invites contempt rather than approval. I have thus far seen no book of importance written by a negro woman and I know of no one among us who can appropriately be called famous.

Southern black women have not only produced quilts of stunning beauty, they have also crafted books of monumental significance, works that have made them appropriately famous. In fact, it has been precisely the appropriation of energy drawn from sagging cabins and stitched remainders that has constituted the world of the quiltmakers' sorority. The energy has flowed through such women as Harriet Brent Jacobs, Zora Neale Hurston, and Margaret Walker, enabling them to continue an ancestral line elegantly shared by Alice Walker.

In a brilliant essay entitled "Alice Walker: The Black Woman Artist as Wayward," Professor Barbara Christian writes: "Walker is drawn to the integral and economical process of quilt making as a model for her own craft. For through it, one can create out of seemingly disparate everyday materials patterns of clarity, imagination, and beauty." Professor Christian goes on to discuss Walker's frequently cited "In Search of Our Mothers' Gardens" and her short story "Everyday Use." She convincingly argues that Walker employs quilts as signs of functional beauty and spiritual heritage that provide exemplars of challenging convention and radical individuality, or "artistic waywardness."

The patchwork quilt as a trope for understanding black women's creativity in the United States, however, presents an array of interpretive possibilities that is not exhausted by

Professor Christian's adept criticism of Walker. For example, if one takes a different tack and suggests that the quilt as a metaphor presents not a stubborn contrariness, a wayward individuality, but a communal bonding that confounds traditional definitions of art and of the artist, then one plays on possibilities in the quilting trope rather different from those explored by Christian. What we want to suggest in our own adaptation of the trope is that it opens a fascinating interpretive window on vernacular dimensions of lived, creative experience in the United States. Quilts, in their patched and many-colored glory offer not a counter to tradition, but, in fact, an instance of the only legitimate tradition of "the people" that exists. They are representations of the stories of the vernacular natives who make up the ninety-nine percent of the American population unendowed with money and control. The class distinction suggested by "vernacular" should not overshadow the gender specificity of quilts as products of a universal woman's creativity—what Pattie Chase in *The Contemporary Quilt* calls "an ancient affinity between women and cloth." They are the testimony of "mute and inglorious" generations of women gone before. The quilt as interpretive sign opens up a world of *difference,* a nonscripted territory whose creativity with fragments is less a matter of "artistic" choice than of economic and functional necessity. "So much in the habit of sewing something," says Walker's protagonist in the remarkable novel *The Color Purple,* "[that] I stitch up a bunch of scraps, try to see what I can make."

The Johnson women, who populate the generations represented in Walker's short story "Everyday Use," are inhabitants of southern cabins who have always worked with "scraps" and seen what they could make of them. The result of their labor has been a succession of mothers and daughters surviving the ignominies of Jim Crow life and passing on ancestral blessings to descendants. The guardians of the Johnson homestead when the story commences are the mother—"a large, big-boned woman with rough, man-working hands"—and her daughter Maggie, who has remained with her "chin on chest, eyes on ground, feet in shuffle, ever since the fire that burned the other house to the ground" ten or twelve years ago. The mood at the story's beginning is one of ritualistic "waiting": "I will wait for her in the yard that Maggie and I made so clean and wavy yesterday afternoon." The subject awaited is the other daughter, Dee. Not only has the yard (as ritual ground) been prepared for the arrival of a goddess, but the sensibilities and costumes of Maggie and her mother have been appropriately attuned for the occasion. The mother day-dreams of television shows where parents and children are suddenly—and pleasantly—reunited, banal shows where chatty hosts oversee tearful reunions. In her fantasy, she weighs a hundred pounds less, is several shades brighter in complexion, and possesses a devastatingly quick tongue. She returns abruptly to real life meditation, reflecting on her own heroic, agrarian accomplishments in slaughtering hogs and cattle and preparing their meat for winter nourishment. She is a robust provider who has gone to the people of her church and raised money to send her light-complexioned, lithe-figured, and ever-dissatisfied daughter Dee to college. Today, as she waits in the purified yard, she notes the stark differences between Maggie and Dee and recalls how the "last dingy gray board of the house [fell] in toward the red-hot brick chimney" when her former domicile burned. Maggie was scarred horribly by the fire, but Dee, who had hated the house with an intense fury, stood "off under the sweet gum tree . . . a look of concentration on her face." A scarred and dull Maggie, who has been kept at home and confined to everyday offices, has but one reaction to the fiery and vivacious arrival of her sister: "I hear Maggie suck in her breath. 'Uhnnnh,' is what it sounds like. Like when you see the wriggling end of a snake just in front of your foot on the road. 'Uhnnnh'."

Indeed, the question raised by Dee's energetic arrival is whether there are words adequate to her flair, her brightness, her intense colorfulness of style which veritably blocks the sun. She wears "a dress so loud it hurts my eyes. There are yellows and oranges enough to throw back the light of the sun. I feel my whole face warming from the heat waves it throws out." Dee is both serpent and fire introduced with bursting esprit into the calm pasture that contains the Johnsons' tin-roofed, three-room, windowless shack and grazing cows. She has joined the radical, black nationalists of the 1960s and 1970s, changing her name from Dee to Wangero and cultivat-

ing a suddenly fashionable, or stylish, interest in what she passionately describes as her "heritage." If there is one quality
that Dee (Wangero) possesses in abundance, it is "style": "At
sixteen she had a style of her own: and knew what style was."

But in her stylishness, Dee is not an example of the
indigenous rapping and styling out of Afro-America. Rather,
she is manipulated by the style-makers, the fashion designers
whose semiotics the French writer Roland Barthes has so
aptly characterized. "Style" for Dee is the latest vogue—the
most recent fantasy perpetuated by American media. When
she left for college, her mother had tried to give her a quilt
whose making began with her grandmother Dee, but the
bright daughter felt such patched coverings were "old-
fashioned and out of style." She has returned at the com-
mencement of "Everyday Use," however, as one who now
purports to know the value of the work of black women as holy
patchers.

The dramatic conflict of the story surrounds the definition of holiness. The ritual purification of earth and expec-
tant atmosphere akin to that of Beckett's famous drama ("I
will wait for her in the yard that Maggie and I made so clean
and wavy yesterday afternoon.") prepare us for the narrator's
epiphanic experience at the story's conclusion.

Near the end of "Everyday Use," the mother (who is
the tale's narrator) realizes that Dee (a.k.a, Wangero) is a *fantasy* child, a perpetrator and victim of: "words, lies, other
folks's habits." The energetic daughter is as frivolously careless of other people's lives as the fiery conflagration that she
had watched ten years previously. Assured by the makers of
American fashion that "black" is currently "beautiful," she
has conformed her own "style" to that notion. Hers is a trendy
"blackness" cultivated as "art" and costume. She wears "a
dress down to the ground . . . bracelets dangling and making
noises when she moves her arm up to shake the folds of the
dress out of her armpits." And she says of quilts she has removed from a trunk at the foot of her mother's bed: "Maggie
can't appreciate these quilts! She'd probably be backward
enough to put them to everyday use." "Art" is, thus, juxtaposed with "everyday use" in Walker's short story, and the fire
goddess Dee, who has achieved literacy only to burn "us with

a lot of knowledge we didn't necessarily need to know," is revealed as a perpetuator of institutional theories of aesthetics. (Such theories hold that "art" is, in fact, defined by social institutions such as museums, book reviews, and art dealers.) Of the two quilts she has extracted from the trunk, she exclaims: "But they're 'priceless.'" And so the quilts are by "fashionable" standards of artistic value, standards that motivate the answer that Dee provides to her mother's question: "'Well,' I said, stumped. 'What would *you* do with them?'" Dee's answer: "Hang them." The stylish daughter's entire life has been one of "framed" experience; she has always sought a fashionably "aesthetic" distance from southern expediencies. (And how unlike quilt frames that signal social activity and a coming to completeness are her *frames*.) Her concentrated detachment from the fire, which so nearly symbolizes her role vis-à-vis the Afro-American community (her black friends "worshipped . . . the scalding humor that erupted like bubbles in lye") is characteristic of her attitude. Her goals include the appropriation of exactly what *she* needs to remain fashionable in the eyes of a world of pretended wholeness, a world of banal television shows, framed and institutionalized art, and Polaroid cameras—devices that instantly process and record experience as "framed" photograph. Ultimately, the framed Polaroid photograph represents the limits of Dee's vision.

Strikingly, the quilts whose *tops* have been stitched by her grandmother from fragments of outgrown family garments and quilted after the grandmother's death by Aunt Dee and her sister (the mother who narrates the story) are perceived in Dee's Polaroid sensibility as merely "priceless" works of an institutionally, or stylishly, defined "art world." In a reversal of perception tantamount to the acquisition of sacred knowledge by initiates in a rite of passage, the mother/narrator realizes that she has always worshipped at the altars of a "false" goddess. As her alter ego, Dee has always expressed that longing for the "other" that characterizes inhabitants of oppressed, "minority" cultures. Situated in an indisputably black and big-boned skin, the mother has secretly admired the "good hair," full figure, and well-turned (i.e., "whitely trim") ankle of Dee (Wangero). Sacrifices and sanctity have seemed in order. But in her epiphanic moment of recognition, she perceives the fire-scarred Maggie—the stay-at-home victim of southern scarifications—in a revised light. When Dee grows belligerent about possessing the quilts, Maggie emerges from the kitchen and says with a contemptuous gesture of dismissal: "She can have them, Mama. . . . I can 'member Grandma Dee without quilts." The mother's response to what she wrongly interprets as Maggie's hang-dog resignation before Dee is a radical awakening to godhead:

> When I looked at her . . . something hit me in the top of my head and ran down to the soles of my feet. Just like when I'm in church and the spirit of God touches me and I get happy and shout. I did something I never had done before: hugged Maggie to me, then dragged her on into the room, snatched the quilts out of Miss Wangero's hands and dumped them into Maggie's lap.

Maggie is the arisen goddess of Walker's story; she is the sacred figure who bears the scarifications of experience and knows how to convert patches into robustly patterned and beautifully quilted wholes. As an earth-rooted and quotidian goddess, she stands in dramatic contrast to the stylishly fiery and other-oriented Wangero. The mother says in response to Dee's earlier cited accusation that Maggie would reduce quilts to rags by putting them to everyday use: "'She can always make some more,' I said. 'Maggie knows how to quilt.'" And, indeed, Maggie, the emergent goddess of New World improvisation and long ancestral memory, does know how to quilt. Her mind and imagination are capable of preserving the wisdom of grandmothers and aunts without material prompts: "I can 'member . . . without the quilts," she says. The secret to employing beautiful quilts as items of everyday use is the secret of crafty dues.

In order to comprehend the transient nature of all wholes, one must first become accustomed to living and working with fragments. Maggie has learned the craft of fragment weaving from her women ancestors: "It was Grandma Dee and Big Dee who taught her how to quilt herself." The conjunction of "quilt" and "self" in Walker's syntax may be simply a serendipitous accident of style. Nonetheless, the conjunc-

162

tion works magnificently to capture the force of black woman's quilting in "Everyday Use." Finally, it is the "self," or a version of humanness that one calls the Afro-American self, that must, in fact, be crafted from fragments on the basis of wisdom gained from preceding generations.

What is at stake in the world of Walker's short story, then, is not the prerogatives of Afro-American women as "wayward artists." Individualism and a flouting of convention in order to achieve "artistic" success constitute acts of treachery in "Everyday Use." For Dee, if she is anything, *is* a fashionable denizen of America's art/fantasy world. She is removed from the "everyday uses" of a black community that she scorns, misunderstands, burns. Certainly, she is "unconventionally" black. As such, however, she is an object of holy contempt from the archetypal weaver of black wholeness from tattered fragments. Maggie's "Uhnnnh" and her mother's designation "Miss Wangero" are gestures of utter contempt. Dee's sellout to fashion and fantasy in a television-manipulated world of "artistic" frames is a representation of the *complicity of the clerks*. Not "art," then, but use or function is the signal in Walker's fiction of sacred creation.

Quilts designed for everyday use, pieced wholes defying symmetry and pattern, are signs of the scarred generations of women who have always been alien to a world of literate words and stylish fantasies. The crafted fabric of Walker's story is the very weave of blues and jazz traditions in the Afro-American community, daringly improvisational modes that confront breaks in the continuity of melody (or theme) by riffing. The asymmetrical quilts of southern black women are like the off-centered stomping of the jazz solo or the innovative musical showmanship of the blues interlude. They speak a world in which the deceptively shuffling Maggie is capable of a quick change into goddess, an unlikely holy figure whose dues are paid in full. Dee's anger at her mother is occasioned principally by the mother's insistence that paid dues make Maggie a more likely bearer of sacredness, tradition, and true value than the "brighter" sister. "You just don't understand," she says to her mother. Her assessment is surely correct where institutional theories and systems of "art" are concerned. The mother's cognition contains no categories for framed art. The mother works according to an entirely different scale of use and value, finally assigning proper weight to the virtues of Maggie and to the ancestral importance of the pieced quilts that she has kept out of use for so many years. Smarting, perhaps, from Dee's designation of the quilts as "old-fashioned," the mother has buried the covers away in a trunk. At the end of Walker's story, however, she has become aware of her own mistaken value judgments, and she pays homage that is due to Maggie. The unlikely daughter is a *griot** of the vernacular who remembers actors and events in a distinctively black "historical" drama.

Before Dee departs, she "put on some sunglasses that hid everything above the tip of her nose and her chin." Maggie smiles at the crude symbolism implicit in this act, for she has always known that her sister saw "through a glass darkly." But it is the mother's conferral of an ancestral blessing (signaled by her deposit of the quilts in Maggie's lap) that constitutes the occasion for the daughter's first "real smile." Maggie knows that it is only communal recognition by elders of the tribe that confers ancestral privileges on succeeding generations. The mother's holy recognition of the scarred daughter's sacred status as quilter is the best gift of a hard-pressed womankind to the fragmented goddess of the present.

At the conclusion of "Everyday Use," which is surely a fitting precursor to *The Color Purple,* with its sewing protagonist and its scenes of sisterly quilting, Maggie and her mother relax in the ritual yard after the dust of Dee's departing car has settled. They dip snuff in the manner of African confreres sharing cola nuts. The moment is past when a putatively "new" generation has confronted scenes of black, everyday life. A change has taken place, but it is a change best described by Amiri Baraka's designation for Afro-American music's various styles and discontinuities. The change in Walker's story is the "changing same." What has been reaffirmed at the story's conclusion is the value of the quiltmaker's motion and strategy in the precincts of a continuously undemocratic South.

---

*African storyteller, guardian of the peoples' history.

But the larger appeal of "Everyday Use" is its privileging of a distinctively woman's craft as *the* signal mode of confronting chaos through a skillful blending of patches. In *The Color Purple,* Celie's skill as a fabric worker completely transmutes the order of Afro-American existence. Not only do her talents with a needle enable her to wear the pants in the family, they also allow her to become the maker of pants par excellence. Hence, she becomes a kind of unifying goddess of patch and stitch, an instructress of mankind who bestows the gift of consolidating fragments. Her abusive husband Albert says: "When I was growing up . . . I use to try to sew along with mama cause that's what she was always doing. But everybody laughed at me. But you know, I liked it." "Well," says Celie, "nobody gon laugh at you now. . . . Here, help me stitch in these pockets."

A formerly "patched" separateness of woman is transformed through fabric craft into a new unity. Quilting, sewing, stitching are bonding activities that begin with the godlike authority and daring of women, but that are given (as a gift toward community) to men. The old disparities are transmuted into a vision best captured by the scene that Shug suggests to Celie: "But, Celie, try to imagine a city full of these shining, blueblack people wearing brilliant blue robes with designs like fancy quilt patterns." The heavenly city of quilted design is a form of unity wrested by the sheer force of the woman quiltmaker's will from chaos. As a community, it stands as both a sign of the potential effects of black women's creativity in America, and as an emblem of the effectiveness of women's skillful confrontation of patches. Walker's achievement as a southern, black, woman novelist is her own successful application of the holy patching that was a staple of her grandmother's and great-grandmother's hours of everyday ritual. "Everyday Use" is, not surprisingly, dedicated to "your grandmama": to those who began the line of converting patches into works of southern genius.

MARGOT ANNE KELLEY ■

Sisters' Choices: Quilting Aesthetics in Contemporary African-American Women's Fiction

Taking a piece of cloth and using it for something other
than defining social status and gender is not an aesthetic
talent. It is a step to social deliverance.
—RADKA DONNELL

when women make cloth, they have time to think . . .
—NTOZAKE SHANGE

In "African-American Women's Quilting: A Framework for Conceptualizing and Teaching African-American Women's History," Elsa Barkley Brown explains that quilts provide an excellent analytic framework for courses by enabling students to "center in another experience, validate it, and judge it by its own standards" (Brown 10). Books like *Double Stitch: Black Women Write about Mothers and Daughters* reinforce the aptness of her model; this anthology of essays, poems, fiction, and personal narratives is organized into six sections: "Threading the Needle: Beginnings," "Piecing Blocks: Identities," "Stitching Memories: Herstories," Fraying Edges:

Tensions," "Binding the Quilt: Generations," and "Loosening the Threads: Separations." The implication that quilting is integral to African-American women's experiences recurs in many recent literary works, including Alice Walker's *The Color Purple*, Gloria Naylor's *Mama Day,* and Toni Morrison's *Beloved*. The quilting images in these works help to place them in a continuum of black women's creative efforts and to clarify the most significant features of that continuum. Perhaps surprisingly, an understanding of the African-American quilting aesthetic and its function in these writings can also help critics to situate them in relation to the novels conventionally labelled "postmodern." Like many postmodern writers, these black women novelists are interrogating the prevailing assumptions about the subject, external reality, and representation. Through their quilting metaphors, however, they venture a step further, suggesting alternative modes of perception and creation and offering new understandings of the relation of art to social life.

In her essay "Aesthetic Inheritances: history worked by hands," bell hooks celebrates her grandmother, noting in the "very first statement . . . about Baba" that she "was a dedicated quiltmaker" and *then* that her name was Sarah Hooks Oldham (116). Hooks points out early in the discussion of Baba's quilts and quiltmaking practices that "the work of black women quiltmakers needs special feminist commentary which considers the impact of race, sex, and class" (118), a need exacerbated by the situation that

> when art museums highlight the artistic achievement of American quiltmakers . . . often the representation at such shows suggests that white women were the only group truly dedicated to the art of quiltmaking. This is not so. Yet quilts by black women are portrayed as exceptions; usually there is only one. The card identifying the maker reads "anonymous black woman."
>
> (115)

Happily, travelling exhibits like "Who'd a Thought It: Improvisation in African-American Quiltmaking," a show organized by the San Francisco Craft & Folk Art Museum in 1988, are correcting the inaccurate impression that hooks decries.[1] At the same time, such shows enable those who cannot rummage through a grandmother's attic or sewing room to view African-American quilts of the nineteenth and twentieth centuries and to understand them in relation to African textiles. This juxtaposition of quilts and West African cloths accentuates the aesthetic commonalities between the two materials, while also underscoring specific cultural significances of quilting itself.

Like some standard-traditional quilts,[2] African-American (or "Afro-traditional") quilts are composed of the scraps of material used in other projects, fabric from outgrown clothing, and pieces given to the quilter by friends and relatives. For the quilter, the diverse fabric sources create histories that are often significant; hooks explains that in her grandmother's case, each quilt had a "story [that] was rooted in the quilt's history" (120) and that

> Baba would show her quilts and tell their stories, giving the history of chosen fabrics to individual lives. Although she never completed it, she began to piece a quilt of little stars from scraps of cotton dresses worn by her daughters. Together we would examine this work and she would tell me about the particulars, about what my mother and her sisters were doing when they wore a particular dress. . . . To her mind these quilts were maps charting the course of our lives. They were history as life lived.
>
> (120–121)

This quilt connects the lives of grandmother, mother, and daughter, providing an opportunity for storytelling and a place to record domestic particulars, to artistically rework women's experiences. Moreover, since quilts are one of the very few sites in which African-American women's creative impulses have been preserved (until recently), such a family heirloom "symbolically identif[ies] a tradition of black female artistry . . . [and] challenges the notion that creative black women are rare exceptions" (121). Indeed, hooks goes on to assert that through quilts like those made by Baba "we are deeply, passionately connected to black women whose sense of aesthetics, whose commitment to ongoing creative work, inspires and sustains" (121).

The "sense of aesthetics" functioning in these quilts has been investigated by a number of scholars interested in both the differences between standard-traditional quilt patterns and Afro-traditional patterns, on the one hand, and the similarities between the latter and West African textiles, on the other. Briefly summarizing these inquiries in their article "Aesthetic Principles in Afro-American Quilts," Maude Southwell Wahlman and John Scully point out that connections have been made between appliquéd quilts (like Harriet Powers's famous Bible quilts) and Fon wallhangings, between strip quilts and Ashanti and Ewe woven textiles from Ghana, and between the wide loom weavings of women in both the United States and Africa (Wahlman and Scully 80–82). The correspondences take into account not only large-scale similarities, but also some more particular shared aesthetic preferences distinct from those manifest in standard-traditional quilts. Wahlman and Scully enumerate five such qualities: in both West African textiles and African-American traditional quilts, strips are used "to construct and to organize quilt top design space"; there is a partiality toward "large-scale designs," as well as one for "strong, highly contrasting colors"; and color and design work together to produce both "off-beat patterns" and "multiple rhythms" (86). To this list, we should add that both cloth-makers and quilt-makers evince a preference for— indeed a reliance on—improvisation. Quoting folklorist John Michael Vlach in the exhibition catalogue for "Who'd a Thought It," quilt collector Eli Leon observes that improvisation is "the basis of Afro-American creativity" and that "there is a use of formal design motifs but not a submission to them. There is a playful assertion of creativity and innovation over the redundancies of disciplined order" (Leon 22).

The strips and "strings" (very narrow strips) in African-American quilts are usually long and rather narrow, running the length of the quilt and often alternating with patched blocks. Sometimes horizontal strips are added, creating a grid effect. In either case, the strips function both to structure the quilt top and "as a time-saving device"—enabling the quilter to make a large quilt with a bit less patching or to repair an ex-

170

isting quilt-top (Wahlman and Scully 86). Whereas the background color of many standard-traditional quilts is often a neutral shade that is not incorporated into the overall design,[3] "the color of the strips in a quilt is also a major element in the visual experience of the quilt. When the colors of the strips are different from the colors in the rows of blocks or designs, two distinct movements can be seen: one along the strips and the other within the designs" (Wahlman and Scully 86). Wahlman, Scully, and others maintain that this preference for stripping entire quilts (rather than just the borders) "reflects a textile aesthetic which has been passed down for generations among Afro-American women who were descendants of Africans" (Wahlman and Scully 86). In West Africa, narrow strips of cloth are woven by men on portable looms and then sewn together, a technique which allows great variety in the final product: "strips can be aligned so as to create regular, plaid-like patterns, checker-board designs, diamond patterns, or open-ended and asymmetrical arrangements" (Wahlman and Scully 83). "Women's Weave," the cloth made by women on large stationary looms, often reproduces these patterns—suggesting that they are not so much an inadvertent by-product of sewing the pieces together as they are a distinct preference. To reinforce their claim that African-American quilt stripping can be associated with West African textile "stripping," Wahlman and Scully asked Pecolia Warner, a quilter who has been the subject of several folklore articles,

> what was the ideal width for a strip. And she said 'the width of my hand,' and laid her hand over a strip in one of her quilts. When presented with a single strip of West African narrow loom cloth, she immediately placed her hand over it, and found to her delight that it was the right width, the width of her hand.
>
> (86)

Afro-traditional quilts are also distinctive in their use of large-scale designs. While tiny, even stitches and myriad, precisely aligned patches are the hallmark of most high-caliber standard-traditional quilts, many African-American quilters employ large, often abstract designs. In the earliest days of the

Freedom Quilting Bee in Alabama, this design preference contributed to the group's success. Francis Xavier Walter, a priest involved in the civil rights movement, bought quilts from women in Gee's Bend and its environs, sent them to New York to be auctioned, and gave the money to the women to support themselves and to re-invest into quilting—thus beginning one of the most successful, longest enduring quilting collectives in the nation. Among the quilts getting high bids at an early auction was "a quilt that was yellow and aqua. It was an amazing abstract design, as though the quiltmaker had taken almost a segment of one block and blown it up to full size" (quoted in Callahan 27). Tom Screven, one of the organizers of the auctions, surmised that this large design "came from a shortage of materials, or maybe they were making [the quilts] quickly to get them to the city [in time for the auction]" (quoted in Callahan 27). While not recognizing the links between this aesthetic preference and the African traditions from which it was derived, many purchasers at the auction liked and purchased the quilts because they "were so original" and "they looked like op art" (27).

Making these large designs all the more striking is a frequent reliance on strong, highly contrasting colors. In the first batch of Freedom Quilting Bee quilts were "two-toned quilts, not just in black-and-white, but blue-, red-, yellow-, even brown-and-white" (Callahan 15–17). Another volunteer who helped with the Bee in its early stages asserted that she could

> tell a Freedom Quilting Bee quilt from an Appalachian quilt as quickly as the snap of a finger because of the color strength in the Freedom quilt. The technical term is "high chroma," the use of primary colors at their most intense contrast. The quilts had a dynamism resulting from their combination of geometry and brilliance in juxtaposition of primary colors. What struck me when I first saw them was that as patchwork quilts so many of them were black-white, red-white, dark blue-white. Such opposition gave them a wonderful, almost Mondrian design.
>
> (53)

Robert Farris Thompson suggests that such juxtaposition of strong colors might be looked at in terms of "something other than decorative intent" (Thompson 21). He notes that the

> Bakongo believe that breaks in pattern, for instance terraced shifts from white to red to black, can symbolize passing through two worlds, the quest for the superior insights and power of the ancestors. I stop to consider how many of the finest quilters in Black America are devout church-goers, believers in the spirit. Then I regard the shimmering shifts of form and size and color spread out upon their children's beds. And I wonder.
>
> (21)

Whether the intent is spiritual or simply decorative, a further consequence of color pairing is a simultaneous emphasis on "both the color and the relationship [between colors]," a concurrent awareness of parts and wholes (Wahlman and Scully 88).

A different but equally eye-catching effect is achieved when quilters interject colors in a random way, seeming to break whatever patterns they have established. Callahan describes such quilts as "less-than-perfect,"

> marred . . . [by] their well intended, hit-or-miss color schemes—showpieces themselves in their crude, almost eerie approach. As one early buyer said of the quilt whose patches were all one color except for the red block at one end, "If Picasso can do it, I guess they can, too."
>
> (17–18)[4]

From a different aesthetic orientation, such an infusion of color can be understood as a way to demonstrate that the quilter has mastered the pattern and then deliberately broken free of it (Wahlman and Scully 89), emphasizing the importance of chance and accident to African-American quilting. While seemingly random insets may be necessitated by the quilter running out of one fabric, as viewers usually presume, Wahlman and Scully explain that "the sporadic use of the

173

same material in several squares when this material could have been used uniformly [suggests that] Afro-American quilters develop variation rather than regularity" (90). Leon argues that such manipulations reflect the paradigm of "flexible classicism" that shapes traditional African art: "There are definite forms to which the artists are bound and within which they work . . . [but] great scope exists for individual expression. Improvisation is always encouraged, however contained within the traditional bounds" (43–44). The misperception that Callahan records is quite understandable, though, since "structural variation in the reproduction of a quilt block, except in the most elementary cases, is an African-American phenomenon unfamiliar in the standard tradition" (Leon 26).

Color is coupled with design to produce both off-beat patterns and multiple rhythms. The dominant light and dark accents in the columns or rows of a quilt can be thought of as "beats," like the beats in music. Wahlman and Scully explain that "when the accents in one row match the accents in another row, the design is 'on the beat.' But when the accents in one row do not match up with the accents in another row, then we have what can be termed 'off-beat' designs" (90). These are often bemoaned by standard-traditional quilters, who prefer more symmetric, balanced, "on the beat" designs. In fact, in Blanche and Helen Young's *The Lone Star Handbook,* they advise novice quilters that "in the Lone Star quilt, the fabrics should blend, or flow, from one diamond to the next, graduating from light to dark. Avoid alternating lights and darks; sudden changes in color intensity will give the Star a choppy, or checkerboard, look" (Young and Young 7). Off-beat patterns may seem choppy, because their asymmetry destabilizes the pattern and propels the viewer into a tension between focussing on the individual colors and concentrating on the pattern. Or, as in the red-block quilt mentioned in the Callahan quote above, an irregularity in the design might prompt a reconsideration of the whole design.

Callahan describes one of the early Freedom quilts that sold for a high bid as "a coral and blue rendering whose pattern could be perceived as two designs" (27), a likely indication that this piece was made by someone with a passion for the medium. Wahlman and Scully point out that while "off-

174

beat patterning occurs in many Afro-American quilts made by women who quilt occasionally for family and friends . . . multiple rhythms usually occur in quilts made by women who 'love' to quilt" (90). One can easily imagine the colors in a two-tone quilt shifting before the eye as one color is regarded first as ground, then as figure. However, improvisational quilts often also manifest both off-beat patterns and multiple rhythms. The presence of these *gestalt* qualities is surprising when one realizes that "many quilts are the result of last-minute aesthetic choices. Often quilters do not plan their quilts, but piece together scraps as they come out of a box or bag. Yet all will say that the patches must 'hit each other right' or 'show off the design well'" (Wahlman and Scully 91). The quilter often does not precisely measure her pieces, either, which means she must make frequent adjustments to the overall design to compensate for differences in size and shape. Eli Leon argues that the improvisational abilities that enable the quilters to work in this way result from their ability to work from "models in their mind," a way of approaching design that some quilters also attributed to their mothers and grandmothers (30). Connecting this approach to that used by the Kuba people of Kongo for making embroidered raffia cloth, Leon quotes art historian and anthropologist Monni Adams: "In textile design the Africans of the Kasai-Sankaru region do not project a composition as an integrated repetition of elements . . . Kuba women use neither sample patterns nor sketches on the cloth; they are working from models in their minds" (26). The effect of these improvisations in both quilts and textiles "is to double, triple, and fragment patterns and rhythms so that one can see multiple accents which disrupt and suspend any regular flow of movement with color or form. . . . One or more patterns fade or fragment without completion" (Wahlman and Scully 91).

In short, then, the aesthetic governing African-American traditional quilting is profoundly different from that implicit in standard-traditional quilting. These preferences are less and less often being displayed by members of groups like the Freedom Quilting Bee, as "the pressures of commercialization force the Bee to discontinue production of several whimsical but labor-intensive patterns" (Callahan 115) and their mainstay accounts (notably one with Sears to produce pillow shams) demand uniformity. Nevertheless, quilt images in noteworthy African-American fiction keep the principles of this aesthetic alive and enable us to ponder the correspondences between them and those evident in much postmodern literature.

Perhaps the most metaphorically resonant quality of quiltmaking is a trait shared by Euro- and Afro-American traditions—the promise of creating unity among disparate elements, of establishing connections in the midst of fragmentation. Quite often, this connectivity applies across time as well as space, uniting the women of different generations who join the pieces of fabric as much as the scraps of material themselves. Bell hooks maintains this in her commemoration of her grandmother, as does Radka Donnell in *Quilts as Women's Art: A Quilt Poetics*. There, she asserts that

> a great many quilts have been made . . . to forge links between daughters, mothers, and mothers' mothers. . . . I want to acknowledge that the strongest single force connecting a quilt-maker to quilts is a woman's connection to other women, and above all her connection to her mother.
>
> (85)

The fiction writers considered here employ quilting images to emphasize the importance of woman-woman relationships to their work. While Gloria Naylor and Toni Morrison do so concentrating on intergenerational connections, Alice Walker uses quilts as a site for establishing relationships among peers.

In Naylor's *Mama Day,* Mama Day/Miranda and her sister Abigail create a double wedding ring quilt for Cocoa, Abigail's granddaughter, as a wedding gift. Mama Day grouses lovingly about having to sew the complicated design: "from edges to center, the patterns had to twine around each other. It would serve her right if it took till next year, and it probably would" (Naylor 135). When Abigail points out that Cocoa "did finally say she'd settle for a simple pattern," Mama Day is no less satisfied, and reminds Abigail that the quilt will "be passed on to my great-grandnieces and nephews when it's time for them to marry. And since I won't be around to defend myself, I don't want them thinking I was a lazy old somebody who couldn't make a decent double-ring quilt" (136). Mama Day is aware that she is sewing herself into the quilt, creating an heirloom that will preserve a part of herself when she is no longer "around," much as she is sewing in the rest of the family through the pieces of fabric she uses:

> A bit of her daddy's Sunday shirt is matched with Abigail's lace slip, the collar from Hope's graduation dress, the palm of Grace's baptismal gloves . . . Her needle fastens the satin trim of Peace's receiving blanket to Cocoa's baby jumper to a pocket of her own gardening apron.
>
> (137)

Mama Day wants to incorporate a piece of "Mother's gingham shirtwaist" as "it would go right nice into the curve between these two little patches of apricot toweling," even though she knows "Abigail would have a fit" (137). Working with the fragile, old cloth, Mama Day's clairvoyant connections to both its wearer and the recipient of the quilt are heightened; she realizes that the piece joins her own unhappy mother to "another woman who could not find peace" but that "it was too late to take it out of the quilt, and it didn't matter no way." She knew before asking that the answer to her rhetorical questions "Could she take herself out? Could she take out Abigail? Could she take 'em all out and start again?" (138) was a resounding "no." Naylor uses the quilt to reinforce the reader's awareness of the interconnections of the women across space and time, and to underscore the potency of these links. Indeed, as Linda Wagner-Martin has put it, "the mystery, the complicity, the inter-relation of women's lives and friendships are here imaged in the quilt . . . reminding [Naylor's] readers that women's lives, and their patterns of experience, are the focus of *Mama Day*" (7).

Explicit in regarding the quilt as a manifestation of familial relationships, Naylor articulates through Mama Day the kinds of connections that Toni Morrison implies in *Beloved*. When Baby Suggs gave up on living, she went to bed in the keeping room and just stayed there. Involved in her own turmoil, daughter-in-law Sethe only understands that in that room Baby is

> starved for color. There wasn't any except for two orange squares in a quilt that made the absence shout. . . . [In the bland room,] the dominating feature, the quilt over an iron cot, was made up of scraps of blue serge, black, brown, and gray wool—the full range of the dark and the muted that thrift and modesty allowed. In that sober field, two patches of orange looked wild—like life in the raw.
>
> (Morrison 38)

This quilt becomes a site for making connections among the many women in 124 Bluestone Road. Like Baby Suggs, the next woman in the narrative to exist in the liminal space between life and death craves the orange of the quilt. At the same time that this parallelism suggests a connection between Baby and Beloved, the quilt itself helps foster a bond between Beloved and Denver:

> It took three days for Beloved to notice the orange patches in the darkness of the quilt. Denver was pleased because it kept her patient awake longer. She seemed totally taken with those faded scraps of orange, even made the effort to lean on her elbow and stroke them. An effort that quickly exhausted her, so Denver rearranged the quilt so its cheeriest part was in the sick girl's sight line.
>
> (54)

Such patience is new to Denver, who strives to keep happy this girl whom she is certain is her sister's ghost.

Beloved's interest in the orange squares is more than just a delight in bright colors, though, for she says that the "yellow flowers in the place before the crouching [from Africa before being crowded into a slaveship's hold]. . . . are on the quilt now where we sleep" (214). This conflation of the bright flowers and the bright patches connects Beloved to Sethe (whom Beloved thinks picked the flowers), to Sethe's own mother (who actually was brought to America on a slaveship) and, more generally, to all slave-women. In "Nameless Ghosts:

Possession and Dispossession in *Beloved*," Deborah Horvitz maintains that Beloved "represents the spirit of all the women dragged onto slave ships in Africa and also all Black women in America trying to trace their ancestry back to the mother on the ship attached to them" (157). Creating this complicated trans-Atlantic chain of women is one of Morrison's aims; she is trying to present the stories and histories of African-American women that have not "been passed on." Beloved's "reading" of the quilt is one of the most specific instantiations of this effort.

Although Beloved and Sethe rework the quilt, adding bright, lively fabrics, the new colors do not change the quilt's literal and symbolic significance, simultaneously connecting them to one another and marking the place where members of this family of women choose between life and death. At the close of the novel Paul D finds a third woman on the life-death brink beneath the bedcovering. Sethe rests in the keeping room "under a quilt of merry colors" in a repose that makes him "nervous" (271). Paul D realizes "what he is reminded of and he shouts at her, 'Don't you die on me! This is Baby Suggs' bed! Is that what you planning?'" Though her literal ghost, Beloved, has disappeared, Paul D will not let Sethe "give up the ghost," and helps her decide instead to live. As representatives of three generations in this family, Baby Suggs, Sethe, and Beloved touch one another through the quilt-with-the-orange-squares, reminding the reader that quilts are not just symbolic, but are inevitably linked to the body—to birth (and rebirth) and death, as well as to the living in between.

For Alice Walker in *The Color Purple,* figurative rebirth occurs through the connections made among women who quilt together. Confronting Celie, who has told her stepson Harpo to beat Sofia for not "minding," Sofia throws the curtains that Celie has made for her back at the other woman in a rage. After talking through the ways that each woman deals with the suffering implicit to her cultural position, the two reconcile by "mak[ing] quilt pieces out of these messed up curtains" (44). Their action recalls one of Radka Donnell's verses, "rage submits to the homing / power of cloth, two equal / two pieces of cloth rock each one / of us back into consciousness, / to self-recognition and rest" (26).

The relationship which is most critical to Celie's re-birth, that with Shug, also begins with the two making blocks for a quilt. As unremarkable as her quilting is, Shug's attempts to stitch mark the beginning of her warmth toward Celie, a change in attitude that Celie is quick to sense:

> Me and Mr. _____ both look up at her. Both move to help her sit down. She don't look at him. She pull up a chair next to me.
>
> She pick up a random piece of cloth out the basket. Hold it up to the light. Frown. How you sew this damn thing? she say.
>
> I hand her the square I'm working on, start another one. She sew long crooked stitches, remind me of that little crooked tune she sing.
>
> That real good, for first try, I say. That just fine and dandy. She look at me and snort. Everything I do is fine and dandy to you, Miss Celie, she say.
>
> (59)

As their relationship develops, Shug donates a yellow dress for the "Sister's Choice" quilt Celie is making, and later enables Celie to establish financial independence through her sewing.

The quilts and quilting reflect a concern with women's relationships to one another central to much recent literature by African-American women. Furthermore, the specific details provided about the quilts indicate that the writers share the "sense of aesthetics" that hooks affirms among black women artists. Understanding the function of quilting images prompts us to think about aesthetics more generally; and in regarding organization and structure from this new perspectives, we can recognize the reconfigurations of the novel undertaken by each woman. Further guiding our re-perception is the novelists' inclusion of characters who consciously associate Afro-traditional quilting aesthetics with African textile aesthetics, as we find in *The Color Purple*.

Among the first things that Nettie reports to Celie about Africa is the fact that the Senegalese wear "brilliant blue robes with designs like fancy quilt patterns" (147). After arriving at the village where she is to work as a missionary, she writes to

Celie that "the Olinka are known for their beautiful cotton fabrics which they handweave and dye with berries, clay, indigo, and treebark" (164) and, in another letter, explains that "the Olinka men make beautiful quilts which are full of animals and birds and people" (192). Nettie's descriptions of Olinka and Senegalese cloths recall both Fon appliqués and West African narrow strip textiles; and she goes on to note that upon seeing those materials, the missionary Corrine "began to make a quilt that alternated one square of appliqued figures with one nine-patch block" (192). M. Teresa Tavormina has read Corrine's quilt keenly, noting that her combination of appliqué and blocks produced "an icon dense with history— personal, familial, artistic, national, racial, human—and with union and reunion. It brings together differences without denying them or subjugating them one to another—here a flowered square, there a checkered bird" (227). That Corrine's quilt also serves to re-establish trust between Nettie and Corrine adds still another facet to the already numerous signification functions in which it participates.

While it is difficult to be certain whether Celie's quilts are stripped like African cloth, or whether they have small or large designs,[5] Walker does indicate that both Celie and Corrine work in blocks (58, 192)—a technique routinely used in making strip quilts, albeit also in many other types. Morrison also intimates that Baby Suggs stripped her quilt when she writes that Sethe and Beloved "tack[ ] scraps of cloth on Baby Suggs' old quilt" (241) for, as Wahlman and Scully argue, their potential for being easily refurbished or augmented in this manner is one of the appealing features of strip quilts.

Whatever the patterns used, the characters in these novels clearly share a preference for bright colors. Celie loves the yellow of Shug's old dress both because it is from Shug and because "the little yellow pieces look like stars" (61). Sethe and Beloved add "carnival colors" to Baby Suggs's quilt (272), presumably leftover scraps from the "blue stripes and sassy prints" (240) they purchase with all of Sethe's savings. And Mama Day and Abigail craft striking rings: "the overlapping circles start out as golds on the edge and melt into oranges, reds, blues, greens, and then back to golds for the middle of the quilt" (137). The circle into which Mama Day works her mother's gingham includes "apricot toweling" and "light red crepe" (138). These bright shades and the variety of fabrics are a dazzling alternative to those found in the traditional "Double Wedding Rings," which were "often made from a kit, pieced of pastel floral prints on a white ground" (Leon 35).[6]

Leon persuasively argues that the "vital force" of Afro-traditional "Double Wedding Rings" distinguishes them from the "fragile perfection" of their standard-traditional counterparts (37). And in an essay entitled "Sea Island Black Quilters," Nan Tournier makes a parallel claim that is especially applicable to *Mama Day*. Tournier argues that the quilts made by African-American women from the islands off the South Carolina shore "often display a highly individual interpretation of a traditional quilt design" (41–42). She goes on to observe that these interpretations can be linked to African aesthetics, in large part because the islands have "large, stable communit[ies]," so that "there is little difficulty in retaining through the generations a creative philosophy which can subtly reflect the African cultural heritage" (46) despite the islanders' proximity to the shore and to Anglo-American culture. The heritage Tournier describes bears marked similarity to that attributed to Naylor's residents of Willow Springs, an island off the coast of the South Carolina–Georgia border, but allowed to remain almost unchanged over time because it is claimed by neither state. Additionally, Mary Arnold Twining notes in her dissertation, "An Examination of African Retentions in the Folk Culture of the South Carolina and Georgia Sea Islands," that the quilters on these islands often combine diverse types of fabric in a single quilt: "they mix velvet, broadcloth, upholstery fabric, nylon, batiste, twills, woolens, rayon all in the same quilt" (187). While this sort of assemblage likely originated as an economic rather than aesthetic choice, Tournier and Twining both note that the stability of the community perpetuates and reinforces certain aesthetic preferences and cultural practices. We may suppose that economic necessity has been transmuted into aesthetic preference on the Sea Islands and in *Mama Day*, for Abigail and Miranda—who are not financially troubled—employ materials as diverse as those on Twining's list.

While Naylor does name the quilt Abigail and Mama Day are making, and Walker mentions the "Sister's Choice" in particular, very few patterns are specified considering the number of quilts in these three novels. Therefore, we must piece together from textual fragments whether or not these characters worked in off-beat patterns or employed multiple rhythms, as is characteristic of much Afro-traditional quilting. Celie, who loves to sew, quite probably did; making the "Sister's Choice" quilt, she asserts that she "work[s] in a piece" of Shug's yellow dress "every chance I get" (61). Celie's words suggest that rather than incorporating the material at regular intervals, as one would expect her to do since she is employing a standard design, she is in fact playing with the pattern to some degree. Analogously, Leon's description of Afro-traditional "Double Wedding Rings" and Tournier's of Sea Island quilts, especially when combined with the color choices Mama Day describes, reinforce our supposition that Cocoa's wedding quilt is a "highly individualized variation" of the traditional design. And much as the red square in the Freedom quilt simultaneously calls attention to itself and to the pattern it disrupts, the orange squares in Baby Suggs's quilt create an impression of both order and interruption, a new pattern made explicitly part of an African aesthetic because it is employed to help forge a link between Beloved and the "sixty million and more" who did not survive the middle passage acknowledged by Morrison in the epigraph.

As many of the descriptions above have implied, the improvisation that is the hallmark of Afro-traditional quilting is also critical to these characters' quilting practices. While working on the "Sister's Choice," Celie decides that "if the quilt turn out perfect, maybe I give it to her, if it not perfect, maybe I keep" (61), an attitude which indicates that she does not know precisely what it will look like when she finishes, even though she is nominally working from a pattern. This perspective recalls the "flexible classicism" Leon ascribed to African aesthetics. Furthermore, even when working from "a basketful of scraps on the floor" (58), Celie is able to generate striking designs, as did many of the quilters Wahlman and Scully described. Mama Day and Abigail also work from scraps; in Abigail's living room, they sit "almost knee-deep in bags of colored rags, sorted together by shades" (137). And like many of the African-American quilters interviewed by folklorists, these two do not measure their scraps precisely; when trying to incorporate a bit of her mother's dress, for example, Mama Day "tries and tries again just for a sliver" (137), which she must eventually baste to a bit of gingham before "she can shape the curve she needs" (137–138). Similarly, as both Baby Suggs's staid color choices and Sethe and Beloved's flamboyant ones suggest, these quilters worked with what they had, creating the most interesting designs possible with limited supplies.

By emphasizing the improvisational qualities and the principles of combination and connection inherent to quilting in their texts, Gloria Naylor, Toni Morrison, and Alice Walker suggest that these qualities are important to creative black women—that they are part of the aesthetic inheritance that hooks makes visible and seeks to perpetuate. Because they are contributing to this tradition through their narratives, we are prompted to look at the structure of the novels in a new way, to try to recognize how these principles contribute to a restructuring of this historically white, bourgeois, European form.

While the three novels are not identical to one another in structure, they all deviate quite clearly from the conventions of the classic realist text. All are "patchworked"; Walker's epistolary form may make this structuring most obvious, but the shift among several narrators and the manipulations of chronology in Naylor's and Morrison's texts achieve a similar result. Discussing *The Color Purple,* Tavormina discusses the efficacy of quilts and epistolary forms in refocussing one's attention away from linear causality and a single perspective on experience, two attributes of the classic realist novel:

> The art—Walker's art—is not only in the creation (or the transmission) of the two lives [Nettie's and Celie's], but also in the arrangement that juxtaposes and interlocks moments of revelation in Africa and America. . . . Letters, like quilts, transcend time's boundaries. . . . yet quilts and correspondence, besides transcending time, record its parts.
>
> (226)

Naylor's use of the voices of Willow Springs, of Mama Day, of Cocoa, and of George after he has died to narrate meld a variety of perspectives while disrupting our customary ontological borders—both a place's "spirit" and a dead man's voice have the same ability to speak and evaluate as do the living individuals, an attribution of agency that is strikingly at odds with the conventions of most serious fiction written for adult readers. Similarly, Morrison overtly defies the boundaries of space and time because she has constructed a ghost story; but Beloved is not the only character for whom the space-time continuum does not conform to our usual understanding of it. Sethe explains to Denver that "rememories" are like afterimages of past events and places, that

> "If a house burns down, it's gone, but the place—the picture of it—stays, and not just in my rememory, but out there, in the world.". . . .
>
> "Can other people see it?" asked Denver.
>
> "Oh, yes. Oh yes, yes, yes. Someday you be walking down the road and you hear something or see something going on. So clear. And you think it's you thinking it up. A thought picture. But no. It's when you bump into a rememory that belongs to somebody else."
>
> (36)

Morrison remembers and (re)constructs through the arrangement of her text: she reaches forward and backward in time, selecting and highlighting details as they become important, clarifying information in ways that accentuate fundamental interrelationships among people and events and the processes of thinking and storytelling.

Although the unwieldy nature of the task prohibits me from demonstrating that *The Color Purple, Mama Day,* and *Beloved* display the literary equivalents to the multiple rhythms and off-beat patterns of Afro-traditional quilts, readers familiar with the three texts will readily recall the presence of these *gestalt* qualities. Similarly, such readers may regard the vibrant, highly individualized characters involved in permutations of primal situations as a writer's analog to the strong, highly contrasting color and design of the quilter's palette.

185

While re-affirming the Afro-traditional quilting aesthetic of their matrilineage, Walker, Naylor, and Morrison also develop an aesthetic in these books that bears some unexpected similarities to that typically labelled "postmodern."

In many of the books that have received academic acclaim during the last four decades, we discern a set of features now termed "postmodern." Some philosophical consensus exists concerning the meaning of this category, as Jane Flax notes in *Thinking Fragments:*

> Postmodern stories about contemporary social transformations have at least one common organizing theme: There has been a breakdown in the metanarrative of Enlightenment . . . [and] ideas that now seem problematic include such independent concepts as the dignity and worth of the "monadic" (socially isolated and self-sufficient) individual and the interconnections between reason, knowledge, progress, freedom, and ethical action.
>
> (7)

The conciseness and relative clarity of this definition notwithstanding, literary critics and theorists have yet to agree upon precisely what is meant by postmodernism, or when it began, or why it has become so pervasive. Most literary theorists, however, do maintain that postmodernism is not limited to specific examples of the elite arts and academic discourse, but is a manifestation of the above-mentioned breakdown in the perceived efficacy of the Enlightenment metanarrative, that it involves a transformation within our cultural matrix. In his article "The Fine Art of Rap," Richard Shusterman emphasizes the ubiquity of postmodern aesthetic when he argues that hip-hop manifests many of the stylistic features that postmodernists use to question the assumptions implicit to earlier forms, including:

> recycling appropriation rather than unique originative creation, the eclectic mixing of styles, the enthusiastic embracing of the new technology and mass culture, the challenging of modernist notions of aesthetic autonomy and artistic pu-

186

rity, and an emphasis on the localized and temporal rather than the putatively universal and eternal.

(614)

This incredulity toward metanarrative and the manners in which it is expressed remind us that the most significant preoccupations postmodern literary writers grapple with concern the subject, history, representation, and space/time—the parameters of "reality." The subject, which used to be understood as individuated, autonomous, and capable of exhibiting agency, is regarded by postmodernists alternatively as dead, fragmented, culturally constructed, or a bourgeois illusion—a point that Fredric Jameson emphasizes in his writings. History, which was once perceived as a single, linear narrative, is understood as one construction among many. Representation, once considered a potentially unbiased depiction of some ontologically prior "reality," is now regarded as necessarily ideologically inflected and not necessarily prior to whatever "reality" it describes. And space and time, rather than being absolute, are being viewed with some uncertainty. While a list like this one can provide only a hasty overview of some of the concerns and techniques of postmodern writers, it does suggest a starting point for making connections between the quilting aesthetic and the postmodern one.

Through the quilting images, the African-American women writers discussed above have been able to concertedly theorize a subject that is not the monadic self of the Enlightenment narrative, but who can nevertheless project a "rational, coherent, effective identity"—the traits most feminist critics find crucial to any new definitions of subjectivity (Waugh 6). This identity is explicitly constructed of fragments that make a strong whole; for example, by aligning her with the double wedding ring quilt that Mama Day and Abigail make, Naylor presents Cocoa as constructed out of a little bit of Abigail, a little bit of Mama Day, and a little bit of her great-grandmother, among others. Naylor does not suggest that Cocoa is simply the sum of her ancestors through a naturalistic calculus; instead she emphasizes that our inevitable constructedness also involves the promise of incorporating new parts that can further strengthen the self—as Cocoa learns after coming to terms with George's death, thereby gaining some of his fortitude.

An analogous patchworking of time also occurs in these narratives. Of the three writers, Morrison most overtly depicts history as not only not a linear narrative, but as constructed out of a multiplicity of stories—many of which have been silenced and are only slowly re-emerging. While one rarely reads in history textbooks about the slave's perspective on slavery, for example, this vantage provides significant information about historical conditions. Yet, Morrison reminds us that history cannot simply be rewritten from the slave's vantage, since Stamp Paid's and Sethe's perspectives, for example, are no more equivalent than are Mr. Garner's and schoolteacher's ideas about being a master. Consequently, she re-presents history through lots of narrative vantages—all of them obviously and inevitably partial. This process stresses the need to combine the fragments in order to have a viable whole, to seam scraps together into a comforting cover.

Morrison's linking of revisionary history with alternative forms of representation closely parallels the postmodernist intermingling of history and representation. Linda Hutcheon discusses this intertwining, noting that "postmodern representational practices . . . refuse to stay neatly within accepted conventions and traditions . . . and [they] deploy hybrid forms and seemingly mutually contradictory strategies" (37). The complicated strategies (re)present "postmodern relativity and provisionality . . . [which are] perhaps the very conditions of historical knowledge. Historical knowledge may thus be seen today as unstable, contextual, relational, and provisional, but postmodernism argues that, in fact, it has always been so" (Hutcheon 67). Despite the doubts postmodern writers evince about the viability of accurately presenting history, many postmodern works are historiographic metafictions—a genre discussed at length by critics of postmodernism Patricia Waugh and Linda Hutcheon. For Morrison, the importance of re-presenting history lies in the artistic and literal remaking it enables. As she explained to Nellie McKay, she tries to tell "the same story again and again. I can change it," she says, "if I contribute to it when I tell it. I can emphasize special things"

188

(McKay 421). In presenting black women's experiences, a new focus in novels, Morrison and the other novelists contribute both to the story and to our awareness of storytelling. They force us to think about the ways in which the stories we tell have, as Fredric Jameson argues, "reflect[ed] a fundamental dimension of our collective thinking and our collective fantasies about history and reality" (1981, 34). Such attention re-presents narrative itself, opening it up to the same scrutiny as do the more conspicuously experimental forms of postmodernism.

Finally, as I suggested above, the disruptions of chronology (through flashbacks, letters, and rememory), and the unsettling of spatial parameters (through the juxtaposition of Nettie's Africa and Celie's United States or George's New York and Cocoa's ambiguously-placed Willow Springs), like the conflation of past and present through the fabrics of an heirloom quilt, encourage the reader to rethink her or his understanding of space and time—both their significance and their relation to what we name "real." In talking about another of her books, *Meridian*, Alice Walker said that she

> wanted to do something like a crazy quilt . . . something that works on the mind in different patterns . . . A crazy-quilt story is one that can jump back and forth in time, work on many different levels, and one that can include myth. It is generally much more evocative of metaphor and symbolism than a novel that is chronological in structure, or one devoted, more or less, to rigorous realism.
>
> (Tate 176)

Like Walker, Naylor and Morrison have also shaped stories that "work on the mind in different patterns."

The correspondences between postmodern practices and these quilting/literary aesthetics are significant for their shared interest in rethinking the subject, in grappling with the subject's relation to space and time, and in finding socially appropriate and viable forms of representation. However, most critical discussions of postmodern texts note that the rethinking in these works involves much more questioning than answering. One of the most important distinctions we can make between postmodern texts and these African-American wom-

189

en's works, therefore, is that the latter take one more step than the former: many of the black women writers whose works are now gaining attention try to offer plausible, non-reactionary rescripting of the terms that postmodernism has undecided.

Just as their mothers employed various colors and sizes of fabric to piece a quilt top, these literary women rely on partial, local, and fragmented knowledges to make a narrative. The writers acknowledge that both the quilts and the narratives—as well as the beings who are their makers—are constructed. However, they regard the need to piece and seam not as a reason for despair but as an opportunity to rework the outmoded, in clothing, novel structures, and conceptions of the self. Similarly, while doubt about the efficacy of history or representation often paralyzes characters in postmodern narratives, the women in the three books I have discussed are liberated through the rescriptings. Shug's and Celie's refusals to conform entirely to someone else's patterns do not, in the long run, inhibit them from creating. Instead, their improvising ability opens new alternatives, as Walker's form does. And while the ghosts of *Beloved,* magic/hoodoo of *Mama Day,* and serendipity of *The Color Purple* remain difficult for some readers to accept because the paranormal cannot be recuperated into their worldview, it does open new ontological possibilities for what we call reality. As Toni Morrison once explained, "birds talk and butterflies cry" in her stories because such things are "not surprising or upsetting to [black people]. These things make the world larger for them" (McKay 428).

The writings of Alice Walker, Toni Morrison, and Gloria Naylor "make the world larger" and more vibrant for their readers by wrapping us in quilts of many colors. Through their images of quilts and their adaptations of the novel form, they simultaneously describe and participate in an alternative aesthetic tradition. This tradition, which can be traced back to Africa, is one that their foremothers perpetuated in the patching and stitching of threadbare, often roughly sewn bedcoverings that bear only a general resemblance to standard-traditional quilts, creating an alternative that "stands," as Houston A. Baker and Charlotte Pierce-Baker assert, "as a signal instance of a patterned wholeness in the African diaspora"

190

(706). And indeed both these African-American writers and the women whom they remember with reverence seem to have discovered that quilts are an apparently innocent means by which "women could send a hidden message to other women" (MacDowell 72), a message that, in this case, preserves and continues their aesthetic heritage. Conscious of, and valuing, this heritage as both women and artists, these novelists incorporate images of quilts and quilting into their works. While arising from different cultural and material conditions, this inheritance enables the novelists to participate in the kind of radical questioning endemic to the postmodern era, and—unlike many of other writers of the times—to suggest some possible ways to resolve the queries that are so often now being raised.

Without insisting that either quilts or quilting aesthetics in narrative offer a solution to all of our literary and existential woes, I would argue that through their reliance on such an aesthetic, the novelists described in this essay have been able to remind us that the assembly of a lowly bedcovering can suggest valuable ways to reconceptualize our senses of self, community, lineage, and the connections between art and its social function. Such reconceptualizations seem to signify that the search for meaning in a postmodern world might well begin at home.

☐ *Notes* ∎

1. Maude Southwell Wahlman and John Scully (1983) mention two other exhibits: one that they organized at the Yale Art and Architecture Gallery in 1979 and another entitled "Something to Keep You Warm" that was organized by Roland Freeman and toured the United States. Elaine Showalter refers briefly to "highly successful museum exhibits [of black women's quilts] in Dallas, San Francisco, New York, Mississippi, and Washington, D.C." (163).

2. Eli Leon distinguishes between the many quilting practices that originated in different parts of Europe and those from Africa—collectively referring to the former as standard-traditional, and to the latter, as Afro-traditional. I find this distinction useful for my discussion.

3. Amish shadows quilts are one important exception to this generalization.

4. One wonders, given the importance of African art to Picasso's work, if perhaps *he* could do it for precisely the reasons that *they* could.

5. The one pattern she specifies, "Sister's Choice," is a block quilt that would typically combine many small blocks. In it, Celie uses many tiny pieces of Shug's dress, an indication that she probably does keep that scale small.

6. Eli Leon highlights the difference between the standard "Double Wedding Ring" and its African-American counterpart through the following anecdote (Leon is showing his collection to five sisters, aged 62 to 75, who all quilt):

> When I got ready to show the "Double Wedding Ring," I asked if everyone was familiar with the patterns. One of them wasn't sure, so I spread out a spellbinding example of a 1930s standard "Double Wedding Ring," the kind that was often made from a kit, pieced of pastel floral prints on a white ground. The quilt was in mint condition, lusciously crisp, exquisitely quilted, a pristine examine of an archetype of Anglo-American femininity at a high point in standard American quiltmaking. The ladies loved it and a chorus of "ain't that nice" in hushed, cooing tones circled the room. Seeing the quilt afresh, through their eyes, I felt the same reverence and, unexpectedly, some fearful anticipation about the reception the Hall "Wedding Ring" would get. This was really a hard act to follow.
>
> But I proceeded to bring out Emma Hall's worn and roughly crafted quilt and was thunderstruck by their reaction. These five stately women, a moment before so sweet and serene, started to hoot and stomp until the house shook. The room became a stadium; the fans gone wild. It was an exhilarating experience and it gave me some information I had been unwittingly seeking about cultural differences in standard- and Afro-traditional esthetic intention. (35–37)

☐ Works Cited ■

Baker, Houston A. and Charlotte Pierce-Baker. "Patches: Quilts and Community in Alice Walker's 'Everyday Use.'" *The Southern Review* 21:3 (Summer 1985): 706–720.

Bell-Scott, Patricia et al., eds. *Double Stitch: Black Women Write about Mothers and Daughters.* Boston: Beacon Press, 1991.

Brown, Elsa Barkley. "African-American Women's Quilting: A Framework for Conceptualizing and Teaching African-American Women's History." In *Black Women in America: Social Science Perspectives.* Edited by Micheline R. Malson et al. Chicago: University of Chicago Press, 1990.

Callahan, Nancy. *The Freedom Quilting Bee.* Tuscaloosa: University of Alabama Press, 1987.

Donnell, Radka. *Quilts as Women's Art: A Quilt Poetics.* Vancouver, Canada: Gallerie Publications, 1990.

Ferris, William, ed. *Afro-American Folk Arts and Crafts.* Boston: G. K. Hall, 1983.

Flax, Jane. *Thinking Fragments: Psychoanalysis, Feminism, and Postmodernism in the Contemporary West.* Berkeley: University of California Press, 1990.

hooks, bell. *Yearning: race, gender, and cultural politics.* Boston: South End Press, 1990.

Horton, Laurel and Lynn Robertson Myers, eds. *Social Fabric: South Carolina's Traditional Quilts.* Columbia, S.C.: McKissick Museum (University of South Carolina), 1986.

Horvitz, Deborah. "Nameless Ghosts: Possession and Dispossession in *Beloved.*" *Studies in American Fiction* 17:2 (Autumn 1989): 157–167.

Hutcheon, Linda. *The Politics of Postmodernism.* London: Routledge, 1989.

Jameson, Fredric. *The Political Unconscious: Narrative as a Socially Symbolic Art.* Ithaca, N.Y.: Cornell University Press, 1981.

———. "Postmodernism, or the Cultural Logic of Late Capitalism." *New Left Review* 146 (July–August 1984): 53–92.

Leon, Eli, ed. *Who'd a Thought It: Improvisation in African-American Quiltmaking.* San Francisco: San Francisco Craft & Folk Art Museum, 1987.

MacDowell, Marsha. "Women, Quiltmaking and Social Change in America." In *Quilted Together: Women, Quilts, and Communities.* Edited by Joyce Ice and Linda Norris. Delhi, N.Y.: Delaware County Historical Association, 1989.

McKay, Nellie. "An Interview with Toni Morrison." *Contemporary Literature* 24:4 (Winter 1983): 413–429.

Morrison, Toni. *Beloved.* New York: Alfred A. Knopf, 1987.

Naylor, Gloria. *Mama Day*. New York: Vintage Contemporaries, 1988.

Shange, Ntozake. *Sassafras, Cypress & Indigo*. New York: St. Martin's Press, 1982.

Showalter, Elaine. 1991. *Sister's Choice: Tradition and Change in American Women's Writing*. Oxford: Clarendon Press, 1991.

Shusterman, Richard. "The Fine Art of Rap." *New Literary History* 22:3 (Summer 1991): 613–632.

Tate, Claudia, ed. *Black Women Writers at Work*. New York: Continuum, 1983.

Tavormina, M. Teresa. "Dressing the Spirit: Clothworking and Language in *The Color Purple*." *Journal of Narrative Technique* 16:3 (Fall 1986): 220–230.

Thompson, Robert Farris. "From the First to the Final Thunder: African-American Quilts, Monuments of Cultural Assertion." In Preface to *Who'd a Thought It: Improvisation in African-American Quiltmaking*, ed. Leon.

Tournier, Nan. "Sea Island Black Quilters." In *Social Fabric: South Carolina's Traditional Quilts*, ed. Horton and Meyers.

Twining, Mary Arnold. "An Examination of African Retentions in the Folk Culture of the South Carolina and Georgia Sea Islands." Dissertation, Indiana University, Bloomington, 1977.

Wahlman, Maude Southwell and John Scully. "Aesthetic Principles in Afro-American Quilts." In *Afro-American Folk Arts and Crafts*, ed. Ferris.

Wagner-Martin, Linda. "Quilting in Gloria Naylor's *Mama Day*." *Notes on Contemporary Literature* 18:5 (1988): 6–7.

Walker, Alice. *The Color Purple*. New York: Pocket Books, 1982.

Waugh, Patricia. *Feminine Fictions: Revisiting the Postmodern*. London: Routledge, 1989.

Young, Blanche and Helen Young. *The Lone Star Quilt Handbook*. Oak View, Calif.: Young Publications, 1979.

Common
Threads

Susan Glaspell's story 'A Jury of Her Peers' (1917) has a Gothic
plot in which the woman takes a desperate revenge. Adapted
from her play *Trifles,* the story begins with two women ac-
companying their husbands to a cold farmhouse where the
local miser, John Wright, has been strangled in his sleep, and
his wife Minnie jailed for the crime. Mrs Peters is the wife of
the sheriff; Mrs Hale is the wife of his deputy; and thus both,
as the sheriff jokes, are 'married to the law.' But this is a per-
plexing case. There seems to be no evidence of a motive for
the crime; the men futilely search the house and barn for
clues, while the women clean up the strangely disordered
kitchen. Gradually, however, the women begin to notice domestic details eloquent of Minnie Foster Wright's troubled
mind and of her oppression in a cruel and childless marriage.
The most telling clues are the blocks of her unfinished quilt,
left in the sewing basket. The 'crazy sewing' of a Log Cabin
block pierced all askew alerts them to the anger and anguish
of a woman who cannot control her feelings enough to create
an orderly art. As Mrs Peters and Mrs Hale discover the other
missing evidence—the body of a pet canary whose neck had
been twisted by the husband—they recognize their own bonds
within a cultural system meaningless to men, and their own responsibility for the isolation and loneliness of a former friend,
long abandoned, who has been driven mad. In a moment

From *Sister's Choice: Tradition and Change in American Women's Writing.*
(Oxford: Oxford University Press 1991), pp. 145–175, 192–195. Copyright
© 1991 by Elaine Showalter.

of silent conspiracy, they resew the pieces and destroy the damning evidence, under the very eyes of their uncomprehending husbands who make fun of their feminine obsession with trifles. 'Have you decided whether she was going to quilt it or knot it?' Mr Hale mockingly asks his wife. 'WE think she was going to—knot it,' Mrs Hale replies. The patchwork would have been knotted as Minnie Wright has knotted the rope around her husband's neck. But also in declaring 'knot it' at the end of the story, the women signal their infidelity to patriarchal law and serve as a jury of Minnie Foster's peers to acquit her of murder.[1]

The conceptual patterns Glaspell represents seem like they might offer a way to address the common threads of American women's culture and writing, and the significance of patchwork as its symbol. Both theme and form in women's writing, piecing and patchwork have also become metaphors for a Female Aesthetic, for sisterhood, and for a politics of feminist survival. In the past two decades especially, they have been celebrated as essentially feminine art forms, modes of expression that emerge naturally from womanly impulses of nurturance and thrift, and that constitute a women's language unintelligible to male audiences or readers.[2] Indeed, for feminist critics of American literature, 'A Jury of Her Peers' has been taken since the mid-1970s as a metaphor for feminist reading itself. As Annette Kolodny observes,

> Glaspell's narrative not only invites a semiotic analysis, but, indeed, performs that analysis for us. If the absent Minnie Foster is the 'transmitter' or 'sender' in this schema, then only the women are competent 'receivers' or 'readers' of her message, since they alone share not only her context (the supposed insignificance of kitchen things), but, as a result, the conceptual patterns which make up her world.[3]

Yet to emphasize quilting as the aesthetic domain of women is to lose sight of the way it has been constructed over time in the contexts of changing ideological definitions of femininity as well as strongly gendered separations of the spheres of craft and art. To perpetuate the idea that women have a *natural* inclination for quilting as an expressive mode can serve as an explanation for their absence from the master-pieces of art history, suggesting that 'women are to patchwork as men are to painting.'[4] Furthermore, as the quilt-maker Radka Donnell argues,

> there is more to the problem than the art/craft contro-versy. . . . More than anything, it is sexism, not just elitism, that has kept quilts from a share of space on museum walls. Quilts, after all, have been and are still made almost exclu-sively by women in a culture where the work, concerns, and accomplishments of women are inexorably dismissed as mean-ingless and unimportant.[5]

Feminizing the quilt, as the feminist art historian Lisa Tickner has explained, 'keeps women's work marginal and identifies it with the characteristics of a reproductive and do-mestic femininity, which are understood not to be the charac-teristics of great art.'[6]

Because of the devaluation, even stigma, of the domes-tic, the feminine and craft within the value systems of cultural history, the incorporation of quilt methods and metaphors in American women's writing has always been risky. Quilts, like those who write about them, are thought to be trifling; they have been seen as occupying a female sphere outside of high culture. Indeed, as Roszika Parker and Griselda Pollock point out in their book *Old Mistresses,* 'any association with the traditions and practices of needlework and domestic art can be dangerous for an artist, especially when that artist is a woman.'[7]

But the history of piecing and writing in the United States, and the literary or rhetorical history of the quilt meta-phor, show that conventions and styles that were originally associated with a women's culture have been gradually trans-formed in new configurations and adapted in the service of new ideological ends. Like other American cultural practices and symbols, quilting has also undergone a series of gender transformations, appropriations, and commodifications within the larger culture. While quilting does have crucial meaning for American women's texts, it can't be taken as a transhistori-cal and essential form of female expression, but rather as a gendered practice that changed from one generation to the next, and that has now become the symbol of American identity at the *fin de siècle*.

To see how the metaphor of quilting has evolved, we might begin by seeing how the history of the quilt identified it with women's culture, and why piecing offered a particularly moving symbolism of the American democratic ideal. While the practice of piecing and quilting was brought to America from its very different sources in England and Africa, it early became a distinctive feature of American society. Quilting was a practical and economic necessity in a country where ready-made bedding could not be easily obtained before the 1890s, and where in the cold New England or prairie winter each family member might need five thick quilts. All American girls were taught to piece and to quilt, and autobiographies of this period 'frequently begin with a childhood memory of learning patchwork' and doing a daily 'stint.'[8] Moreover, early art, writing, and mathematical exercises taught to little girls emphasized geometric principles of structure and organization, and such lessons were applied practically to the design of quilts. An American girl was encouraged to finish her first small quilt in time for a fifth birthday, and by the time she was engaged, she aspired to have a dozen quilts in her dower chest; the thirteenth quilt of the trousseau was the Bridal Quilt, made of the most expensive materials the family could afford, and stuffed, backed, and quilted by the bride's female relatives and by the most expert needlewomen of her community at a special quilting bee.

Furthermore, the social institutions of quilting helped forge bonds between women. At the quilting bee women celebrated a birth or an engagement; they shared rituals of grief as well when they pieced funeral quilts to line a baby's coffin or to commemorate a friend. Quilting bees were also places where women came together to exchange information, learn new skills, and discuss political issues; it was at a church quilting bee in Cleveland, for example, that Susan B. Anthony gave her first speech on women's suffrage. Even when they rebelled against the task of learning to quilt, American women had internalized its aesthetic concepts and designs, and saw it as a fundamental part of their tradition.[9]

Moreover, American quilt-making crossed racial, regional, and class boundaries, and its immense aesthetic vitality came from its fertilization by other design traditions. Black women in the South adapted design elements from West African textiles, including strips, bright colors, large figures, multiple patterns, asymmetry, and improvisation.[10] The quilts made by slaves for their own use were different from those made according to the patterns prescribed to them as seamstresses; as Houston and Charlotte Baker point out, 'the hands that pieced the master's rigidly patterned quilts by day were often the hands that crafted a more functional design in slave cabins by night.'[11] African-American quilt-making took from its sources 'a percussive manner of handling textile color,' and an exuberant 'acceptance of accident and contingency.'[12] Native American quilt-makers incorporated traditional patterns from Navaho or Sioux rugs. The non-representational Amish and Mennonite traditions contributed strikingly modern color-field designs. In Hawaii, quilt-making in the 1820s was supervised by the Queen dowager, and only aristocratic women were allowed to participate in making quilts with strongly colored floral and flag patterns.

To the appliqué and string techniques brought from England and Africa, American women added the piecing technique which would become the dominant feature of quilting. Making a patchwork quilt involves four separate stages of artistic composition. The quilt-maker first selects her colors and fabrics, traditionally using recycled clothing or household material with emotional associations; and cuts out small, geometrically-shaped pieces. These fragments are then 'pieced' or joined together in a particular pattern to form a larger square unit called a 'patch' or 'block.' The patches are joined together into an overall pattern, usually a traditional one with a name that indicates its regional, political, or spiritual meaning. Finally, the entire fabric is stitched to a padding and heavy backing with a variety of large-scale embroidery motifs.

Piecing is thus an art of making do and eking out, an art of ingenuity, and conservation. It reflects the fragmentation of women's time, the scrappiness and uncertainty of women's creative or solitary moments. As the art critic Lucy Lippard observes, 'the mixing and matching of fragments is the product of the interrupted life. . . . What is popularly seen as "repetitive," "obsessive," and "compulsive" in women's art is in fact a necessity for those whose time comes in small squares.'[13]

But piecing also presents a triumph over time and scarcity. As a Texas quilter explains,

> You're given just so much to work with in a life and you have to do the best you can with what you got. That's what piecing is. The materials is passed on to you or is all you can afford to buy . . . that's just what's given to you. Your fate. But the way you put them together is your business. You can put them in any order you like. Piecing is orderly.[14]

This metaphor is central to the historical tradition of American women's writing, and is deeply connected to the creative vision American women writers have shared. For American women, housekeeping, as Lydia Maria Child said in *The American Frugal Housewife* (1829) 'is the art of gathering up all the fragments so that nothing be lost.' Piecing these fragments together into a beautiful design, Harriet Beecher Stowe explains in her novel *The Minister's Wooing,* is an emblem of 'that household life which is to be brought to stability and beauty by reverent economy in husbanding and tact in arranging the little . . . morsels of daily existence.'

Moreover, piecing is not a repetitious recycling of design elements, but a series of aesthetic decisions that involve the transformation of conventions. Even when working with such well-known patterns as the Star, Sun, or Rose, 'the quilt artist exploited the design possibilities through her colors, contrasts, and inventive variations on the original pattern.'[15] In the African-American quilt tradition, improvisation has also led to distinctive and unique designs. As Stowe comments in *The Minister's Wooing,* quilting gave women an outlet for their originality: 'Many a maiden, as she sorted and arranged fluttering bits of green, yellow, red, and blue, felt rising in her breast a passion for somewhat vague and unknown, which came out at length in a new pattern of patchwork.' And piecing and quilting were not anonymous or collective arts. As Patricia Mainardi has pointed out, 'The women who made quilts knew and valued what they were doing: frequently quilts were signed and dated by the maker, listed in her will with specific instructions as to who should inherit them, and treated with all the care that a fine piece of art deserves.'[16]

Finally, the quilt process corresponds to the writing process, on the level of the word, the sentence, the structure of a story or novel, and the images, motifs, or symbols that unify a fictional work. Parallels between piecing and writing emerge in the earliest days of the Republic. In the 1830s and 1840s, album quilts, today the most prized and expensive examples of American quilt art, were the dominant genre of female craft. Album quilts are composed of pieced or appliquéd squares 'that are entirely different, even if their construction has been carefully planned and orchestrated by a single quilter. The effect is as if each square were a page in a remembrance book.'[17] They were made to be presented to young men on their 21st birthdays (known as Liberty quilts), or exchanged among women friends (Medley or Engagement quilts), and were signed square by square (Friendship quilts). Many, like the Betsy Lee Wright quilt made in 1851, had poems and messages written on their squares. The most elaborate album quilts were made beginning in 1846 by a small community of Methodist women in Baltimore, among whom were the master quilt-makers Acsah Goodwin Wilkins and Mary Evans, professional needlewomen who worked on commission and whose work now brings between $70,000 and $100,000 at auctions.

A number of nineteenth-century women's texts discuss the problem of reading a quilt, of deciphering the language of piecing like pages in an album. In 'The Patchwork Quilt,' an anonymous essay by a factory girl printed in *The Lowell Offering* in 1845, the author's quilt is described as 'a bound volume of hieroglyphics.' But only a certain kind of reader can decipher these female signifiers. To the 'uninterested observer,' the narrator declares, it looks like a 'miscellaneous collection of odd bits and ends,' but to me 'it is a precious reliquary of past treasure.' She locates the significance of the quilt in the individual piece, as if it were a textile scrapbook. The quilt's pieces, taken from the writer's childhood calico gowns, her dancing school dress, her fashionable young ladies' gowns, her mother's mourning dress, her brother's vest, are thus a record of the female life cycle from birth to death.[18]

During the same period the standard genre of American women's writing was the sketch or piece written for annuals, which became popular in the 1820s, and which often accepted only American materials.[19] While the sustained effort of a novel might be impossible for a woman whose day was shattered by constant interruption, the short narrative piece, quickly imagined and written, could be more easily completed. Harriet Beecher Stowe's literary career, for example, began in the 1840s with a series of pieces written for Christmas gift annuals, ladies' albums, and religious periodicals. A 'piece' could be written in a day, and bring in $2.00 a page, and Stowe thought of her writing in terms of temporal blocks which could be set aside when financial pressure demanded. 'When the family accounts wouldn't add up,' Stowe recalled, 'Then I used to say to my faithful friend and factotum Anna . . . Now if you will keep the babies and attend to the things in the house for one day I'll write a piece and then we shall be out of the scrape.'[20] Working with the piece or story, Judith Fetterley has argued, freed American women from the pressures of the novel form, the one 'most highly programmed and most heavily burdened by thematic and formal conventions.' Short story forms allowed them more freedom, for 'in territory less clearly marked, the woman's story that these writers wished to tell could perhaps be better told.'[21] As the book and novel form became more important in the American market, women gathered their pieces together in books such as *Fern Leaves from Fanny's Portfolio*, a model Whitman would later borrow and masculinize in *Leaves of Grass*. At first simply gatherings of disparate pieces, these collections evolved in some cases into novels with narrative structures developed out of the piecing technique.

By the mid-nineteenth century, the most popular American pieced-quilt pattern was the Log Cabin. It begins with a central square, usually red to represent the hearth; and its compositional principle is the contrast between light and dark fabric. Each block is divided into two triangular sections, one section executed in light-colored fabrics, the other in dark. When the blocks are pieced together to make the quilt, dramatic visual effects and variations such as Light and Dark, Barn Raising, Courthouse Steps, and Streak of Lightning can be created depending on the placement of the dark sections.

When she began to write *Uncle Tom's Cabin,* serialized in short weekly installments, Stowe continued to think of her writing as the stitching together of scenes. Uncle Tom's log cabin, first described in the fourth chapter, is a metanarrative marker of the Log Cabin quilt, which in its symbolic deployment of boundaries, is particularly apt for Stowe's novel of the borders and conflicts between the states, the races, and the sexes. In the novel, Uncle Tom's cabin becomes the iconographic center upon which narrative blocks are built up. Each block of the novel is similarly centered on a house, and around it Stowe constructs large contrasts of black and white society. The novel does not obey the rules which dictate a unity of action leading to a denouement, but rather operates through the cumulative effect of blocks of event structured on a parallel design.

The coded formal considerations which lie behind Stowe's novels can also be seen in other women's literary genres of the American Renaissance, especially in the poetry of Emily Dickinson. Dickinson's famous use of the dash for punctuation makes her poems resemble patches, and emphasized the way she joined her poems together in stitched booklets called fascicles. Barton St Armand has suggested that while Dickinson's poetic sequences follow no traditional literary models, 'the art of quilting offers an alternative model for coherence and design.' St Armand argues that 'the discipline of the pieced quilt is as rigorous as that of the sonnet,' and that it provides us with a 'model or metaphor for Dickinson's art that is visual rather than verbal, yet that was also . . . firmly a part of her own culture.'[22] In the heyday of the female world of love and ritual, the woman's rite had serious meaning and dignity.

But by the 1860s, piecing had begun to seem old-fashioned, an overly-moralized exercise in feminine decorum. Louisa May Alcott's children's story, 'Patty's Patchwork,' which appeared as part of her series *Aunt Jo's Scrap-Bag,* shows how tendentiously the process was allegorized to teach feminine behavior. Ten-year-old Patty, visiting her Aunt Pen while her mother has a new baby, grows impatient with her patchwork, and flings the pieces into the air, declaring that 'something dreadful ought to be done to the woman who invented it.' But Aunt Pen has a different point of view. The quilt, she explains, is a 'calico diary,' a record of a female life composed of 'bright and dark bits . . . put together so that the whole is neat, pretty, and useful.' As a project, Patty sets out to make a 'moral bed-quilt' for her aunt to read and decipher, while she herself is learning to become a 'nice little comforter,' the epitome of female patience, perseverance, good nature, and industry. When the infant sister dies, Patty none the less goes on to finish the quilt, which Aunt Pen not only reads and interprets as a journal of her psychological maturity, but which she also inscribes—that is, writes upon—with verses and drawings that became a textual criticism of both the work and the life. Ironically, Aunt Pen is a figure for Alcott herself in her role as dispenser of moral pap to the young, a role she particularly loathed and deplored.[23]

By the *fin de siècle* changes in technology as well as in attitude influenced the ideology and aesthetics of the quilt. In 1870 Singer sold 127,833 sewing machines, which both transformed the time invested in quilts and could also be a 'boon, a challenge, and inspiration' to quilters: 'The machine's speed and its technical possibilities,' along with aniline dyes, the availability of commercial cotton batting, and other technological developments, acted as a stimulus to ambitious designs, especially since home-made quilts were no longer a domestic necessity.[24] Styles in quilts had changed as well. The 'calico patchwork quilt had become associated with the past and with backward rural regions,'[25] and the new trend was for the virtuoso techniques of the crazy quilt, which flourished during the 1880s and 1890s, and which reflected a more cosmopolitan awareness. The styles of crazy quilting, otherwise known as puzzle, mosaic, kaleidoscope, or Japanese patchwork, were inspired by oriental ceramics, textiles, and prints displayed at the Centennial Exposition of 1876 in Philadelphia. Embroidery, the use of silver and gold, and especially the 'jagged patterns in which irregular, triangular and circular patterns overlap' linked Eastern art with Western crazy-quilt design; the combination of many patterns was influenced by a form of Japanese textile called 'kirihame,' and alluded to the crazing in the ceramic glazes used in China and Japan.[26] Crazy quilts incorporated ribbons, commemorative images, photographs, masonic emblems and symbols of religious and sororal societies, and machine-made appliqués. Designs were embroidered on the individual pieces with silk floss, metallic thread, or ribbon; inscriptions were also handwritten, printed, or painted on the cloth.

By the 1880s quilting became identified with an older, dying generation, and especially with the temperance movement. In 1878 the Crusade quilt made by 3,000 Temperance women was shown at the national WCTU convention in Baltimore, testifying to 'women's patience in matters of detail' as well as their hatred of the Demon Rum.[27] To many New Women, such as the suffragist Abigail Duniway, bed-quilts were 'primary symbols of women's unpaid subjection.'[28] Filled with 'a profound horror of the woman's life,' the suffragist Inez Haynes Irwin vowed as a student at Radcliffe in the 1890s that she would 'never sew, embroider, crochet, knit;—especially would I never learn to cook.'[29] Parallels between piecing and women's writing were being more self-consciously, but often negatively or satirically, explored by American women writers wishing to assert themselves as artists. The stories of the local colorists are often more explicitly about the frustrations of the woman writer struggling to create an appropriate form for her experience within a literary culture increasingly indifferent or even hostile to women's domestic lives. These are stories that represent women's culture as sour or comic, and that frequently end in its defeat.

We can see the generational contrast in two related stories about the quilting bee, Ann S. Stephens's 'The Quilting-Party,' written in the 1850s, and Mary Wilkins Freeman's 'A Quilting-Party in Our Village,' written in 1898. In Stephens's story, the 'quilting frolic' is an all-day festival of female bonding; a bevy of girls in silk dresses stitch merrily away on a rising-sun pattern, while they sing romantic ballads. At night there is a lavish feast, and the gentlemen arrive to dance in a room filled 'with a rich fruity smell left by dried apples and frost grapes.' In this story, women's culture is at its ripest and most romantic moment of plenitude, comfort, and harmony.

In Freeman's story, however, the quilting bee takes place on the hottest day of a July heatwave. Wearing their oldest dresses, the quilters set grimly to their task, gossiping among themselves about the bride's age, ugliness, and stinginess. The supper is sickening in its vulgar abundance, and when the gentlemen arrive for a sweaty dance, the women nearly come to blows competing for their attention. The rising-sun pattern which they also quilt now seems like a mocking allusion to the setting sun of women's culture, and to the disappearance of its sustaining rituals.[30]

Similarly, in 'Mrs. Jones's Quilting' (1887) by Marietta Holley, the quilting bee for the minister's wedding is an occasion for ripping up other women's reputations rather than sisterly solidarity or communal piety:

> The quilt was made of different kinds of calico; all the wimmen round had pieced a block or two, and we took up a collection to get the batten and linin', and the cloth to set it together with, which was turkey red, and come to quilt it it looked well; we quilted it herrin' bone and a runnin' vine round the border. After the post-master was demorelized, the school-mistress tore to pieces, the party to Ripleys scandelized, Miss Brown's baby voted an unquestionable idiot, and the rest of the unrepresented neighborhood dealt with, Lucinder Dobbs spoke up, as sez she: 'I hope the minister will like the bed-quilt.'

When sisterhood has unravelled, it takes more than a quilt to stitch it up.

'Elizabeth Stock's One Story,' by Kate Chopin, takes up the issue of piecing and narrative design, originality, and appropriation. Elizabeth Stock is a postmistress in a secluded town who longs to be a writer, but is stymied by her inability to imagine a narrative both in conformity with a patriarchal literary tradition and in creative relation to it: 'Since I was a girl I always felt as if I would like to write stories,' but 'whenever I tried to think of one, it always turned out to be something that some one else had thought about before me.' Despairing of her efforts to imitate male traditions of plot that are 'original, entertaining, full of action, and goodness knows what all,'

206

Elizabeth Stock turns to the female tradition which seems to offer a more authentic, but also less orderly plot: 'I . . . walked about days in a kind of a dream, twisting and twisting things in my mind just like I often saw old ladies twisting quilt patches to compose a design.' After her death of consumption at the age of thirty-eight, Elizabeth Stock's desk is found to contain 'scraps and bits of writing.' Out of this 'conglomerate mass,' the male editor, who may be either her nephew or her longtime suitor, assembles the only pages which seem to resemble a 'connected or consecutive narration.' Finally her scraps and bits of writing, her stock of experience, will be edited, condensed, and preserved according to the consecutive and linear models of the male tradition, with all their craziness and originality lost.[31]

Following the introduction of Cubism to the United States at the New York Armory Show in 1913, the *New York Sun* published a cartoon of the crazy quilter as the 'original Cubist.' Dorothy Canfield Fisher's story 'The Bedquilt,' published in 1915, describes the design and creation of a magnificent quilt, a great work of art, by an elderly spinster. At the age of sixty-eight, Aunt Mehetabel suddenly conceives a great artistic project: a spectacular quilt, pieced according to a dramatically difficult and original design. As Fisher writes,

> She never knew how her great idea came to her. Sometimes she thought she must have dreamed it, sometimes she even wondered reverently, in the phraseology of her weekly prayer-meeting, if it had been 'sent' to her. She never admitted to herself that she could have thought of it without other help. It was too great, too ambitious, too lofty a project for her humble mind to have conceived. . . . By some heaven-sent inspiration, she had invented a pattern beyond which no patchwork quilt could go.

As Aunt Mehetabel becomes absorbed in the 'orderly, complex, mosaic beauty' of her pieces, so too her family begins to give her recognition, praise, and a sewing table of her own. The story of Aunt Mehetabel's prize-winning quilt is obviously applicable to Fisher's own literary fantasies. A Columbia Ph.D. who had abandoned academia to become a writer, Fisher confessed her anxieties about 'the enormous difficulties of story telling, often too great for my powers to cope with.' Her ambitions to create an extraordinary new form for the novel are figured in the image of the ultimate quilt. The literary masterpiece Fisher feared was beyond her as a woman writer is transformed into the mastery of pieces in the great quilt; and her sense of alienation from narrative convention takes shape in the form of a new and inspired pattern, whose 'mosaic beauty' suggests both complex form and spiritual liberation.[32]

Yet modernism, despite its celebration of the fragment in Cubism and in such poetic epics as Eliot's *Waste Land,* disparaged and suppressed women's fragmented art. Women's poetry, Theodore Roethke observed, was largely 'the embroidery of trivial themes.' At the same time art historians, despite the impact of Cubism, belittled even the most basic elements of quilt practice as feminine, trivial, and dull. In one 1925 treatise, for example, the authors proclaimed that

> the geometric style is primarily a feminine style. The geometric ornament seems more suited to the *domestic,* pedantically tidy, and at the same time superstitiously careful spirit of women than that of men. It is, considered purely aesthetically, a petty, lifeless, and despite all its inventiveness of colour, a strictly limited mode of art.[33]

Thus we should not be surprised that many serious women writers scorned needlework metaphors in an effort to dissociate their work from the insulting imputations of feminine triviality. Beginning her career in the mid-1920s, Genevieve Taggard disparaged much women's lyric poetry as 'literary needlework.'[34]

Piecing and quilting underwent an aesthetic revival only after the women's movement in the late 1960s had encouraged a new interest in women's art. In 1971 the curator Jonathan Holstein broke through the barrier that had relegated quilts to the level of craft when he organized a major exhibit on 'Abstract Designs in American Quilts' at the Whitney Museum in New York. Several American women artists such as Judy Chicago and Miriam Schapiro 'found new artistic inspiration and self-validation in women's needlework.'[35]

Indeed, the pieced quilt has become one of the most central images of the new feminist art lexicon. As the art critic Lucy Lippard explains, 'Since the new wave of feminist art began around 1970, the quilt has become the prime visual metaphor for women's lives, for women's culture.'[36]

In feminist literary theories of a Female Aesthetic, piecing became the metaphor for the decentered structure of a woman's text. According to Rachel DuPlessis, a pure *écriture feminine* would be 'nonhierarchic . . . breaking hierarchical structures, making an even display of elements over the surface with no climactic place or moment, having the materials organized into many centers.' In the 'verbal quilt' of the feminist text, she argued, that is 'no subordination, no ranking.'[37] Radka Donnell-Vogt, a Bulgarian quilt-maker living in Boston who was featured in the documentary 'Quilts in Women's Lives,' wrote about piecing as a primal women's art form, related to the body, to mother–daughter bonding, to touch and texture, and to the intimacy of the bed and the home.[38] Using a vocabulary from psychoanalysis, feminism, and poststructuralism, Donnell-Vogt has been the Kristeva of quilting.[39]

Most of the women writers adopting quilt imagery in their poems and novels, however, were not quilt-makers themselves. In contemporary American women's writing, Elaine Hedges has written, the quilt often stands for an idealized past, 'a way of bridging the gulf between domestic and artistic life that until recently women writers have found such difficulty in negotiating.' Textile imagery, 'especially imagery associated with quilts, the piecing together of salvaged fragments to create a new pattern of connections, and integrated whole . . . provides the elements . . . for a new transformative vision.'[40] This imagery is nostalgic and romantic. Marge Piercy's 'Looking at Quilts' describes

> Pieced quilts, patchwork from best gowns,
> winter woolens, linens, blankets, worked jigsaw
> of the memories of braided lives, precious
> scraps: women were buried but their clothing wore on.

Joyce Carol Oates's poem 'Celestial Timepiece' sees quilts as women's maps and history, 'their lives recorded in cloth.' In

209

Adrienne Rich's poem 'Natural Resources,' the humble 'things by women saved' become

> scraps, turned into patchwork,
> doll-gowns, clean white rags
> for stanching blood
> the bride's tea-yellow handkerchief,
> that have the power to 'reconstitute the world.'

In 'Transcendental Etude' the 'bits of yarn, calico, and velvet scraps' along with objects from the natural world, such as 'small rainbow-colored shells,' 'skeins of milkweed,' and 'the dry darkbrown lace of seaweed,' become the substance of what Rich calls 'a whole new poetry beginning here,' a poetry as much 'whole' as 'new,' that is, that makes an effort to remember, reconstruct, and remake. The imagery of common threads in American women's quilts offers Rich a model for her 'dream of a common language' of women.

At the same time, the 'common language' of American women's quilting was being challenged by the rediscovery of black women's quilts, which were displayed in highly successful museum exhibits in Dallas, San Francisco, New York, Mississippi, and Washington, D.C. Houston and Charlotte Baker have argued that the patchwork quilt is 'a trope for understanding black women's creativity in the United States.' Piecing represents 'a signal instance of a patterned wholeness in the African diaspora.'[41] As the Bakers conclude,

> In order to comprehend the transient nature of all wholes, one must first become accustomed to living and working with fragments. . . . Finally it is the 'self,' or a version of humanness that one calls the Afro-American self, that must, in fact, be crafted from fragments on the basis of wisdom gained from preceding generations.[42]

The patchwork quilt appealed not only to black women artists but also to a new generation of African-American intellectuals, artists, and critics seeking powerful and moving symbols of racial identity. In the context of the Black Aesthetic movement, blues and jazz had been posited as the definitive

Afro-American art forms; by the late 1970s scholars began to argue that quilts too incorporated the improvisational techniques important to African-American music. In 1979 Maude Wahlman and John Scully organized an exhibition of 'Black Quilters' which emphasized analogies between piecing and the blues. Elements of spontaneity and novelty in the work of twentieth-century black quiltmakers were cited as crucial to 'Afro-Atlantic aesthetics,' just as 'fresh' was the 'all-purpose encomium on the streets of black and Puerto Rican New York.'[43]

For Alice Walker, piecing and quilting have come to represent both the aesthetic heritage of Afro-American women and the model for what she calls a 'womanist,' or black feminist, writing of reconciliation and connection. In her essay 'In Search of Our Mothers' Gardens,' Walker identified the quilt as a major form of creative expression for black women in the South. 'In the Smithsonian Institution in Washington, D.C.,' Walker writes,

> there hangs a quilt unlike another in the world. In fanciful, inspired, and yet simple and identifiable figures, it portrays the story of the Crucifixion . . . Though it follows no known pattern of quiltmaking, and though it is made of bits and pieces of worthless rags, it is obviously the work of a person of powerful imagination and deep spiritual feeling. Below this quilt I saw a note that says it was made by 'an anonymous Black woman in Alabama a hundred years ago.'

The quilt Walker is describing from memory is in fact one of two extant narrative quilts by Harriet Powers (1836–1911), born a slave in Georgia. The Powers quilt at the Smithsonian illustrates Bible stories, while the one in the Boston Museum of Fine Arts mingles Bible tales with folklore and astronomical events such as shooting stars and meteor showers.[44] For Walker, genuine imagination and feeling can be recognized without the legitimacy conferred by the labels of 'art' or the approval of museums. Paradoxically this heritage survives because it has been preserved in museums; but it can be a living art only if it is practiced.

The theme of Walker's quilt aesthetic is most explicitly

presented in her early story 'Everyday Use.' Like much of her work, it uses a contrast between two sisters to get at the meaning of the concept of 'heritage': a privileged one who escapes from Southern black culture, and a suffering one who stays or is left behind. The younger daughter, Maggie, has stayed at home since she was horribly scarred in a house fire ten years before. Dee is the bright and confident sister, the one with 'faultfinding power.' Dee has learned fast how to produce herself. 'At sixteen she had a style of her own: and knew what style was.' Now having chosen the style of radical black nationalism, her name changed to 'Wangero,' and spouting Swahili, Dee returns to claim her heritage from her mother in the form of 'folk art': the worn benches made by her father, the butter churn whittled by an uncle, and especially the quilts pieced by her grandmother. 'Maggie can't appreciate these quilts,' Dee exclaims. 'She'd probably be backward enough to put them to everyday use.' Walker thus establishes a contrast between 'everyday use' and 'institutional theories of aesthetics.'[45] In a moment of epiphanic insight, the mother, who has always been intimidated by Dee's intelligence and sophistication, decides to give the quilts to Maggie. 'She can always make some more,' the mother responds. 'Maggie knows how to quilt.' Maggie cannot speak glibly about her 'heritage' or about 'priceless' artifacts, but unlike Dee, she understands the quilt as a process rather than as a commodity; she can read its meaning in a way Dee never will, because she knows the contexts of its pieces, and loves the women who have made it. The meaning of an aesthetic heritage, according to Walker's story, lies in continual renewal rather than in the rhetoric of nostalgia or appreciation. In writing *The Color Purple*, Walker herself took up quilt-making as well as using it as a central metaphor in the novel.

The issues of cultural heritage, female creativity, and order are differently explored in Bobbie Ann Mason's 'Love Life,' which appeared in the 29 October 1984 *New Yorker*, and is the title story of her recent collection. Like Walker, Mason is a Southern writer, from western Kentucky, a region in which most of her powerful and disturbing fiction is set. But for Mason, the legacies of Southern women's culture are not simply healing; they also have a darker side that speaks of

212

secrecy and repression, of women's self-destructive commemoration of the patriarchal traditions in which their own freedoms had been thwarted, and of commodification within a sentimentalizing ideology of American womanhood.

In 'Love Life,' two unmarried women represent two generations of women's culture—Aunt Opal, the retired schoolteacher, the old woman who is the caretaker of tradition; and her niece Jenny, the New Woman of the 1980s, whose casual love affairs and backpack existence suggest the dissolution of the female world and the loss of its cultural traditions. Returning to Kentucky, Jenny pleads with Opal to see the family's celebrated but secret and hidden burial quilt. Mason here alludes to a regional quilt genre which flourished in nineteenth-century Kentucky, as a version of the funeral-quilt tradition. Funeral quilts were rituals of mourning in which family members and friends, and sometimes even the dying person, worked together in making a memorial quilt out of fragments recalling the person's life. Burial quilts, however, were more like records of mortality. The best-known surviving example is Elizabeth Roseberry Mitchell's Kentucky Coffin Quilt, done in Lewis County in 1839, and now in the collection of the Kentucky Historical Society. When a member of Mitchell's family died, she would remove a labelled coffin from the border and place it within the graveyard depicted in the center of the quilt.

Aunt Opal's burial quilt is made of dark pieced blocks, each appliquéd with a named and dated tombstone. Its 'shape is irregular, a rectangle with a clumsy foot sticking out from one corner. The quilt is knotted with yarn, and the edging is open, for more blocks to be added.' According to family legend, a block is added whenever someone dies; the quilt stops when the family name stops, so 'the last old maids finish the quilt.' Who will be the last old maid? Ironically, Aunt Opal has rejected the cultural roles of the past. To her, the quilts mean only 'a lot of desperate old women ruining their eyes.' The burial quilt is a burden, 'ugly as homemade sin,' a depressing reminder of failure, loneliness, and servitude. Opal plans to take up aerobic dancing, to be modern; meanwhile she spends all her time watching MTV. 'Did Jenny come home just to hunt up that old rag?' she thinks about the burial quilt.

Jenny, however, plans to learn how to quilt. She will use the burial quilt to stitch herself back into history, to create her context.

Using the familiar nineteenth-century women's narrative model of an emotional interaction between aunt and niece, Mason brings us back, through Aunt Opal's Scrap Bag, to a sense of continuity and renewal in an American female literary and cultural tradition. But the story also suggests that these traditions may be burdens rather than treasures of the past, and that there may be something morbid, self-deceptive, and even self-destructive in our feminist efforts to reclaim them. Is it time to bury the burial quilt rather than to praise it?

The stories by Walker and Mason both reflect the commodification of quilts in the 1970s, and the popularity that made them available as cultural metaphors to many different groups. In 1976 the celebration of the Bicentennial led to a regendering of the quilt aesthetic in relation to American identity. Every state commissioned a Bicentennial quilt, and many towns and communities made their own album quilts with patches by schoolchildren, senior citizens, women's groups, and ethnic groups. By 1984 a survey indicated that fourteen million Americans had made, bought, sold, or had something to do with a quilt. The bonding activities of quilting had great appeal to Americans wishing to come together after the traumas of Watergate and Vietnam. The 1980s, as Annette Kolodny points out, 'were to be the decade of healing and consolidation . . . three presidents in a row—Gerald Ford, Jimmy Carter, and Ronald Reagan—called upon the country to bind up its wounds, heal its divisions, and commit itself anew to shared traditions.'[46] Both communal quilts and collective literary histories seemed to represent the endurance of American traditions.

But the 1980s were also the decade which questioned the monolithic concepts of American exceptionalism. As Sacvan Bercovich notes,

> now it is said, in reaction against those who speak of an American literature or a national culture, that this country is sheer heterogeneity. The ruling elite has an American ideology; the people have their own patchwork-quilt (rather than

melting-pot) American multifariousness: 'America' is—many forms of ethnicity, many patterns of thought, many ways of life, many cultures, many American literatures.[47]

The melting-pot, with its associations of alchemy, industry, and assimilation, had 'shaped American discourse on immigration and ethnicity' for most of the twentieth century. Its major literary source was Israel Zangwill's 1909 melodrama *The Melting-Pot*, which proclaimed, 'America is God's crucible, the great Melting Pot where all the races of Europe are melting and reforming.' The Ford Motor Company dramatized this image too in the graduation ceremonies for their English School, in which male factory workers in their ragged native garb marched into a huge caldron on the company athletic field, merging on the other side in natty American suits waving little American flags. Sometimes plant managers stirred the giant pot with huge ladles, while the Ford band played patriotic songs.[48]

But since World War II, the image of the melting-pot had carried unpleasant associations, not only the macabre echoes of cannibalism and the crematorium, but also distasteful connotations of processed identical robots. Americans needed a new metaphor of national identity, one that acknowledged ethnic difference, heterogeneity, and multiplicity, that incorporated contemporary concerns for gender, race, and class.

Thus the patchwork quilt came to replace the melting-pot as the central metaphor of American cultural identity. In a very unusual pattern, it transcended the stigma of its sources in women's culture and has been remade as a universal sign of American identity. Like other national symbols, the quilt can be adopted and transformed by many groups. Thus, while on the one hand quilts have come to signify a kinder, gentler upper-class Republican America as they appear in fashions by Ralph Lauren, on the cover of the Horchow catalog, and on the boxes of high-fiber cereals, their potential for a more radical political symbolism has also been recognized. It was most fully expressed in Jesse Jackson's speech before the Democratic National Convention in Atlanta in July 1988, when he called for a Democratic 'quilt of unity'.

America is not a blanket woven from one thread, one color, one cloth. When I was a child growing up in Greenville, South Carolina, and grandmomma could not afford a blanket, . . . she took pieces of old cloth—patches—wool, silk, gaberdeen, crockersack—only patches, barely good enough to wipe off your shoes with. But they didn't stay that way very long. With sturdy hands and strong cord, she sewed them together into a quilt, a thing of beauty and power and culture. Now, Democrats, we must build such a quilt.

Jackson's unity quilt called for patches from farmers, workers, women, students, Blacks, Hispanics, gays and lesbians, conservatives and progressives, 'bound by a common thread' in a great multicolored quilt of the American people.[49]

In a tragic irony Jackson had not anticipated, the phrase *Common Threads* has become best known as the title of a documentary about the NAMES Project, usually called the AIDS Quilt, which has become the material embodiment of Jackson's metaphor. In 1987 the San Francisco gay activist Cleve Jones had the vision of a 'unifying quilt in memory of those who had died of AIDS.' As Jones has explained, he saw the quilt both as a memorial which demonstrated the magnitude of the epidemic, and 'a way for survivors to work through their grief in a positive, creative way. Quilts represent coziness, humanity, and warmth.'[50] The national monument to the holocaust of AIDS, then, like the Vietnam War Memorial, would not be an anonymous abstraction, but a space that would allow personal mourning and remembrance. All the names of the dead would be included, in quilt blocks made by their friends, families, and lovers. Working out of a store on Market Street in the Castro, San Francisco's gay neighborhood, NAMES Project volunteers raised money, sewed, and received quilt panels sent to them by grieving friends of those who had died. In many respects, the AIDS Quilt draws on the traditions and rituals of burial quilts developed in women's culture.

But the AIDS Quilt is also very different from those pieced by American women, and its differences suggest the transition from private to public symbols, from women's culture to American culture, from feminine imagery to masculine imagery, and from separate spheres to common threads. First of all, there is its enormous scale. Quilt panels are each three by six feet long, and thus about twenty-five times as large as a standard quilt block. By October 1987 there were 1,920 panels that had been attached with grommets to white fabric walkways. When it was first displayed on the Mall of the Capitol in Washington, the quilt, according to news releases, covered an area the size of 'two football fields' and weighed 6,890 pounds. By 1988, as the AIDS Quilt was exhibited in twenty-five major American cities, usually in parks or huge convention halls, it had to be lifted by cranes, and was transported from city to city by an air cargo company called the Flying Tigers. By fall 1989 it weighed thirteen tons, and included 11,000 panels. Now it is so huge that it can no longer be shown in its entirety.

Secondly, the quilt panels themselves are not pieced. They are made out of every conceivable material from baby clothes to black leather and gold lamé, and are 'laden with mementos, possessions, and final farewells'—medals, locks of hair, jock straps, toys, messages.[51] Most are cloth rectangles to which shapes have been appliquéd or glued; they are painted and written on with crayons and marking pens, often only with names of the dead, but also with phrases and slogans. In contrast to traditional burial quilts, which take several months to make, and become part of the work of grieving, the AIDS Quilt blocks are so simply designed and crudely made that they are very rapidly completed, over periods ranging from a few hours to a few weeks at most.

Folklorists have debated whether the AIDS Quilt belongs to the authentic tradition of women's quilt-making, or whether it reflects the immensity and distance more characteristic of masculine monuments. The AIDS Quilt cannot be treasured, stroked, held, used to solace sleep. It is not an 'intimate object.'[52] Its attendant metaphors of football, sales conventions, and cargo planes evoke a normative American masculinity, perhaps in a deliberate effort to counter the stigma of homosexuality associated with AIDS. To some, the promotional rhetoric of the Project seems commercial; to others, sentimental.

Yet the AIDS Quilt has clearly added its own symbols, rituals, and images to the tradition, and must be read in its own new terms. Its pieces are a solace for grief not because they are made privately in a slow process, but because they link individual mourning to a national loss. The funerary elements seen as morbid in stories like Mason's 'Love Life' take on different meanings in the NAMES Project as making the quilt block became for some a way of preparing for death, a farewell letter and last testament. The large blocks are the size of coffins, and represent the missing graves of AIDS, like a national cemetery of those fallen in war. This symbolism is especially important for the San Franciscans who began the Project, since most of the people who have died there of AIDS

> have no grave or headstones; they are cremated and their ashes are scattered over the mountains or in San Francisco Bay. Even those who are buried disappear—to the cemetery town of Colma, just to our south—because an old law forbids graveyards within the city limits. After the memorial service, the scattering of ashes, and the garage sale, there isn't much left.[53]

The scale and visibility of the quilt testifies to remembrance of lost lives too easily forgotten.

Moreover, the AIDS Quilt has evolved its own powerful rituals and ceremonies: the blessing and unfolding of the huge segment of the quilt by volunteers dressed in white; the reading aloud of the names in each segment by the bereaved. What is perhaps most moving and impressive about this project initiated within the gay community is its refusal to privilege the loss of any individual or group over another. Love and grief are the common threads that bind mothers, fathers, wives, lovers; here hemophiliac children, gay men, straight women, the famous and the obscure, the addicted and the caretakers, are equally remembered and mourned. The British AIDS theorist Simon Watney is one of many witnesses whose initial cynicism about the quilt was overcome by its emotional power:

> I was skeptical about it before I saw it. Falling back on a rationalist perspective, I thought, Oh, God, this is so sentimental. But when I finally saw it, despite the ghastly New Age music

218

booming overhead, it was a completely overwhelming experience. To have this social map of America. To have Liberace
alongside Baby Doe, to have Michel Foucault alongside five
gay New York cops. In many ways it's a more accurate map of
America than any other I've ever seen.[54]

What is important about the AIDS Quilt is not its 'au-
thenticity' in folklore terms, or its fidelity to the feminine traditions of piecing. In it we see the continued vitality of the
quilt metaphor, its powers of change and renewal, and its potential to unify and to heal. Like the literary traditions that
have grown out of American women's culture, the quilt tradition created and nurtured by American women has never
been more meaningful, even as it ceases forever to belong to
us alone.

Are there still common threads that bind American women's
writing, despite the changes which have opened it to the
world? If American women are 'unequal sisters' divided by the
multi-cultural force fields of racial, regional, religious, economic, and erotic difference, do we still share a conversation
and a correspondence?[55]
    Surely one element which unites us and which perme-
ates our literature and our criticism is the yearning for community and continuity, for the bonds of even an unequal
sisterhood. To a striking degree, American women writers
have rejected the Oedipal metaphors of murderous 'originality' set out as literary paradigms in Harold Bloom's *Anxiety of
Influence;* the patricidal struggle defined by Bloom and exem-
plified in the careers of male American writers has no matri-
cidal equivalent, no echo of denial, parody, exile. Instead, Alice
Walker proclaims, 'each writer writes the missing parts to the
other writer's story.'[56] Similarly, Joyce Carol Oates has said,

> The living are no more in competition with the dead than they
> are with the living. . . . All of us who write work out of a
> conviction that we are participating in some sort of communal
> activity. Whether my role is writing, or reading and respond-
> ing, might not be very important. . . . By honoring one anoth-

er's creation, we honor something that deeply connects us all and goes beyond us.[57]

Virginia Woolf's image of a room of one's own, so enabling for women modernists in England seeking privacy and autonomy, seems somehow isolated and remote for American women writers, especially black writers, today. In the writer's need to reach her audience, the room of one's own, writes Hortense Spillers, 'explodes its four walls to embrace the classroom, the library . . . conferences, the lecture platform, the television talk show, the publishing house, the "best seller," and collections of critical essays.'[58] Moreover, as the work of Alice Walker suggests, 'Art, and the thought and sense of beauty in which it is based, is the province not only of those with a room of their own, or of those in libraries, universities, and literary Renaissances.' The power of creating also belongs to those who 'work in kitchens and factories, nurture children and adorn homes, sweep street or harvest crops, type in offices or manage them.'[59]

To recognize that the tradition of American women's writing is exploding, multi-cultural, contradictory, and dispersed is yet not to abandon the critical effort to piece it together, not into a monument, but into a literary quilt that offers a new map of a changing America, an America whose literature and culture must be replotted and remapped. Indeed, that work of exploration and assembly must be carried on, for until feminist critics took up their cause, few American women writers, black or white, were seen as part of the national literary landscape at all. The pages of the ongoing history of women's writing to which this book is a contribution will have to give up the dream of a common language and learn to understand and respect each sister's choice; but we can still choose to read American women's stories and to ask American questions about their past and future.

☐ *Notes* ∎

1. When Glaspell published the story and also produced it as a one-act play called 'Trifles,' it was taken to refer to the sensa-

tional Lizzie Borden case, with its all-male jury. It also served an indirect threat that voteless American women would reject the patriarchal law that had declared their rights and rites to be only trifles. See Susan Gubar and Anne Hedin, 'A Jury of Her Peers,' *College English* 43 (December 1981), 179–89; Karen Alkaley-Gut, 'Jury of Her Peers: The Importance of Trifles,' *Studies in Short Fiction* 21 (Winter 1984), 1–10; and Elaine Hedges, 'Small Things Reconsidered: Susan Glaspell's "A Jury of Her Peers,"' *Women's Studies* 12 (1986), 89–110.

2. See e.g. Patricia Mainardi: 'Women not only made beautiful and functional objects, but expressed their own convictions on a wide variety of subjects in a language for the most part comprehensible only to other women'. 'Quilts: The Great American Art,' *Radical America* 7 (1973), 56.

3. 'A Map for Rereading: Gender and Interpretation of Literary Texts,' in Elaine Showalter, ed., *The New Feminist Criticism* (New York: Pantheon, 1985), 42.

4. Lisa Tickner, 'Feminism, Art History, and Sexual Difference,' *Genders* 3 (1988), 96.

5. Quoted in Pattie Chase, 'The Quilt as an Art Form in New England,' in *Pilgrims and Pioneers: New England Women in the Arts* (New York: Midmarch Arts, 1987), 81. There is always a great fuss when a man enters a traditionally feminine field, and usually a claim that he has outperformed all the women. In 1886 one Charles Pratt declared himself quilt-making champion of the world. See also the work of Lloyd Blanks, 'He's Raised Needlework to the State of an Art,' *New School Observer*, March 1984. Thanks to Carol Barash for this article.

6. *The Spectacle of Women: Imagery of the Suffrage Campaign 1907–14* (Chicago: University of Chicago Press, 1988), 278 n. 13.

7. *Old Mistresses: Women, Art, and Ideology* (New York: Pantheon, 1981), 78.

8. Elaine Hedges, 'The Nineteenth-Century Diarist and Her Quilts,' *Feminist Studies* 8 (Summer 1982), 295.

9. For the history of American quilts, see Pat Ferrero, Elaine Hedges, and Julie Silber, *Hearts and Hands: The Influence of Women & Quilts on American Society* (San Francisco: Quilt Digest Press, 1987).

10. See Maude Southwell Wahlman and Ella King Torrey,

Ten Afro-American Quilters (Center for the Study of Southern Culture, University of Mississippi, 1983).

11. 'Patches, Quilts and Community in Alice Walker's "Everyday Use,"' *Southern Review* 21 (July 1985), 713.

12. Robert Ferris Thompson, preface, 'From the First to the Final Thunder: African-American Quilts, Monuments of Cultural Assertion,' in Eli Leon, *Who'd A Thought It: Improvisation in African-American Quiltmaking* (San Francisco Craft & Folk Art Museum, 1987), 17, 21.

13. 'Up, Down, and Across: A New Frame for New Quilts,' in Charlotte Robinson, ed., *The Artist and the Quilt* (New York: Knopf, 1983), 18.

14. Quoted in Patricia Cooper and Norma Buferd, *The Quilters: Women and Domestic Art* (New York: Doubleday, 1978), 20.

15. Parker and Pollock, *Old Mistresses*, 71.

16. Mainardi, 'Quilts,' 37.

17. Ron Pilling, 'Album Quilts of the Mid–1880s,' *Art & Antiques*, November–December 1982, 72.

18. 'Annette,' 'The Patchwork Quilt,' in Benita Eisler, ed., *The Lowell Offering* (New York: Harper, 1977), 150–4.

19. Judith Fetterley, *Provisions* (Bloomington: Indiana University Press, 1985), 3.

20. Mary Kelley, *Private Woman, Public Stage: Literary Domesticity in Nineteenth-Century America* (New York: Oxford University Press, 1984), 169.

21. Fetterley, *Provisions*, 14–15.

22. *Emily Dickinson and Her Culture* (Cambridge: Cambridge University Press, 1984), 9, 10.

23. Louisa May Alcott, 'Patty's Patchwork,' in *Aunt Jo's Scrap-Bag* (Boston: Roberts, 1872), i. 193–215. Thanks to Elizabeth Keyser for bringing this story to my attention; my analysis is indebted to her presentation in our NEH Summer Seminar on 'Women's Writing and Women's Culture,' 1984.

24. Ferrero, Hedges, and Silber, *Hearts and Hands*, 37.

25. Ibid., 96.

26. Susan R. Finkel, *New Jersey Crazy Quilts 1875–1900* (Trenton, New Jersey State Museum, 19 November 1988–8 January 1989).

27. Ferrero, Hedges, and Silber, *Hearts and Hands*, 87.

28. Ibid., 94.

29. 'The Making of a Militant,' in Elaine Showalter, ed., *These Modern Women* (New York: Feminist Press, 1989).

30. Ann S. Stephens, 'The Quilting Party,' in John S. Hart, ed., *The Female Prose Writers of America* (Philadelphia: E. H. Butler, 1857), 204–10; and Mary Wilkins Freeman, 'A Quilting Bee in Our Village,' *The People of Our Neighborhood* (Philadelphia: Curtis, 1898), 113–28.

31. Kate Chopin, 'Elizabeth Stock's One Story,' in Sandra M. Gilbert, ed., *The Awakening and Selected Stories* (New York: Penguin, 1984), 274–80.

32. Dorothy Canfield Fisher, 'What My Mother Taught Me,' and 'The Bedquilt,' in Susan Cahill, ed., *Women and Fiction 2* (New York: New American Library, 1978).

33. Quoted in Parker and Pollock, *Old Mistresses*, 68.

34. In Showalter, ed., *These Modern Women*.

35. Elaine Hedges, 'The Needle or the Pen: The Literary Rediscovery of Women's Textile Work,' in Florence Howe, ed., *Tradition and the Talents of Women* (Urbana: University of Illinois Press, 1991).

36. 'Up, Down, and Across,' 32.

37. DuPlessis, 'For the Etruscans,' in Showalter, ed., *The New Feminist Criticism* (London: Virago, 1986), 278.

38. Lynn Miller and Sally Swenson, eds., *Lives and Works* (Metuchen, N.J.: Scarecrow Press, 1981).

39. Donnell-Vogt believes that the basic quilt patterns are archetypal representations of the female body. In her own art, she explains, quilt-making 'was essential in giving me a base for exploring my situation as a woman and as an artist . . . quilts became for me a confirmation and restatement of women's toils in child-raising of the physical labor in the cultural shaping and maintenance of persons. . . . Finally, I saw quilts as the bliss and the threat of the womb made visible, spread out as a separate object shaped by the imaginative wealth of women's work and body experience.' Ibid., 12.

40. 'The Needle and the Pen,' in Howe, ed., *Tradition and the Talents of Women*. Hedges argues in this essay that needlework and writing are antagonistic in women's literature, but her concern is with sewing as domestic task rather than the quilt metaphor.

41. Baker and Baker, 'Patches,' 706.

42. Ibid., 718.

43. Thompson, in Leon, ed., *Who'd A Thought It*, 13, 17.

44. See Marie Jean Adams, 'The Harriet Powers Pictorial Quilts,' *Black Art* 3 (1980), 12–28; Gladys-Marie Fry, 'Harriet Powers: Portrait of a Black Quilter,' in Anna Wadsworth, ed., *Missing Pieces: Georgia Folk Art 1770–1976* (Atlanta: Georgia Council for the Arts and Humanities, 1976), 16–23.

45. Baker and Baker, 'Patches,' 716.

46. 'The Integrity of Memory: Creating a New Literary History of the United States,' *American Literature* 57 (May 1985), 291–2.

47. 'Afterword,' *Ideology and Classic American Literature* (Cambridge: Cambridge University Press, 1986), 438.

48. See ch. 3, 'Melting Pots,' in Werner Sollers, *Beyond Ethnicity: Consent and Descent in American Culture* (New York: Oxford University Press, 1986), 66–101.

49. 'Excerpts from Jackson's Speech: Pushing Party to Find Common Ground,' *New York Times,* 20 July 1988, A18.

50. Cindy Ruskin, *The Quilt: Stories from the NAMES Project* (New York: Pocket Books, 1988), 12.

51. Ibid., 13.

52. Dr Beverly Gordon, quoted in 'When an Object Evolves from an It to a He or She,' *New York Times,* 16 Nov. 1989.

53. 'Notes and Comment,' *The New Yorker,* 5 Oct. 1987, 31.

54. Simon Watney, quoted in John Seabrook, 'The AIDS Philosopher,' *Vanity Fair,* December 1990, 111.

55. See Ellen Carol DuBois and Vicki L. Ruiz, *Unequal Sisters: A Multi-Cultural Reader in U.S. Women's History* (New York: Routledge, 1990).

56. Alice Walker, quoted in Henry Louis Gates, Jr., ed., *Reading Black, Reading Feminist* (New York: Meridian, 1990), 11.

57. Robert Phillips, 'Joyce Carol Oates: The Art of Fiction LXXII,' *Paris Review,* Winter 1978, 225–6.

58. Hortense Spillers, 'Cross-currents, Discontinuities: Black Women's Fiction,' in Marjorie Pryse and Hortense Spillers, eds., *Conjuring: Black Women's Fiction and Literary Tradition* (Bloomington: Indiana University Press, 1985), 250.

59. These are the words of Barbara Christian, writing about Walker in 'The Highs and Lows of Black Feminist Criticism,' in Gates, ed., *Reading Black, Reading Feminist,* 44.

☐ Selected Bibliography ∎

Works by Alice Walker

Once: Poems. New York: Harcourt Brace and World, 1968.

The Third Life of Grange Copeland. New York: Harcourt Brace Jovanovich, 1970.

In Love and Trouble: Stories of Black Women. New York: Harcourt Brace Jovanovich, 1973.

Revolutionary Petunias and Other Poems. New York: Harcourt Brace Jovanovich, 1973.

Langston Hughes, American Poet. New York: Harper and Row, 1974.

Meridian. New York: Harcourt Brace Jovanovich, 1976.

Good Night Willie Lee, I'll See You in the Morning. New York: Dial, 1979.

"Zora Neale Hurston: A Cautionary Tale." Introduction to *I Love Myself When I Am Laughing . . . And Then Again When I Am Looking Mean and Impressive: A Zora Neale Hurston Reader*. Old Westbury, New York: Feminist Press, 1979.

You Can't Keep a Good Woman Down: Stories. New York: Harcourt Brace Jovanovich, 1981.

The Color Purple. New York: Harcourt Brace Jovanovich, 1982.

In Search of Our Mothers' Gardens: Womanist Prose. New York: Harcourt Brace Jovanovich, 1983.

Horses Make the Landscape Look More Beautiful: Poems. New York: Harcourt Brace Jovanovich, 1984.

Living By the Word. New York: Harcourt Brace Jovanovich, 1988.

To Hell With Dying. Illustrated by Catherine Deeter. New York: Harcourt Brace Jovanovich, 1988.

The Temple of My Familiar. New York: Harcourt Brace Jovanovich, 1989.

Her Blue Body: Everything We Know: Collected Poems. New York: Harcourt Brace Jovanovich, 1991.

Possessing the Secret of Joy. New York: Harcourt Brace Jovanovich, 1992.

Suggested Further Reading

Abramson, Pam. "Alice Walker Makes the Big Time with Black Folk Talk." *California Living* (August 15, 1982): 16–20.

Appiah, Anthony, and Henry Louis Gates, Jr., eds. *Alice Walker: Critical Perspectives: Past and Present*. Cambridge: Harvard University Press, 1993.

Banks, Erma Davis and Keith Byerman, *Alice Walker: An Annotated Bibliography*. New York: Garland, 1989.

Bloom, Harold, ed. *Alice Walker.* New York: Chelsea House, 1989.

Bradley, David. "Novelist Alice Walker: Telling the Black Woman's Story." *New York Times Sunday Magazine* (January 8, 1984): 25–37.

Christian, Barbara T. "Alice Walker: A Literary Bibliography." *Dictionary of Literary Biography, Vol. 33: Afro-American Fiction Writers After 1955,* ed. Thadious Davis and Trudier Harris. Detroit: Gale Research Company, 1984: 257–270.

———. "The Contrary Women of Alice Walker." *The Black Scholar* 12 (March–April 1981): 21–30, 70–72.

———. "Novels for Everyday Use." *Black Women Novelists: The Development of a Tradition, 1892–1976.* Westport, Conn.: Greenwood Press, 1980: 180–238.

———. "We Are the Ones That We Have Been Waiting For: Political Content in Alice Walker's Novels." *Women's Studies International Forum* 9 (Winter 1986): 421–426.

Cooke, Michael. "Intimacy: The Interpenetration of the One and All in Robert Hayden and Alice Walker." *The Achievement of Intimacy.* New Haven: Yale University Press, 1984: 133–176.

Erickson, Peter. "'Cast Out Alone/To Heal/And Re-Create Ourselves': Family-Based Identity in the Works of Alice Walker." *CLA Journal* 23 (September 1979): 71–94.

Featherston, Elena. "Alice Walker on Alice Walker." *San Francisco Focus* 32 (December 1985): 95.

Freeman, Alma. "Zora Neale Hurston and Alice Walker: A Spiritual Kinship." *Sage: A Scholarly Journal on Black Women* 2 (Spring 1985): 37–40.

Homans, Margaret. "Her Very Own Howl: The Ambiguities of Representation in Recent Women's Fiction." *Signs* 9 (Winter 1983): 186–205.

Kirschner, Susan. "Alice Walker's NonFictional Prose: A Checklist, 1966–1984." *BALF* 18 (Winter 1984): 162–163.

Pratt, Louis and Darnell Pratt. *Alice Malsenior Walker: An Annotated Bibliography, 1968–1986.* Westport, Connecticut: Meckler, 1988.

Richards, Mary Margaret. "Alice Walker." *African American Writers.* Edited by Valerie Smith. New York: Scribners, 1991: 441–458.

Ross, Jean. "Interview with Alice Walker." *Contemporary Authors,* 229. New Revision Series, Vol. 27, ed. Hal May and James G. Lesniak. Detroit: Gale Research, 1988: 471–74.

Sadoff, Diane. "Black Matrilineage: The Case of Alice Walker and Zora Neale Hurston." *Signs* 11 (Autumn 1985): 4–26.

Spillers, Hortense J. "'The Permanent Obliquity of an In[pha]llibly Straight': In the Time of the Daughters and the Fathers." In *Daughters and Fathers,* ed. Lynda Boose and Betty Flowers. Baltimore: John Hopkins University Press, 1989: 157–176.

Steinem, Gloria. "Do You Know This Woman? She Knows You—A Profile of Alice Walker." *Ms.* 10 (June 1982): 35–37, 89–94.

Tate, Claudia, ed. "Alice Walker." *Black Women Writers at Work.* New York: Continuum, 1983: 175–187.

Washington, Charles. "Positive Male Images in Alice Walker's Fiction." *Obsidian* 2 (Spring 1988): 23–48.

Willis, Susan. "Alice Walker's Women." *Specifying: Black Women Writing the American Experience.* Madison, Wisconsin: University of Wisconsin Press, 1987: 110–128.

❑ Permissions ∎

"Everyday Use," by Alice Walker, from *In Love and Trouble: Stories of Black Women*, by Alice Walker (New York: Harcourt Brace Jovanovich, 1973). Reprinted by permission of Alice Walker and Harcourt Brace & Company.

"In Search of Our Mothers' Gardens," by Alice Walker, originally published in *MS* (May 1974), from *In Search of Our Mothers' Gardens: Womanist Prost*, by Alice Walker (New York: Harcourt Brace Jovanovich, 1983). Reprinted by permission of Alice Walker and Harcourt Brace & Company.

"For My Sister Molly Who in the Fifties," by Alice Walker, from *Revolutionary Petunias and Other Poems*, by Alice Walker (New York: Harcourt Brace Jovanovich, 1972). Reprinted by permission of Alice Walker and Harcourt Brace & Company.

"Interview with Alice Walker," by John O'Brien, from *Interviews with Black Writers*, by John O'Brien (New York: Liveright, 1973). Reprinted by permission of John O'Brien and Liveright Publishing Company.

"An Essay on Alice Walker," by Mary Helen Washington, from *Sturdy Black Bridges: Visions of Black Women in Literature,* ed. Roseann P. Bell, Bettye J. Parker, and Beverly Guy-Sheftall (Garden City, N.Y.: Anchor/Doubleday, 1979). Reprinted by permission of Mary Helen Washington.

"Alice Walker's Celebration of Self in Southern Generations," by Thadious M. Davis, from *Southern Quarterly* 21.4 (Fall 1984). Reprinted by permission of Thadious M. Davis and *Southern Quarterly.*

"Alice Walker: The Black Woman as Artist as Wayward," by Barbara T. Christian, from *Black Women Writers (1950–1980): A Critical Evaluation,* ed. Mari Evans (Garden City, N.Y.: Anchor/Doubleday, 1984). Reprinted by permission of Barbara T. Christian and Anchor/Doubleday.

"Patches: Quilts and Community in Alice Walker's 'Everyday Use,'" by Houston A. Baker, Jr., and Charlotte Pierce-Baker, from *The Southern Review* 21 (Summer 1985). Reprinted by permission of Houston A. Baker, Jr., Charlotte Pierce-Baker, and *The Southern Review.*

"Common Threads," by Elaine Showalter, from *Sisters' Choice: Tradition and Change in American Women's Writing*, by Elaine Showalter. The Clarendon Lectures, 1989. (Oxford and New York: Oxford University Press, 1991). Copyright © 1991 by Elaine Showalter. Reprinted by permission of Elaine Showalter and Oxford University Press.

CPSIA information can be obtained at www.ICGtesting.com
Printed in the USA
LVOW12s2012180216

475682LV00001B/129/P